Banking on the Truth

A Ruby Finch Mystery

Ruby Finch Mystery Series

- Last Will and Puzzlement (Book 1)
- Banking on the Truth (Book 2)
- Render at Your Own Risk (Book 3 — coming 2027)

Banking on the Truth

A Ruby Finch Mystery

MELISSA NORDHOFF

Nordhoff Publishing
Lancaster, PA

Banking on the Truth
A Ruby Finch Mystery

ISBN: 9798995413103 (paperback)
ISBN: 9798995413110 (ebook)

MelissaNordhoff.com

Printed in the United States of America

Dedicated to my family, who continues to support me through drafts, rewrites, and the occasional writer meltdown.

And to my readers, who waited (so patiently!) for this second adventure in Lancaster County. Your excitement nudged me back to my writing desk again and again. I swear the third book will arrive much faster.

2004

1 ~ Ruby

My heart hammers against my ribs as I pull the ski mask over my face. The wool itches my skin. My hot, panting breath dampens the fabric releasing a sour smell that makes me queasy. The interior of the van is oppressive, but the summer heat isn't the cause of the sweat coating my body.

My twin brother Roddy inches the van down a narrow alley, parking beside the First National Bank in Marietta.

"I'm anxious." My sweaty palms make slipping into my black leather gloves a challenge.

He ties a red bandana over the lower half of his face, covering his strong jaw and blond stubble, pops a cowboy hat onto his head, and squeezes between the seats, joining me in the back of the van. "Me too."

I hold up a trembling hand. "My hand's not the only thing shaking. My legs feel like Jello. Do you think Gigi and Pop felt this way when they robbed the Ephrata National Bank?"

He shrugs. "Who knows? Pop probably, but you know Gigi. I bet she was reveling in the challenge."

Thoughts of our beloved grandmother cut through the nervous tension. She made life (and even her funeral, for that matter) thrilling. Chores were games of make-believe. Grocery shopping was a scavenger hunt. And learning became an entertaining competition. Though Roddy and I only found out about her and my grandfather's bank heist four years ago, we always knew she was one-of-a-kind.

I smile. "She never shied away from a temerarious adventure."

Roddy lands a playful punch on my shoulder. "Oh, look at you using a favored word. Points for you."

To increase our vocabulary, Gigi chose a variety of "favored words." When Roddy and I used them correctly, we scored points towards a reward. We still played in adulthood (a testament to our nerdiness).

I laugh. "I bet she's still counting in heaven."

He nods. "Indubitably."

I suck in a huge inhale, refocusing on the job at hand. "Okay, brother, let's go rob a bank."

We hop out the back of the van. The soupy air, heavy with the smell of rotting food from an overflowing dumpster, does nothing to ease my roiling stomach. I swallow and sigh out my anxiety. Looking up into the cloudless summer sky, I try to channel Gigi's fearless spirit.

Roddy slings the tool bag over his shoulder and stuffs his fingers into a pair of rubber gloves. "Are you ready?"

I check my wristwatch. "We've got forty-five minutes to empty the safe and get out. Let's do it!"

Hugging the red brick building, we make our way to the side entrance. The thick wood door is padlocked. Roddy digs out lockpicks from the tool bag and jiggles them into the bottom of the lock. Within minutes the lock clicks open.

"Nice job, Roddy. Clearly, you've been practicing."

We slide through the open door into an expansive lobby and are immediately confronted with crisscrossing red laser beams.

The heavy wool mask feels claustrophobic. "Remind me not to wear a winter ski mask next time. I'm suffocating."

Roddy shakes his head. "I told you to wear a bandana."

I roll my eyes at him. "I'm channeling international jewel thief, not stagecoach robber."

He gives me the once over. "Hence the black catsuit."

"Correct. Perfectly streamlined to get through the lasers."

Roddy motions to the maze of lights. "Have at it."

I slowly bend, slide, shimmy, and step, over and under the beams. Tension spasms my leg muscles as I struggle not to set off the alarm. "Jeez. I wish I would've kept up with yoga classes."

"You're almost there," Roddy says. "Keep going."

Fifteen minutes later, panting and drenched in sweat, I have conquered the first security hurdle. Behind the tellers' booths I find a shut-off switch. Once I hit it, the beams disappear and sliding glass doors open to management's office area. Six desks sit side by side in front of a huge metal cage. Roddy joins me.

He pinches the bridge of his slightly-crooked nose, broken by his buddy Allen Marsdale in a weekly pick-up basketball game. "We've got to open the cage to get to the safe."

I point to the numbered keypad on the metal door. "Yep. Ideas on breaking the code?"

He lifts his cowboy hat to run his gloved fingers through his sweaty blond hair. "Maybe in one of these desks or the Rolodexes?"

I check the time. Adrenaline surges through my body. "Crap, Roddy, we've only got twenty minutes before the alarm sounds. We've got to hustle." I wave my hand over the desks on the right. "You search those three. I'll look at these."

I rifle through the Rolodexes searching the Cs for code and the Ps for password with no luck. I fling open file drawers, my fingers flying over the tabs looking for anything useful. Still no luck.

Time is ticking. We're not going to make it. My breath changes to shallow pants. Sweat rolls into my eyes.

I dump out pencil holders looking for scraps of paper with code numbers. Nothing. I flip through the pages of daily planners. I skim logs of accounts.

Shoving my hand under my mask, I wipe the stinging sweat from my eyes. "Roddy, any luck?"

His brows are puckered with worry. "Nothing."

"It's got to be here." I scan the room hoping for inspiration. My eyes land on a time clock. The date reads January 3, 1967—nowhere close to today's date. "Roddy, I think I've got it. Try 1, 3, 1, 9, 6, 7."

Roddy punches in the numbers and the gate swings open. He pumps his fist in the air. "That's what I'm talking about!"

We dash to the safe door. Roddy studies the intricate combination lock.

I check the time. "Only three minutes left."

He shakes his head. "I don't even know where to start."

"Just dial in some numbers. Try anything."

His hands tremble as he tries different numbers. The seconds tick by.

My mouth is dry. "We're not going to make it."

Wee-woo! Wee-woo! The alarm blares. Seconds later, the front doors of the bank swing open. Two sets of boot heels click on the floor as a sheriff and her deputy barrel into the lobby, raised guns pointed at our chests.

My stomach drops. It's over. Roddy and I throw our hands in the air and surrender.

2 ~ Ruby

"Your robbery is over!" Sheriff Stephanie, the owner of the First National Heist, yells, dangling the plastic handcuffs from her fingers. "You've failed."

Roddy and I collapse to the restored wide-planked wood floor of the 1875 bank. His hat topples from his head when he plops down onto his back. I whip my ski mask off and lay my damp cheeks against the wood, appreciating its coolness.

Laughing, I sit up, raking my fingers through the red curls sweat has plastered to my head. "That was brilliant! An actual bank turned into a pretend heist—what a great concept! Does anybody ever manage to pull off the burglary?"

Stephanie lays her fake gun, and cuffs on one of the desks. When she removes her Sheriff's hat, long blonde hair cascades around her shoulders. "There's a seventy-five percent completion rate."

I shrug. "Well, guess we're in the bottom twenty-five."

Roddy stands and shoves his gloves and bandana into the pocket of his Levi's. He offers me a hand, pulling me up. "Ethan is going to love this."

Ethan Hall is turning the big five-o. His wife Clarice hired my one-person company, Make A Splash! Event Planning, to organize a surprise bank heist and costume party.

Stephanie enters the cage and points out numbers made of wires attached to the back of the cage door. "These are the combination numbers."

Once the numbers are pointed out, they're obvious. "Can't believe I missed them."

She dials in the combination, but the safe doesn't open. "Two keys, turned at the same time, are required to unlock the safe."

I bump Roddy's shoulder. "Kind of like the teak box the lawyer delivered after Gigi died. Whew, we had no idea what was coming."

My grandmother's customized funerary adventure uncovered all kinds of secrets, including the biggest of all—our father's real identity. I've embraced Donald as my dad. Except for the occasional growing pains, we have a great relationship. Roddy, on the other hand, is skittish in the relationship department. His divorce—well, more specifically Clara's cheating—did a real number on him. Gigi's lies about our parentage didn't help. And Dad's sketchy behavior—prior to reentering our lives—just topped things off.

Dad was our mom's (much older) boss and a raging alcoholic. Booze made him do some pretty terrible things. But people change. When he stopped drinking, he begged Gigi to let him into our lives. Even though she refused, he showed up (unbeknownst to Roddy and me) at the big events in our lives. And now he's been sober for over twenty years. If Dad keeps putting in the time, like he has these past four years, I know Roddy will come around.

Roddy sucks in a breath and shakes his head. "No idea is an understatement." He says to Stephanie, "When we turn the keys, we're not in for any huge surprises, are we? I don't need any more bombshells in my life."

Stephanie laughs. "Nope. Nothing's gonna pop out at you. I promise."

She collects one key from its hiding spot on the bottom ledge of the cage, and her "deputy" Janelle grabs another hanging on the wall from a wooden paddle that says restroom. They hand them to us. Roddy and I insert the keys and turn. The safe door releases, and I swing the heavy beast open.

I clap my hands together, delighted with the interior. "This is the perfect place to have his money-bag-shaped birthday cake and champagne! And maybe even a few of his friends waiting to surprise him."

Stephanie shakes her head. "No can do on the friends. It's airtight. Don't want to risk anyone asphyxiating."

"Jeez, that would be horrific! Okay, just champagne and cake."

Roddy's chuckle rumbles like a deep bass note. "Good choice."

Stephanie motions towards the actual office. "Now that you've done the dry run of the heist, let's talk about any remaining details."

"Perfect. Let me grab my notes from the catering van."

Roddy fishes the keys from his pocket. "I'll get them."

When he stands, his T-shirt pulls across his chest, and I catch Janelle giving him the full once over. He has that effect on women—young, old, married, single. He insists I'm imagining it whenever I tease him, which only makes it funnier.

I press my lips together to hide an amused smile as he heads for the side entrance.

Janelle's silky brown hair sways as she runs after Roddy. "I'll open the door for you. Otherwise, you'll have to pick the lock again."

Stephanie and I walk into the cramped office. I point at her clothes. "Will you and Janelle wear the costumes during the event?"

Stephanie nods. "You bet."

Stephanie sits on one side of a massive oak desk, and I sit on the other. The light odor of pine-scented air freshener almost hides the smell of musty money impregnating the historic building.

Stephanie clasps her hands in front of her. "I got your extremely, ah, comprehensive fax about the table and chair placement."

Roddy laughs at the doorway. "I bet she's got it down to the minute and inch."

I admit, I could organize a hamster circus within an inch of its life. I even make lists of my to-do lists. But honestly, it serves me well in my job as an event planner.

I sigh dramatically, lifting the curls from my forehead. "I don't like to leave anything to chance."

Stephanie grins. "I can tell you two are siblings." She taps the edge of the fax onto her desk. "I actually appreciate the details. That way we know exactly what you need from us."

As Janelle squeezes past me to stand behind Stephanie, I refrain from throwing Roddy a smug look when he hands me my oversized, cheery, yellow bag with the Make A Splash! logo.

I point to the paper. "As you can see by my schedule, as soon as Ethan opens the safe or the alarm goes off, we can bring in the tables and chairs while Roddy begins to set up for the buffet. The guests arrive an hour and fifteen minutes after the Halls, so unless Ethan and his crew crack the safe quickly, we'll only have about thirty minutes to prepare for them."

Stephanie nods. "Completely doable. If you want, I could have a few bank-themed puzzles in the safe to keep the Hall family entertained while we're setting up."

"Great idea. Ethan is a mystery and puzzle buff, so that's perfect."

Stephanie scribbles a note on her planner. "Done. Also, Janelle and I will clear tables during the event and help with clean up after."

"Wonderful."

Roddy hitches his thumb towards the bank's lobby, and says to Stephanie, "I'd like to use the tellers' booth as the buffet table, if that works for you. I'll cover it with thick, clear plastic so no food is spilled on the wood, and a heat-resistant mat will be under the chafing dishes."

Roddy's catering the Halls' shindig. Starting Chef's Secret was a huge step for him. Always the practical one, he never would've quit his steady job as a high school accounting teacher without the safety net of his inheritance. I'm so happy he's finally chasing his dream.

Stephanie nods. "That's fine. Do any of your guests need special accommodations?"

I dunk my hand into my bag and dig for my notes. "As for the heist portion of the evening, only Ethan, his wife, and two sons will be attempting to rob the safe, so no adjustments are needed for that."

Janelle crosses her arms. "Ethan's son David is a nice kid. He and my son were on the same football team at Myerstown." She clears her throat. "Excuse me for a minute."

Roddy scoots his chair closer to me to let Janelle exit.

I pull a copy of the guest list from my bag. "I do have a few folks with special requests." I slide the paper across the desk to Stephanie, and tap the first couple's names. "Ed and Connie Baker. Connie is gluten-free, but that doesn't affect you, only Roddy." I slide my finger down the list. "Liza Abrams has an emotional support dog. Any issue with that?"

Stephanie shakes her head. "Is this my list?" I nod and she writes dog beside Liza's name. "No problem at all."

Janelle chimes in from the doorway of the office. "Liza is my hairstylist. Her dog is the sweetest miniature poodle named Shampoodles."

Turning to face her, I chuckle. "How cute. I bet you and Stephanie will know a bunch of the guests. Most of them are from Marietta."

Janelle nods. "Most likely. It's a small town."

I turn back to Stephanie and move down the list to the next starred names. "This special need is crucial."

"For Isaac and Amanda Stone?" Stephanie asks.

"Yes. Isaac Stone is deathly allergic to peanuts. Nothing with peanuts should come into the bank. No candy bars with peanuts, no protein bars, nothing. We don't want a festive event to turn into an ER visit."

Stephanie adds another star and underlines the name, writing *NO PEANUTS* beside it. "Noted. What else?"

I move further down the list to Oscar and Tabitha Reed. "Tabitha uses a wheelchair. I didn't notice an accessible entrance."

"Janelle," Stephanie says. "The portable ramp is in the utility closet. Would you pull it out to show Ruby and make sure it's suitable?"

I turn to face Janelle. Her neck and cheeks are red. Her jaw and fists are clenched, and her brow is furrowed. She's clearly not happy with Stephanie's request.

"Janelle?" Stephanie says. "The ramp?"

Janelle blinks and pinches the bridge of her nose. "Yeah. Um, let me get it."

I wave my hands. "No, no. If you have used it before, it's not necessary to drag it out. I'll just peek at it before I leave."

She nods. The boots of her deputy's uniform clicks on the wood floor as she walks towards the closet.

Stephanie leans back in her chair. "Anything else?"

I look at Roddy and raise my brows. "Do you have any questions for Stephanie?"

He shakes his head. "All good."

I stand. "I think we're set. I'll call if anything comes up."

Stephanie extends her hand shaking mine then Roddy's. "Thanks for choosing First National Heist. We'll do all that we can to make your event memorable."

3 ~ Millicent

My tan Ford Taurus sputters into Amanda's circular, stamped concrete driveway, seemingly as pooped as I am. Between volunteering at the Historical Society and Violet House, and helping Ruby and Roddy with their events, the activity is wearing me out. Don't get me wrong, I love being involved, but I'm more of a social slug than a butterfly.

As I'm parking, a dented, black pick-up truck, belching thick smoke from its muffler, pulls out of the driveway. I unbuckle my seatbelt, adjust my red-rimmed glasses, and stare after the disappearing truck. My wiry, salt-and-pepper brows draw together. Was that Donald? Hmm. I'll have to ask Amanda why he was here.

Reaching over to the passenger seat, I grab the freshly baked oatmeal raisin cookies—favorites of Amanda's son Ian—and a pain flies into my hip. Darn bursitis. My hip hasn't been the same since a few years back. I fell on it when my identical twin sister Myrtle and I decided we should take up racquetball. Let me tell you, over the age of sixty is not the age to take up new sports. I ease out of the car and limp up the bricked stairs.

Before I can ring the doorbell, Amanda flings the door open. Her normally sleek blonde bob is frizzier than my hair on a Deep-South-sticky summer day. And that's saying a lot. My kinky gray curls attract birds to nest on a good day, add in humidity and it could house a flock.

"Are you okay?" I ask.

"Fine. Fine." She turns and motions for me to follow her inside. Her blouse is untucked and her trousers are wrinkled, like she threw on clothes to answer an unexpected knock at the door.

I lift the tin of cookies. "For Ian."

"He's watching his dad coach today. Set them on the island, won't you?"

Poor Ian. I know he'd love to play football—any sport, really—but he's sidelined because of his hemophilia.

I detour into the massive kitchen of Amanda's suburban McMansion. She and Isaac bought it eight years ago, when he was promoted to head coach of the Marauders, Myerstown University's football team. Though I covet her double ovens, I prefer my cramped but quirky, mustard-yellow saltbox house. The homes in Amanda's Whispering Winds country-club-adjacent development, though stately, are one of two styles. With a little too much wine (which is half a glass for me), I could easily walk into the wrong house.

When I drop the cookies on the counter, I notice a highball glass of melting ice and an open bottle of Woodford Reserve bourbon. Nine in the morning seems a bit early for a tipple. I press my lips together and scold myself. It's not my place to judge.

I limp into the sitting room and settle my size-fourteen bottom into a plush side chair.

"Why are you limping?" Amanda asks.

I pat my ample hip. "Old sky-diving injury."

I expect her to laugh or at least roll her eyes, but she responds like she didn't hear me. "Oh dear, I forgot to offer you a drink."

I wave my hand. "I'm fine. Drank so much coffee my eyes are floating." I prop an embroidered throw pillow under my butt to ease the ache. "So, how do you know Ruby and Roddy's dad, Donald?"

Amanda's eyes widen and her swallow is visible. "Why would you think I know him?"

"I saw him pulling out when I pulled in."

She furrows her brows and shakes her head. "Um … uh … no, no. You're mistaken. That must have been the arborist. Yes, that's who you saw. He's working on a quote to have our birch trees trimmed."

I shrug. "Oh, okay."

When Amanda grabs the manila folder from the glass-topped coffee table, I notice her hand is trembling. "Down to Violet House business. I can hardly believe we're less than four months away from the Friendsgiving Gala. It's a shame Liza couldn't join us. I wanted to confirm she'll offer her services to the women pre-event, and see if she made any headway on formal wear."

Amanda, Liza, and I are an interesting trio. We're like a sundae. Amanda is the vanilla ice cream—classic and traditional. I'm the caramel sauce—oozing with comforting sweetness (a little goes a long way). And Liza is the sprinkles—colorful and chaotic, without which the sundae would be ordinary.

We met at Violet House, a local shelter devoted to empowering women to move forward. Though I love being a docent at the Historical Society—and still do it once a week—I wanted to do more. Twice a week, I fix dinner and offer on-site childcare to the residents. Liza, owner of Mystic Mane hair salon, donates her services and provides a listening ear. And Amanda serves on the board of directors. Our shared passion to help women get back on their feet has sealed our friendship.

"Liza's in for the hairdos. And the owner of Ooh La La Consignment is willing to donate the gowns. Ooh La La is where my sister Myrtle used to get her girls' prom dresses. With nine kiddos, she couldn't be paying bridal shop prices.

"You know, I watch that show, *Say Yes to the Dress,* and could just fall out at the prices. Ten thousand dollars and more for a dress you're going to wear for a few hours, I just can't even imagine spending—oh, mercy me! I'm rambling again. Anyway. Hairdos, check. Dresses, check. And I've got the food covered. Roddy has offered to donate his time. Chef's Secret, his catering business, is still young, so he's hoping to get his name out there. You'll get to taste his food at Clarice's birthday bash for Ethan."

Amanda's face turns ghost-white, and she squeezes her temples.

"Are you sure you're okay? You seem really out of sorts today."

She rubs her forehead. "I'm dreading the party."

"Why? Costume parties are right up your alley."

"Connie and Ed Baker will be there."

"So?"

"So, I just found out Isaac has been sleeping with Connie. And it's not a one-time thing. I don't think I can fake being civil."

I have to lift my jaw off the ground. No wonder the bourbon bottle is out. It's not that Isaac is cheating—from what Amanda has told Liza and me, he canoodles a different co-ed each year—it's who he's cheating with. The Baker's also live in Whispering Winds. But they're not only neighbors, Amanda and Connie run in the same circles. They are both active in the Women's Club. They attend the same church. They play tennis and golf at the country club. And Connie is also an occasional volunteer at Violet House.

I move to sit beside Amanda on the couch and reach for her hand. "I'm so sorry, Amanda."

She pulls away from me, crossing her arms. Anger flares in her cheeks. "I can't live like this anymore. He's flaunting it in front of my face. I'm done. Isaac is an embarrassment. And I don't deserve it."

I sigh. "No, you don't. You deserve someone who will give you all their love."

I never did care for Isaac. He swaggers around like a banty rooster, acting like he's king of the roost. Too full of himself for my taste. I think Amanda has put up with his airs and unfaithfulness all these years because of Ian. She didn't want to disrupt his life any more than his illness already does.

She stands and paces the room. "I met someone."

My eyebrows jump to my hairline. "You have?"

She nods. "Yes. A kind, handsome, attentive, loving man. We've been seeing each other for a few months now. Unlike Isaac, I've remained faithful to my marriage vows, but I'm wavering. I could use a fresh start, and I really could see myself spending the rest of my life with him."

I may as well leave my jaw on the floor. The shocks just keep coming.

Amanda stares at her fidgety fingers. "You must think I'm horrible."

I shake my head. "I don't. What's good for the goose …"

She drops down on the couch. Her heavy exhale lifts her wispy bangs. "That's the thing, Millicent. I don't want to commit adultery."

"Are you thinking of divorce?"

"Yes. No. I don't know." Sighing, she presses her palms together in prayer position and lifts them in front of her mouth. "Ian would be torn between the two of us. The house would have to be sold. I'd need to get a job. It's not fair. My life shouldn't have to change. He's the one who has broken our vows—repeatedly."

"Well, I guess you could stay married, but each, uh, go your own way …"

"A marriage in name only? Hard pass. It may sound naïve, but I still want the white-picket, happily-ever-after dream." She runs her hands through her hair, skinning it back against her head. "I've got to figure out some other option. His philandering has punished me enough. It's his turn."

4 ~ Millicent

Tonight is the final planning dinner for Ethan Hall's surprise birthday party. Amanda might not be looking forward to it, but I am. I love costume parties. Myrtle hosts a Halloween shindig every year, and in the darn near sixty-five years since our first trick-or-treat night, we've been everything from Green Eggs and Ham to the Doublemint Twins. We've worn so many outfits over the decades we could probably open our own pop-culture museum. For the Hall party, Liza and I—oh, and I can't forget Shammie, her emotional support Poodle—are going as the Merry Men. Liza's going as Robin Hood and I'm Little John. Disney's portly bear version, naturally.

Tan pea gravel crunches under my tires as I pull into the driveway. The sun highlights the curves of the clay tile roof on Mirabella, Ruby's name for her childhood home. I swear, that girl names everything, houses, cars, trees, even tea kettles. I don't know if it's comforting, making your stuff feel like friends, or if it's just her playful creativity getting into mischief. We all thought when she got her Basset Hound, Lucy, she'd stop naming things, but we were wrong.

This time, I've put the tin of chocolate chip cookies in the back seat, making getting them easier on my hip than stretching across to the passenger seat. I ease out of my sedan and open the back door. As I'm bending to collect the cookies, blaring rock music and the rumble of a motor startles me and I bang my head against the side of the door.

"If they're not already deaf, they will be," I grumble, rubbing my head. I turn, cookies in hand, and glare at the thump-thump-thumping Jeep.

Jed Stone, Amanda's brother-in-law, sits in the driver's seat, drumming his hands on the steering wheel in time to the booming beat. His long brown hair flops around his bobbing head.

He switches off the ignition and hops out. "Hey Millie! How's it hanging?"

"Heavens to Betsy, Jed. You have that music so loud you'll burst your eardrums."

"It's classic Stones. You gotta rock out to it."

I roll my eyes. "If you say so."

Much to the dismay of his conservative father, Ivan, and practical older brother, Isaac, Jed is in a band. Isaac's always telling him to get a real job, probably because Jed has "spot-me-a-twentied" him to death. Jed's concession is a side hustle as a deejay. Ruby hired him for Ethan's birthday bash.

Noticing my limp, Jed offers me his arm. I rest my hand in the warm crook of his elbow, breathing in his scent of leather and wood. He guides me up the walkway lined with yellow impatiens.

Though both twins inherited the house, Ruby—perfectly content in her own cottage with her named companions—insisted Roddy move out of his "Eeyore apartment," as she called it, and be the one to live here. With their beloved Gigi's ashes resting beneath the dogwood tree in the backyard, selling Mirabella was never an option. Roddy used part of his inheritance to build an outbuilding for his commercial kitchen, designed to blend seamlessly with Mirabella's Spanish Mission style. But other than that, he's barely changed a thing. He claims it's practicality. I sense, much like Ruby with her things, the décor holds memories he isn't ready to disturb.

"So, Millie, what's your job for this gig?" Jed asks as we walk through one of the three arches spanning the front of the stucco house.

"I'm the baker. Dozens of hundred-dollar-bill cookies."

"Hmph. How 'bout you bake me up a couple dozen? I could use the cash." He rubs his fingers together. "Egg donors and surrogates are expeeeeeeensive!"

Jed's husband, Felix Choi—from what Amanda tells me, yet another sore spot between Jed and Ivan—is dead-set on having a baby. Sooner rather than later. I guess men can have ticking biological clocks, too.

"How's that process going?"

He sighs. "The process is fine. Felix has narrowed it down to a few potential bio-moms. Coming up with the funds is the problem."

"I would think picking out the egg donor would be kind of exciting."

He shrugs. "I'm letting it up to Felix."

"You sound about as thrilled as if you were heading to the dentist."

The right side of his mouth lifts, scrunching his cheek towards his eye. "Meh. I could do without a kid. I like my freewheeling lifestyle. Besides, much as I hate to admit it, I'm old. When the kid is ten, I'll be in my sixties. But I always knew it was a deal breaker for Felix." He chuckles. "The downside of marrying a much-younger hottie."

The thick wooden front door creaks when it opens. Ruby, wearing the strawberry-red, daisy-printed romper she picked up from Country Gift and Thrift Shoppe on our last thrift shopping excursion—now, shopping is a sport I *can* handle—stands in the doorway. Droopy-eyed Lucy sits beside her, wagging her tail as she waits to greet us.

Ruby claps her hands together. "Come in. Come in. The gang's all here."

I hand her the cookies as we step inside. The air-conditioning is a welcome relief from the summer humidity. Lucy sniffs Jed's threadbare jeans and he bends to pet her velvety ears. I lean in to hug Ruby. Her unruly red curls tickle my nose.

Jed stands, wiping dog drool on his Led Zeppelin T-shirt. "Something smells delicious."

Ruby waves us into the kitchen. "It's almost ready."

The scent of garlic, lemon, and basil makes my mouth water. "What are you cooking?" I ask Roddy.

He stands in front of bubbling pots and sizzling pans, smiling and calm, his white chef's apron spotless despite the spritzes and splatters on the stove top. The kitchen is his happy place; give that man a pot to stir and he's like a cat soaking up the sun on a warm windowsill.

"Pesto chicken and lemon herb-roasted asparagus."

I dip my finger in the sauce. "Yum."

Donald, dressed in an emerald-green polo shirt that matches his eyes, leans against the butcher block countertop sipping an iced tea.

Ruby introduces Jed to Donald. "Dad, this is Jed, our deejay for the event."

Donald extends his hand to Jed. "You're Amanda's brother-in-law, right?"

Jed grins as he shakes Donald's hand. "If she said good things about me, then yes."

Ruby's eyebrows crunch together. "Dad, how do you know Amanda?"

Donald freezes like a deer caught in headlights. "I, uh, I don't."

His nervousness is odd and triggers an image of the black truck leaving Amanda's driveway. Could he be the new man in Amanda's life?

Donald takes a sip of his tea. "I mean, I know her name in passing. I must've heard you or Millicent mention Jed's connection to her." He points to the beverage refrigerator. "Anyhow, can I get you two a drink?"

"I'd take a beer, if you have it," Jed says.

Donald nods. "Sure do. Millicent? How about you?"

I shake my head. "No beer for me. I have such a low tolerance for alcohol, I swear even the smell of it makes me tipsy. Now, I will have the occasional tipple—if I'm not driving—especially when my sister Myrtle and I get together. We really whooped it up last New Year's Eve.

"Rick, Myrtle's husband, always wanted to go to Times Square for New Year's Eve, and decided he better do it before he got too old. Myrtle refused to join him. She's like me. Crowds make us nervous. I think maybe because one time, when we were little, she and I got lost at the Harrisburg Farm Show Complex. It took the police hours to reunite us with our parents. So, anyway, she stayed home and we celebrated together. We had the paper 2004 crowns and the noisemakers, and cranked up her old record player. After too many bottles of bubbly, we danced till our knees gave out and laughed till we peed. Oh, good gracious, there I go again. Yackety-yakking. I'll just have lemonade, please."

Donald hands Jed a beer and pours me a glass of lemonade. "Millicent, we'll teetotal together. Twenty-three years sober this month."

"Well, cheers to that," I say, raising my glass of lemonade. After Donald and I clink glasses, I turn to Roddy. "What can I help with?"

"Not a thing. It's all ready, we're just waiting for Gail."

Gail suits Roddy to a tee. He tends to be overly serious, but she—and Ruby—have a way of teasing the sunshine right out of him.

"Oh, that reminds me," Ruby says, grabbing a bouquet of sunflowers from the brightly- colored, Talavera-topped kitchen island. "Where are your vases?"

Roddy juts his square jaw towards the creamy white cabinet above the fridge. "In there. That was sweet of you to bring flowers, Ruby."

"What's the occasion?" I ask.

Ruby grabs a stepstool from the humongous pantry and retrieves a vase. "They're for Gail. To celebrate her new position with Ronks Large Animal Vet Center."

I clap my hands together. "Aah! She got the job! That's fantastic."

As if our words conjured her, Gail sails through the door. Her chestnut-brown hair fans out behind her as she hurries in. "Am I late?"

Roddy clicks off the stove. "Nope. Right on time."

Gail rolls up the sleeves of her western-cut shirt and washes her hands at the kitchen sink. "There was an emergency with a birthing cow."

"An udder day, and udder dollar," Ruby jokes as she arranges the sunflowers.

Roddy groans. "That's a Marty joke if I ever heard one." His eyes widen and he slaps his hand over his mouth. "Oh jeez, Ruby. I'm sorry. I didn't mean to bring him up."

Last September, Ruby and Marty were all set to live together. He gave up the lease on his apartment. A U-Haul was rented. Marty's sister Becky and her husband Bart, Roddy, Gail, Donald, and I volunteered to help. An official moving day was planned. And the night before, Ruby called it off. I never heard why. I'm not sure if Roddy even knows. What I do know is Ruby was inconsolable for weeks. Ever since, we've been pussyfooting around anything that so much as rhymes with Marty.

That's how Lucy came into the picture. Ruby's pain nearly gave Roddy an ulcer. Myrtle and I were like that, too. Cut one of us and we both bled. I think it's a twin thing. Anyhow, Lucy was the only way he could think of to get Ruby out of her funk. It helped some, but nearly a year later, her feelings are still tender.

The air in the room evaporates and everyone—even Jed—freezes in place. Ruby's hands drop by her sides and tears well in her eyes. She bends down and snuggles her face into Lucy's fur. Donald moves to her side, resting his hand on her back.

Ruby rises and kisses him on the cheek. "It's okay, Dad. I'm okay." She offers everyone a wobbly smile, then grabs the vase and hands it to Gail. "Congratulations on your new job!"

Breathing returns to the room and celebratory chatter replaces the awkwardness.

Jed leans close to my ear and whispers. "That Marty dude must be a real piece of work for everyone to freak out like that."

"Bad break-up," I whisper back, shrugging off his comment.

Marty is delightful. Funny, smart, lovable, and kind. He and Ruby are—were—the perfect match. Two quirky, fun, self-described geeks. It was baffling when it ended. I was holding out hope they'd get back together, but a few months ago I ran into him coming out of the *Intelligencer Journal* building, arm around a bubbly young woman. He dropped his arm when he recognized me and introduced her as a work colleague. He asked about Roddy and Ruby and sent his regards—which I did *not* relay. Maybe it was a casual hug for a fellow news reporter, but it looked cozier than that.

Roddy slips out of his chef's apron. "Time to eat!"

Gail sets the vase of flowers at the end of the twelve-foot reclaimed wood table. "Thanks again, Ruby. I can't wait to take these home. They'll be the perfect pop of color on my kitchen counter."

Gail lives in a two-story townhouse in Lincoln Gardens, but as far as I can tell, spends most of her time at Mirabella. Things aren't like they used to be. When I was young, moving in together without being married was still frowned upon. But now it's no big deal. Why not combine your resources rather than keeping two households going? Myrtle even encouraged a few of her kids to *shack up* (her words, not mine). Mostly, I think she was just good and ready for a few of them to move out of the house. With nine of them, who could blame her? Anyhow, after four years of dating, I think *shacking up* should be on Roddy and Gail's horizon, too.

"Have a seat everyone," Roddy says.

I choose one of the ten vintage, leather and wood dining chairs a few down from the head of the table. Jed slides in to my right and Gail to my left. Donald sits across from me. Roddy plates the food and Ruby serves.

"Wow," Jed says as Ruby slides the meal in front of him. "I didn't know I was in for fine dining. Did you help cook this?"

The rest of us titter with amusement. Ruby's got plenty of talents, but cooking sure isn't one of them. She's mastered exactly two dishes: eggs and spaghetti.

Ruby's freckled nose crinkles. "Not a chance. It would be inedible. I'm such a bad cook I use the smoke alarm as a timer. This is all Roddy."

When she and Roddy are seated, she lifts her glass of tea and offers a toast. "To the most amazing crew ever! Roddy and I are very grateful for your help."

I'd do anything for Roddy and Ruby. I met them at the Historical Society right after their grandmother died. They took her death hard, especially Ruby. Even after they solved Evie's grand funeral puzzle, Ruby found excuses to visit me. Despite being in her thirties, I could tell she needed some momma-bear loving. With no kids of my own—though I completely adore Myrtle's nine—I have plenty to give.

Over time, cookies and coffees turned to lunches, lunches turned to dinners, and dinners turned to weekend outings. We sort of adopted each other and now I consider Ruby and Roddy family.

*****

After a lovely dinner full of good food and good conversation, we get to work. The demands of owning your own business can be overwhelming, so we all try to help Ruby and Roddy when we can. For this event, Gail will keep her tips as bartender, but Jed is the only one receiving pay. Neither Donald or I are tech savvy enough to be the deejay, so Ruby had to enlist paid help.

Ruby digs a file folder and notepad from her yellow Make A Splash! bag. “So first off everyone. Themed costumes aren’t required, but it would add to the ambience if you all were dressed up.”

Roddy shakes his head. “Nope. I can’t have a costume flapping around when I’m preparing food. Chef’s jacket for me.”

Gail pouts at Roddy. “Party pooper. Well, I’m dressing up.”

“Let me guess,” Roddy says. “Something western. Bandit Queen?”

She presses her lips together in a coy smile. “Not even close. You’ll just have to wait and see.”

Donald strokes his short, white beard. “I’m sure I can come up with something.”

Ruby smiles. “Thanks, Dad.”

Jed takes a swig of his beer, then wipes his mouth with the back of his hand. “Ruby, you may not require us to dress up, but my husband Felix? That man lives for a theme. He’s had our costumes planned for weeks.”

“Me too,” I say. “Liza, Shampoodles, and I have ensemble costumes, and they are humdingers!”

Ruby laughs. “Oh, that is fantastic! Even the dog will be dressed up. That’s so awesome everyone. Everyone but stick-in-the-mud Roddy, that is.” She sticks her tongue out at him and he responds in kind. “This party is going to be one for the books!” She opens her file folder. “Okay, let’s go over the details. Jed, do you want to start with your plans for music?”

“Sure.” He pulls a crumpled paper from the front pocket of his jeans. “Here are a couple of my suggestions. *Smooth Criminal* by Michael Jackson. *Money* by Pink Floyd. *Gimme the Loot* by The Notorious B.I.G. And *Bank Robber* by The Clash.”

Ruby’s green eyes twinkle and her wide smile puffs up her cheeks like apples. “I love it! Who knew there were so many bank robbery related songs? That’s exactly what I’m looking for. Will you have enough music to make it through the event?”

“Yep. I’ve got it covered.”

“Perfect.” Ruby flips through her notes and slides a stack of index cards across the table to Gail. “I’ve created recipes for some criminally delicious signature cocktails: The Getaway, Silent Alarm, and Safecracker. And two tasty mocktails: Alibi and the Copper.”

“Fun names.” Gail scans the cards. “Easy to make, too. I’ll have no problem.”

Roddy kisses her cheek. “Thanks, babe. We appreciate the help.”

Gail rubs her hands together like a greedy cartoon villain. “Hopefully the tips will be generous. School loans, you know.”

Ruby laughs. “It’s mostly the country-club crowd, so fingers crossed.”

Roddy turns to Donald. “Donald, Ruby said you’re down with helping with food service.”

Donald pats the top of Roddy’s hand. “Of course, son. Whatever I can do to help.”

Roddy pulls his hand back quick as a wink, then rakes it through his shaggy blond hair in a clumsy attempt to hide how jumpy Donald's touch—and the word *son*—makes him.

Ruby dove head first into her new father/daughter relationship. *Dad* rolls off her tongue like she's been saying it her whole life. Roddy and Donald's paths have been bumpier. From what Ruby told me, Roddy—thanks to Evie's encouragement—built up Roderick Finch, the dead soldier he thought was his father, to be a hero. When Roddy learned that his "real" father was a drunk who more or less sold him and Ruby to Evie, it knocked the wind right out of him. Rightfully so.

Ruby said that unpacking all the baggage between them is taking longer than she expected. But from my view, Roddy and Donald respect and like—if not love—each other. Sure, there's still work to be done. Roddy's not the trusting type, so it'll take more time. But I think they're moving in the right direction.

Roddy shoots me a loving smile. "And now to my star baker. Millicent, in addition to the dozens of hundred-dollar-bill cookies, we'd like a massive money-bag-shaped birthday cake. Are you game?"

I wave my hand dismissively. "I'm happiest when I have a dusting of flour on my face."

Ruby interjects. "About the flour. We do have two gluten-free guests, so you'll have to accommodate for them."

"One of my nieces is allergic to gluten. Poor child. Well, not so much of a child anymore, she's nearly forty and is a family doctor, which really comes in handy. We all call her for free medical advice. With as big as the family is, if she kept a running tab, we'd probably owe her millions. Just last week, I had a … Oh, mercy me! Here I am, babbling again. Gluten-free is no problem."

Ruby makes a check mark on her paper. "Great, just one more allergy. Jed's brother Isaac is severely allergic to peanuts. So, no peanut products anywhere near where you're baking for the party."

My mind flies back to Amanda's upset over Isaac's gallivanting. Anger bubbles up in my flabby belly. My nostrils flare and my face scrunches up like a shriveled potato. A little scare might knock some sense into him. The second I think it, guilt nips at me. It's not right to wish trouble on anybody. No matter how much of a rat fink he is.

"In fact, no peanuts, period," Ruby says, emphatically tapping the point of her pen into the paper. "Not even on your breath. Got it, everyone?"

"Yeah, wouldn't want my *dear* brother to have an allergic reaction. Might ruin his night," Jed says.

His sarcasm hangs sour in the air, like milk gone bad. I'm guessing he knows about Connie. Jed and Amanda are close; closer than Jed and Isaac. Isaac's cheating would definitely rile him.

Ruby tenses her jaw and her forehead lines with wrinkles. "Don't even joke, because it would sure ruin mine and Roddy's. We want the night to be memorable for the right reasons."

Everyone nods along, but a little knot tightens in my belly. With things already touchy between Amanda and Isaac, I just hope "memorable" means fun and not the kind of thing folks whisper about later.

5 ~ Millicent

I'm feeling twitchy after a restless night's sleep. Ruby and Roddy's pre-party nerves rubbed off on me. I never get worked up over baking, but now I've got butterflies. But Liza's company and some comfort food ought to calm me down.

The Revere Tavern's enclosed porch is filled with wispy ferns and hanging spider plants. Each white-clothed table has a vase of delicate pink roses. Piano music floats into the space like the warm breeze flowing through the screens. Liza and I eat here often. I come for the Kennett Square stuffed mushrooms and the Snapper Turtle soup. She comes for the spirits that haunt the historic 1740 building.

After settling Shampoodles in her carrier under the table, Liza flips her shiny, gunmetal-gray tresses over her shoulder. My gray curls look like tarnished silver in comparison. Maybe I should have her spruce them up. I don't have much experience with hair salons. My color is au naturel and I cut my own hair, but Myrtle's been bugging me to get a makeover. She jokes that I look too old to be her twin.

The waiter brings Liza's summer salad and my mushrooms and soup. Shampoodles' ears perk up.

Liza points a burgundy fingernail at her fur baby. Her silver bangles clink as they slide to her wrist. "See, she feels the presence of those who crossed over, too."

"Mmm," I say, squeezing a squirt of fresh lemon juice onto the chunky crab imperial stuffing.

I'm betting Shampoodles smells the food, but whatever Liza wants to believe. Despite her woo-woo ways, Liza and I are good friends.

The spicy scent of Old Bay seasoning encourages me to dig in. Nothing like the earthiness of mushrooms paired with crab.

"Have you talked to Amanda this week?"

Liza nods as she chews. "I have. She was surprisingly calm."

My jitters start to settle with the first spoonful of soup. "Oh, that's good." I take another few slurps for good measure. "Calm is an improvement, I think. Amanda was pretty frazzled when she first found out about Connie. I suppose after a while you become immune."

Liza slips a bit of celery to Shampoodles. "It's good for her breath." She wipes her fingers on her cloth napkin. "You know, I expected this. When I did Amanda's tarot reading months ago, the cards alluded to it."

I didn't need tarot cards to predict Isaac's behavior. Once a cheater, always a cheater.

"Did your cards tell you it'd be with Connie? I mean, that's too close to home."

She sighs. "The cards aren't *that* specific, Millicent. But I agree. At least when he dallied with coeds the scandal didn't spread throughout Amanda's peer group. Connie is one of my clients."

"She is? Did you have any idea she was sleeping with Isaac?"

Liza twists one of her silver rings. "Not an inkling. She mostly gossips about the other country club women."

"Hmm. The tables have turned, haven't they? I bet collagen-plumped lips are flapping all over town about Connie. Do you think Ed knows?"

Liza shrugs her shoulders and raises her sculpted eyebrows. "No idea. You'd think he'd want to ring Isaac's neck if he did."

"Hmm." I let out a little huff. "I've got to admit; the thought's crossed my mind. Ed better get in line."

"Behind me, too!" Liza agrees.

Shampoodles yips from the carrier.

We laugh in unison. Liza's ends with her typical snort, a quirk that makes her even more endearing to me.

"Shammie wants a spot in line too," I say with a chuckle.

Liza grins. "That or she has to pee. Better be on the safe side. I'll be right back."

The wide legs of Liza's flowing jumpsuit billow as she hurries out the side door into the small yard of the restaurant. As I watch Shammie sniff every blade of grass, I think about Amanda's revelation that she met someone. Once Shampoodles completes her business, Liza scoops her up and carries her inside, tucking her back into her carrier.

After scooting her chair in, Liza lays the napkin on her lap. "You know what other card I pulled in Amanda's reading?"

I cut into my last mushroom. "What?"

"The death card."

I choke on the crab meat and glower at Liza. "Holy Toledo, Liza! That's horrible. And morbid."

"No, it's not. Not at all. Sure, the death card can bring unexpected, difficult, or even traumatic events—"

"Hmph. Yeah, I'd say death is pretty traumatic."

Her irritated sigh lifts her long, white-streaked bangs off her forehead. "Millicent, after all these years, have I taught you nothing about tarot? Readers never predict physical death. The death card indicates a time of change and new beginnings. And Saturday is a new moon, perfect for a new beginning."

"Okay? What am I missing?"

"Change and newness are coming to Amanda's life. I think it may mean a new man."

I drop my fork and it clatters to the ground. "Shut the front door. Did the cards really say that?"

Liza's elegantly contoured eyebrows furrow. "Yes. Why is your mouth hanging open, Millicent?"

"Amanda told me she's met someone. Someone she wants to pursue, maybe even spend her life with."

Liza's smile is wide, showing off bright white teeth. "The cards never lie."

An eeriness settles over my shoulders. It's not the first time Liza's predictions have come true. I eat more hot soup to rid me of my chill.

Liza dives back into her salad. "So, who is this mystery man?"

I finish off the last of the dark, rich broth. "She didn't tell me." The memory of a black truck and Donald's strange behavior when Amanda was mentioned pops into my head. "Do you know Donald Fraser?"

"Roddy and Ruby's dad?"

"Uh-huh."

Shampoodles raises her head and stares adoringly at Liza. Liza gives her a slice of strawberry. "It's packed with nutrients." The waiter brings me a clean fork and fills our water glasses. Liza downs half of hers. "I know of him, but haven't met him. Why?"

"Does Amanda know him?"

"Unless he's a member of the country club, I doubt it. That's the crowd she and Isaac run with. Again, why?"

I shake my head and dab the corners of my mouth. "Never mind."

Liza rests her hand on mine. "Millicent, your jittery energy is flowing into me. Spill. Why did you ask about Donald?"

I twist my linen napkin. "I thought I saw him leaving Amanda's house, but she claimed it was the gardener."

Her dark-chocolate eyes dance with intrigue. "You think her new man is Donald?"

I shrug. "The thought crossed my mind."

"He'll be at the party, won't he?"

"He will."

She pushes up her sleeve, showing me the raised hair on her arms. "I can feel it, Millicent. Ethan's party is going to be an unforgettable event."

6 ~ Ruby

Now that the guests have started to arrive, my pre-event jitters shift into adrenaline-laced efficiency. This is my payoff (and the money's not bad either). I thrive on watching weeks of ideas, lists, and ridiculously detailed seating charts come to life exactly the way I pictured them. Every little detail I worried and fussed over is doing its job, shaping the exact atmosphere I envisioned. Seeing my clients and their guests light up makes it all worth it.

Though the way I ended up here was disheartening—unchecked sexual harassment and a boss basically telling me to "suck it up, buttercup"—owning your own business isn't for the faint of heart, I wouldn't trade it for anything. Indulging my creativity, having my borderline obsessiveness be an asset, and channeling my take-charge attitude (sometimes referred to as bossiness) into my super-power—I custom-tailored this career just for me.

With the help of Sheriff Stephanie and her deputy, Janelle, the tables and chairs are arranged, Roddy and Donald are preparing the buffet to be set up, and Gail (sporting a super short, curly brown wig, and a machine gun strapped on her shoulder) is mixing signature cocktails for the arriving guests.

I mosey over to Jed's makeshift deejay booth. He's wearing a blue boilersuit, white helmet, and goggles, and flipping CDs as skillfully as a longtime short-order cook flipping pancakes. And his husband Felix, inky-dark hair slicked back (with added 1960's long sideburns that surprisingly suit his Korean features), looks dashing in a bespoke pink suit, white silk shirt and white tie, as he grooves to the bank-robber themed playlist.

I hazard a guess at their costumes. "*Italian Job*?"

"Nailed it," Felix says, preening.

Jed rolls his eyes. "Yeah, I didn't even rank high enough to be a real character. No, no. I get to be a Mini Cooper driver."

Felix pastes on a patronizing, but loving grin. "But, Jed, the drivers were vital to the plot."

Jed dons a scowl and grumbles, "Don't think I don't know you used this costume party as an excuse to buy yourself a pink suit, Felix."

Felix tilts his head, then spreads his arms wide. "But you have to admit, I do look fabulous."

Jed's grumpy expression melts into a smile. "That you do."

I chuckle at their banter. "Well, clearly you two have got this covered. The tunes are fantastic. Keep 'em coming."

Their easy affection leaves me smiling as I head toward Clarice and Ethan at the bank's front door.

Ethan, Clarice, and their sons were able to break into the safe in less than thirty of the allotted forty-five minutes. Unlike Roddy and me, loitering in the bottom twenty-five percent. (Gigi would be so disappointed.)

"And here are the safecrackers. Are you considering a career switch?" I joke.

Ethan's laugh is hearty. "Only if it comes with health insurance."

I notice traffic piling up on Market Street as folks try to find street parking, not realizing the bank has its own lot in the back.

"Clarice, I'm going to step outside and direct cars."

The summer night is sultry, and the long-sleeved, black-and-white striped jumpsuit I'm wearing sticks to my skin. My hair is damp under my orange wig and wide-brimmed black hat, and sweat pools behind the black mask covering my eyes. I wave cars into the alley leading to the parking lot.

Raised voices catch my attention. About a half a block down, Amanda and Isaac Stone, wearing Bonnie and Clyde costumes are in a heated discussion. He lays his hand on her forearm and she pulls away, slamming the door of their sleek Mercedes.

Her words carry. “Don’t touch me, Isaac.”

I can’t hear his response, but he shoves his hands in his pockets and bows his head.

She adjusts her tan beret and smooths her skirt. “I can’t wait to get this night over with.”

I turn at a tap on my shoulder.

Liza and Millicent have arrived, channeling Robin Hood and Little John respectively. Even Shampoodles is wearing a green felt jacket and green wool bycocket with a jaunty feather.

My wide smile crinkles the corners of my eyes. “You look amazing!”

Millicent bows. “I told you they were humdingers.”

Liza twirls in a circle to give me the full effect. Shampoodles yips as Amanda and Isaac storm towards the entrance.

“Ladies,” Isaac says, tipping his Fedora.

Liza sucks in her breath, then shoots Millicent a look that I can’t quite read. Millicent’s jaw clenches. Both women turn their backs on Isaac, chatting with Amanda too quietly for me to hear.

“I’m heading to the bar,” Isaac announces to me, and heads inside.

Millicent squeezes Amanda’s arm. “We’re here if you need us.”

Liza cocks Amanda’s beret at a jaunty angle and winks. “Remember, new moon. New beginnings.”

Amanda gives one sharp nod.

Tense energy radiates from the Merry Men crew like a cloud discharging lightning. I lean in and whisper to Millicent. “Are you okay?”

She waves her hand pooh-poohing me. “Fine. Fine. Just social anxiety.”

Millicent Wagner does not suffer from social anxiety. What in the world is going on?

Before I have a chance to question her more, the Joker and Catwoman are standing in front of me. Despite the painted-on smile, Joker looks anything but happy and Catwoman's claws are out.

"Ed and Connie Baker." His introduction is clipped.

Millicent's nose crinkles, like she smells something rotten. Liza's smile looks fake. "Hi Connie, nice to see you."

Connie digs her mini appointment book from her purse. "Oh, Liza. I've been meaning to call. I need to get in for a color touch-up and trim. I have an awards banquet—"

Red creeps up Ed's beefy neck, and he pulls Connie's arm towards the entrance. "Do that later. I need a drink."

What's with all the drama? It's not even a full moon.

Connie drops her planner back into her purse and says to Liza, "I'll call you."

I smile and motion Joker and Catwoman to the front door. "Feel free to head inside. Cocktails and mocktails are being served."

"I'll be at the bar," Ed says, striding ahead of his wife into the bank. She hurries after him.

With all the sniping that's going on, I'm thinking I could use one, too. And the night hasn't even begun. I dash inside and, regardless of my urge, grab an Alibi (basically a virgin Moscow Mule). The copper cup is icy cold and I press it to my temple on my way back outside.

"Clarice, this is amazing," I hear Ethan say to his wife as I pass them.

"Ruby has done an excellent job," Clarice agrees.

Happiness ripples through me. A thrilled customer is the best reward for my hard work (and it's great for word-of-mouth, too).

I return to my post on Market Street and take a long swallow of my cold Alibi. The spicy ginger beer offers just the right amount of bite. Gail's doing a terrific job as a mixologist. Though Roddy has decreed pushiness is verboten (that's good for at least a point, Gigi), I'd love to have Gail as a sister-in-law. Of course, Roddy used to say the same about Marty.

A sharp pang of regret lodges in my stomach. The trauma around Roddy's divorce from Clara is his reason for taking it snail slow with Gail. Catching his wife and his best friend tangled in his own sheets really did a number on him. Plus, discovering Gigi's lie—tearing the storybook pages of our war-hero dad right out of their binding and replacing them with tattered scraps of a struggling man who bartered us away—didn't exactly help him gain traction in the trust department.

My reasons for derailing my relationship with Marty are more complicated. Despite a shelf full of self-help tomes and eleven months of soul searching, I don't fully understand them myself. Roddy and Dad (well, most people I know) claim I wear rose-colored glasses. They're right. I'm an optimist, and I admit my sunny outlook can sometimes border on being unrealistic. But from what I've gleaned from Dr. Lauter's enlightening *Relationship Repair Manual*, when it comes to romance, I'm a relationship saboteur. I allow my fear of hurt and abandonment (cue the my-mom-died-in-childbirth violins) to control the narrative. Instead of waiting for the other shoe to drop, I drop it myself, feeling safer when I control the fall rather than risking a surprise crash.

So, when I was with Marty, I kept looking for his fatal flaw; the one quirk or habit that would send me running for the hills. For three years, Marty tolerated my nitpicking and constant insecurity. He was patient with my fears and uncertainty. But when I panicked and backed out of having him move in with me, that was the straw that broke Marty's back. I had worn him down. He was done with me waiting for the you-know-what to hit the fan and broke up with me. Apparently, I am really good at getting in my own way. But I'm working on it.

A chorus of female voices singing the Powerpuff Girls' theme song interrupts my wallowing, and three superheroes step in front of me, escorted by the Bank Robbing Gang. Their costumes are on the money (pun intended).

I flip a thumbs up. "If we were having a best costume contest, you'd win!"

The orange-haired superhero looks me up and down. "You're Hamburglar, right?"

I give my best impression. "Robble! Robble!"

She lifts her hand for a high-five. "You did it justice."

"Thanks!" I escort the three couples to the door of the bank. "Clarice, Ethan, the Power Puff crew has arrived."

"Ah, my book buddies." Ethan chuckles. "Cartoon characters? I thought your costumes would be more … historic. Like theirs," he says pointing to a pair of female pirates sauntering up the sidewalk.

"Ahoy mateys," the pirates chime in unison as they reach the group.

Ethan claps his hands, clearly delighted at his friends' costumes. "*Pirate Queens* in the flesh. I see our current book club read has inspired your costumes. Bravo!"

The red-haired pirate tips her leather tricorn hat. "Aargh. At your service."

The dark-haired pirate swishes a fake sword. "Happy Birthday, Ethan. May your blade always be wet and your powder dry."

I'm super stoked about the creativity in costumes. I really thought we'd have a bank full of Bonnie and Clydes.

Speak of the devil … A fuming Bonnie/Amanda marches out the door, with a stormy-faced Clyde/Isaac trailing close behind.

"Amanda, Isaac," Ethan says, stopping their huffy exit. "I want to introduce you to my book club friends."

After a quick round of introductions, Ethan and Clarice show his book club friends to the bar and Amanda and Isaac continue around the side of the bank, still within my earshot.

"You kissed her. Right in front of me. Right in front of everyone. Have you not humiliated me enough?" Amanda hisses at Isaac.

"It was a peck on the cheek, for god's sake, Amanda. Don't be so dramatic."

"Dramatic? Dramatic?" Amanda's volume and pitch rise with each word. "Isaac Stone, you haven't begun to see drama. I promise you that."

Tension clamps down on my shoulders, and the hair on the back of my neck stands on end, like it does when something's about to go sideways. Booze and bickering couples can be a party planner's worst nightmare. Anxiety prickles my skin, but I push it down. It's just a spat. They'll work it out. I'm just being a worrywart.

Everything will be fine.

7 ~ Millicent

Liza—carrying Shammie in a bag she whipped up to resemble Robin Hood's quiver—and I mosey over to the bar, where Gail mixes drinks like a pro.

"Why, if it isn't the infamous Machine Gun Molly in the flesh," I say to Gail. "Should I tip my bycocket or dive for cover?"

Chuckling, she wipes her hands on a white bar towel. "The only shots I'm making tonight are booze filled." Spotting Shammie, her eyes dance with delight. "Oh my! Who is this adorable fluff ball?"

Liza waves Shammie's paw at Gail. "Her name is Shampoodles."

Shammie preens as Gail fusses over her. "What a sweet pup. It's so nice to meet you Shampoodles. Look at those eyes. You're just the cutest little thing."

"Gail," I say. "This is my friend Liza."

Gail drags her focus from Shammie. "Hi Liza. Your dog is absolutely wonderful."

Liza smiles like a proud mama. "I agree."

After a few more air kisses for Shammie, Gail asks, "Does this little cutie need some water?"

Liza shakes her head. "That's so sweet to think of her, but she's good. I brought her own special bowl."

I lean against the bar to take a little weight off my hip. "Yoohoo. I could use something to wet my whistle."

Gail blushes. "Oh brother. Sorry, Millicent. You know me, once I spot an animal, I've got tunnel vision."

I hitch my thumb towards Gail. "Liza, this one just landed a job at a large animal vet clinic. Fits her, don't you think?"

Liza offers a knowing little smile. "I would've guessed that. Gail, your aura has this lovely, calm, green-gold energy that would make an animal trust you instantly. Works for bar-tending, too. Tame the human beasts."

Gail snickers. "There are a few here tonight that need taming, for sure."

Liza notices my grimace as I shift my weight to my other foot. "We better find you a seat, Millicent. I can tell you're uncomfortable. Maybe a little alcohol will dull the pain."

I shake my head. "I'll stick with ibuprofen. Don't want to trade hip pain for a hangover. So, Molly, have you got something sweet with no liquor?"

"One Copper coming right up." She turns to Liza. "And for you."

"The absolute opposite of Millicent."

Gail's grin is edged with amusement. "A Safecracker it is."

I sneak a twenty into the tip jar as she's making our drinks. She would fuss if she saw me do it.

Liza smuggles an orange slice from the bar's garnish station into Shammie's carrier. "Boosts her immunity." She points her chin towards the tellers' counter turned buffet table. "Roddy is certainly in his element, isn't he?"

Roddy's arms and hands move fast, the way a bandleader might wave his baton, as he sets out plate after plate of small, tempting bites on sleek black serving trays. The blond hairs on the back of his neck curl up, covering the edges of his chef's hat.

My bycocket shifts when I nod my head, and I pin it back in place. "It's hard to believe he used to teach accounting. I think he was born with butter in his veins."

Gail, overhearing my comment, laughs. "My expanding waist will attest to that." She hands us our drinks.

I roll my eyes and take a sip of my mocktail. "Pshaw. You're barely a wisp."

Iris, an old friend of Amanda's and a new volunteer at Violet House, saunters up to the bar, wearing a curve-hugging police uniform, a sturdy-looking fellow with a weathered sort of charm at her side. She squeezes my shoulder. "Millicent. Liza. Great to see you." She points at the man dressed in a black and white striped jumpsuit. "This is my husband, Hank."

"Prisoner 7784. Pleased to meet you, both. I'd shake hands but …" He lifts his arms to show handcuffed wrists.

Liza wags her finger. "Iris, I didn't know you had a thing for bad boys."

Iris titters. "Don't we all?"

My cheeks burn like city streets on a summer day when thoughts of my Italian fiancée pop into my head. Four passionate months. Mercy me, I'm getting hot and bothered just thinking of him. I press the cold cup to my face. Closest I ever came to marriage … Aah, best to tuck that story away for another time. My temperature settles as I push my memories back where they belong and return to today.

Prisoner Hank stuffs a ten in the tip jar, thanks Gail, and, using two handcuffed hands, guzzles half his drink. He juts his stubbled chin towards Roddy. "Oh, there's the Rodster."

"You know Roddy?" I ask.

"Yeah. I've played basketball with him a couple times." He jerks his head in Roddy's direction. "C'mon Officer Cutie, let's go say a quick hi."

Iris collects her drink. "I'll talk with you later."

I nod. "Want us to save you and Hank a seat?"

Her slicked back hair doesn't move when she shakes her head. "No thanks. We'll probably sit with Amanda and Isaac."

Hank snorts. "Not a snowball's chance in hell."

"Hank!" Iris snaps, reprimanding her husband.

He shrugs and says, "Nice to meet you," to me and Liza before heading over to Roddy.

Iris's cheeks are red from embarrassment. "Sorry about that."

Liza and I wave it off.

"Iris," Hank calls, holding up his hands. "Unlock me."

She sighs. "If only I could put a lock on his mouth, before he shoves his foot in it again." She says goodbye and hurries over to her husband.

"Wonder what his issue with Amanda and Isaac is?" I say to Liza as we make our way to a table.

She pulls Shampoodles out from her carrier and settles her under the table. "Well, his aura is dark orange, so …"

I stifle my eye roll. "You're going to have to give me more than that, Liza."

"Orange can mean jealousy, bitterness, or a bruised ego."

"Jealousy? You think Isaac was diddling with Iris, too? Amanda and Iris are really close friends. I think they were even college roommates. Would Iris really be so cold?"

Liza adds a coating of shiny gloss to her lips. "It's not out of the realm of possibility. Even nice people can be cruel. Or maybe Hank is Amanda's new man."

I'm taken aback. "No way. He's married and too young." I cast my eyes to Donald, looking debonair in a black vest over a crisp white shirt with sleeve garters and a bow tie, and an old-time green banker's visor. "He's a much more logical option."

Liza follows my gaze. Donald moves the prepared trays into the warming towers, twisting and turning the platters to just the right position, before dusting them with what I assume is some kind of exotic, punchy spice. Roddy's food, after all, is known for its bold, unusual flavors. To attempt to match his style, I even upped my cookie game, using orange zest and cardamom for the hundred-dollar-bill batter, and root beer and white chocolate in the fifty-dollar-bill batter. And the money-bag cake is strawberry champagne. All pretty darn tasty, if I do say so myself.

Liza taps gold fingernails on her chin. "Hmm. Fit and trim. Strong jaw. Mesmerizing green eyes. Elegant white hair and fashionable super-short Balbo beard. I can see why Amanda would be interested."

I wrinkle my nose, irritated at this whole conversation. "Like I said, Donald is more likely than Hank, but I still don't see it. Donald is unassuming, not country-club, and a homebody rather than a social climber. Reserved, professorial, just not Amanda's type."

Liza crosses her arms. "What's her type? Self-important cheater?"

"Good point."

"Ladies," Clarice says, fluttering over to our table. "Love your costumes. You too, Shampoodles," she coos, bending down to pet Liza's poodle. "And Millicent, the cake and cookies look fabulous. I can't wait to taste them. I'm sure none will be left by the end of the night."

I get all warm and gooey inside, like the center of a chocolate lava cake. "Glad you're happy with them."

She squeezes my hand. "Thank you so much for recommending Ruby and Roddy. So far, the party has been better than I could've imagined and I can't wait for the guests to taste Roddy's food. From the samples he provided when I booked him, I know it's to die for."

Now I'm feeling downright bubbly with pride. Last time I felt this way, my niece got accepted at Harvard Law School. "That's wonderful, Clarice. They really do give it their all."

She smiles. "That's obvious in the quality of their work."

A red-faced Amanda is making a beeline for the bar.

"Amanda," Clarice calls. "Join us for a moment. I wanted to chat about the Violet House Friendsgiving event."

Amanda's jaw tightens, but she pastes a bright smile on her face, and she and Clarice air kiss. "Clarice, this party is spectacular. Fresh and fun, and so Ethan."

Clarice's botoxed forehead barely moves with her smile. "He's loving it. I was just telling Millicent how pleased I am with Make A Splash! Event Planning. I'd use Ruby again in a heartbeat."

"Good to know," Amanda says, looking longingly at the bar.

Clarice leans her manicured hands on the back of the folding chair. "I must get back to mingling, but I did want to let the three of you know, Kids Haven Daycare will be donating childcare for the night of the gala."

Liza claps her hands in delight. "Brilliant!"

I stand and hug Clarice. "Thanks so much for making that happen. The women deserve a special night for themselves."

"Yes, thanks. That's wonderful." Amanda says with less exuberance than expected. It's clear her marital troubles are weighing heavily on her.

Clarice waves. "Well, gals, enjoy! I'll visit with you again later."

"How are you holding up?" I ask Amanda, when Clarice is out of earshot.

Though Amanda's makeup is artfully applied, she can't hide the toll of her distress. "He had the audacity to kiss her. Can you imagine? He has pushed me too far. Way too far."

My mouth drops open. "What? He kissed her? Here?"

Amanda's jaw clenches. "Yes, and then he had the nerve to say, 'You're overreacting. It was just a peck on the cheek.' A peck that sent rumors rippling through the guests, mind you. I look like such a fool."

I wrap my flabby arms around her thin frame, inhaling the scent of her signature citrusy bergamot perfume. "Oh honey, we haven't heard a word of gossip, but you don't have to stay. I'll take you home if you want."

Her body tenses and she pulls out of my hug. “No! I refuse to let him ruin one more minute. I’m done with his philandering.” She smooths her blonde bob. “I need a drink. I’ll talk to you later.” Spine held ramrod straight, she strides to the bar.

I shake my head, wishing I could offer more than a hug. “Poor Amanda.”

Liza tilts her head towards the bar. “Look who’s joining her.”

Donald saunters over to Amanda, resting his hand on the small of her back. He whispers something in her ear. Amanda drops her face into her hand and squeezes her temple, then nods. Donald collects two copper mule cups, and they walk out the side door of the bank, into the alley.

My eyes feel too big for my sockets.

Liza flips her palms up and shrugs. “I told you; the cards don’t lie. New moon. New man.”

Heavens to Betsy. I think she may be right.

8 ~ Ruby

My worries have quieted as the guests relax into the evening, sipping their cocktails and swaying to Jed's clever choice of music. As I stroll over to Clarice, I tune into the chatter, listening for anything that might need attention. When Clarice spots me, I ask if she's ready for Roddy to open the buffet.

She checks her rose gold Cartier watch. "Not quite yet. In ten minutes or so. I want to offer a toast to Ethan and then announce it's open. Can I use the microphone?"

"Of course. I'll tell Jed. Just let him know when you're ready."

She nods and resumes mingling.

Catching snippets of conversations as I go, I head to the deejay booth.

One woman says, "Marjorie is pregnant at age forty-two. Can you believe it?"

Her friend groans. "Good God, no! Just shoot me if that ever happens to me."

Joker Ed downs his Silent Alarm and sets the glass beside two other empties. He sways when he stands, grabbing the chairback to steady himself. "I need another whiskey."

"Ed," Catwoman Connie says, hesitance clear in her voice. "Don't you think you've had enough?"

"What I've had enough of is you," he grinds out between clenched teeth.

Connie glares at her husband. "I'm sorry your ego is bruised, but there's no need to make a fool of yourself."

I pretend not to have heard and hurry past the table.

Pink-suited Felix lounges against the wall beside Jed's set up. "We're running out of time, Jed. Since *you* can't make it happen, I will."

Jed adjusts a few buttons on his song mixer, adding more bass to Clapton's *I Shot the Sheriff*. "Now is not the time to discuss this, Felix. I'm working."

Felix huffs. "A gig here and there isn't going to pay for what we need."

This party has enough relationship drama to fill an issue of *Soap Opera Weekly*. If I hadn't already bitten my nails to the quick, I'd be gnawing on them now.

Jed spots me and reaches out for a lifeline. "Ruby, I bet you have some job that Felix can help with."

"Well," I say scanning the room. "Maybe Gail could use some help. Or Roddy. We're about to open the buffet."

"Roddy it is. I'll help that gorgeous hunk of a man anytime," he says, sticking his tongue out at his husband teasingly.

Jed laughs and flips his hand towards the buffet. "Go drool over there." He takes off his white helmet. "Better," he says, mopping his sweaty head. "Felix is adamant I stay in full costume, but I'm sweating like Mick Jagger in leather pants."

I chuckle. "If you start swaggering and strutting like Jagger, I might have to add 'crowd control' to my job title."

"Don't worry. I'm too old to move my hips like that."

"Good. I don't have a contingency plan for a pulled groin. Anyway, Clarice would like to use your microphone to offer a toast."

Jed gives me a thumbs-up (definitely *not* a Jagger move). "Not a problem," he says, queueing up the next song.

I wander over to the food. Felix is wiping dribbles from the platters, Dad is checking the heat source under the warming trays, and Roddy is beaming as he surveys all his creations.

Even though I'm still on the fence about using Gigi's inheritance—it's just sitting in my savings account—I'm glad Roddy used it to launch Chef's Secret. He was meant to cook. We may have shared a womb, but clearly, he hogged all the culinary genes.

He opens his arms, presenting his buffet. "We're ready when you are, Ruby."

My mouth waters at the tempting scents wafting from the table. "As soon as Clarice toasts Ethan, she'll announce the buffet is open. Just a few more minutes."

He joins me in front of the tellers' booth and snaps a few photos for advertising, then wraps his arm around me. "We did good, Sis. This one will go down in the books as a win."

I hug him back. He's right. I got organization—he got seasoning. We make a good team.

Out of the corner of my eye, I catch Clarice waving at me. "Duty calls." I hurry over to her. "What's up?"

"Ruby, this is Tabitha. A 60th anniversary party for her parents is on her horizon and I told her she must meet you."

Tabitha reaches her hand up from the armrest of her wheelchair. "If you're half as good as Clarice's gushing, you're excellent."

My hand flutters to my chest and I blush. "Thank you so much, Clarice. I really appreciate it."

Clarice waves her hand around the room. "You earned the recommendation. I'll leave you to it."

I pull up a chair and sit beside Tabitha. "So, how do you know Clarice?"

"I only know Clarice in passing, but our husbands, along with Isaac and Bob are poker buddies. They have a monthly game. I swear the guys only invite Oscar—that's my husband—because they can clean him out." She smiles. "We could probably pay off our mortgage with all his losses over the years."

I wince, my eyebrows lifting in sympathy. "Yikes. Expensive hobby."

She waves her hand dismissively, then laughs, twisting a tennis bracelet on her wrist. "I can't really complain, since diamonds are mine."

I never understood lapidary lust (I deserve at least ten points for that one, Gigi). Give me quirky vintage earrings or a bracelet that looks like it was made during a family craft night. At least those come with stories.

"Anyway," Tabitha says. "I'd like a creative party for my parents. About a hundred guests—all ages from newborns to golden oldies. Believe it or not, even though they're both in their eighties, my folks are Revolutionary war reenactors, so maybe some kind of historical theme?"

Mop caps and powdered wigs pop into my brain, along with Paul Revere races and musket duels. Excitement at the prospect of planning a colonial era party ripples through me. "Ooh! I'm all about that!"

"Obviously, I'll need a caterer, too. Can your brother do themed menus?"

For a hundred-person job, I'm sure Roddy can figure it out.

"Oh, absolutely. Tell you what, give me your number. Roddy and I will work up a proposal in the next week or two and send it over to you."

"Perfect."

I type Tabitha's number in my phone and thank her for the opportunity to pitch my ideas. As I'm making my way over to mention the job to Roddy, I see Isaac grab the back of Janelle's deputy costume as she's passing his table. She turns and glares at him.

"You work here, don't you?" He waggles his empty cocktail glass in front of her. "How about you get me a drink?"

Her jaw clenches and the veins at her temples pulse. "Get it yourself, *Coach*." She almost spits his title at him.

He draws back, stunned at her rudeness. I'm shocked too. Granted, he was ill-mannered, but if you're in the service industry, dealing with demanding customers is part of the job.

I swoop in to do damage control. "Thanks Janelle, I'll take it from here."

Her nostrils are flared and her free hand is clenched in a fist. From the icy stare she trains on Isaac, it's good her gun doesn't shoot real bullets. She nods to me and storms away.

When I'm standing at the bar getting Isaac a refill, I see Janelle dart into the bathroom. Once Isaac has his drink in hand, I duck into the ladies' room to check on her.

She's splashing cold water on her face.

"Are you okay?" I ask.

"Yeah. Yeah. Fine. Sorry I was rude. It's just, he, uh, he …" Tears well in her eyes and she dabs them with a paper towel. "I just need a minute. It won't happen again."

I nod, but something tells me this wasn't just about a drink.

Isaac and Amanda, Ed and Connie, Felix and Jed, and now Janelle. With all the sparks flying, I'm starting to wonder if Machine Gun Molly spiked those cocktails with a little extra ammunition.

9 ~ Millicent

Liza and Shampoodles are dancing with one of the Bank Robbery Gang, so I amble over to the buffet table to see if I can be of help.

Felix, looking sharp in his pink suit, is wrapping silverware into red linen napkins.

"So, now you're part of the crew, too," I say.

He jumps at my voice.

"Sorry, I didn't mean to startle you."

His eyes dart around and he looks edgy. Where's Liza when you need an aura color deciphered?

Felix straightens his silk tie and fakes a chuckle. "Girl, I was off in my own little fantasy, you know how it is. How *are* you, Millicent? It's been forever."

"Yes, since Amanda's Kentucky Derby luncheon."

He rests his hand on his collarbone. "Oh, those mint juleps were divine."

"And potent."

He wraps another silverware bundle. "If I remember correctly, you slayed the best hat contest."

"My twin sister Myrtle made me that hat. You know, I came up in the day where you still wore hats to church. And gloves—white ones. I had this fancy pair edged with pearlescent beads. Myrtle and I used to sneak candies into church tucked inside our gloves. Tootsie Rolls, Mary Janes—though they were so chewy they always got stuck in my teeth. One time a Mary Jane pulled a filling plum out of my molar. Oh ho! My mother was not happy about that.

"Anyhow, one Sunday I popped a cherry Jolly Rancher into my mouth right before it was time to sing. I didn't want my mother to catch me, so I shoved the sticky, slobbery candy back into my glove mid-hymn. Well, the red dye seeped through the white fabric and looked just like blood. The congregation thought they were witnessing a stigmata miracle. And when the truth came out, my mother was mortified. No more candies. No more gloves."

Felix's laugh makes me happy. His tension is gone. I bet if Liza saw him now his aura would be sunny yellow.

"Why Millicent, what a clever costume," Donald says as he walks up to me. He bows, puts his hand over his heart, and recites a quote from The Merry Adventures of Robin Hood. "Little John, mine own dear friend, and him I love better than all others in the world."

Hmm. Very suave. I can see Amanda falling for his charms. But what do I know about romance? The last date I went on—fifteen years ago, when Myrtle set me up swearing I'd wither like a rose in saltwater if I didn't get out and date—was with a philosophy professor. He spent the entire seven-course dinner at the swanky Log Cabin Restaurant ranting about the evils of money, then stuck me with the bill.

I tip my hat to Donald and reply with a different quote. "Let us be merry, for the day is sweet and the ale is tingling."

The crash of Isaac's chair hitting the floor interrupts our literary repartee and silences the room. Ed has Isaac's tie twisted in his fist. His Joker makeup makes his scowl look downright terrifying. "I thought we were friends."

Uh oh. Looks like Ed knows about Connie and Isaac.

Roddy runs over to the men. "Hey, fellas, let's calm down."

"After what he did?" Ed growls.

Guests cluster together and whispers skitter through the room like centipedes.

Isaac grabs Ed's hands, trying to pry them loose from his tie. His voice is strained. "I don't know what you're talking about."

Connie grabs her husband's arm. "Let him go, Ed. Please. This isn't the place or time. Just settle down."

Ed shoves Connie and she stumbles into the neighboring table, spilling cocktails onto the Powerpuff Girls.

Donald and Roddy spring into action, each grabbing a man and guiding him outside. Janelle and Stephanie give towels to the Powerpuff Girls and right the table and chairs. After collecting the wallet and keys that fell out of Isaac's pockets in the crash, Ruby returns them to his double-breasted suit jacket and drapes it over his chair. Then she signals Gail to help a crying Connie to the ladies' room.

Clarice's face is bright red. I can't tell if she's holding back tears or anger. Maybe both. Ruby hurries to her side and whispers something in her ear, while patting her hand reassuringly. Clarice nods.

Then Ruby grabs the microphone. "Just a little misunderstanding. Nothing to be concerned about. Please, go back to enjoying yourself. We'll be opening the buffet in a few minutes."

When Jed cleverly starts playing, *A Good Old Fashioned Saturday Night Honky Tonk Barroom Brawl,* laughter ripples through the room and the tension is lightened.

A few minutes later, the men reenter the bank. Donald escorts Ed to his seat. Roddy and Isaac head towards the restroom.

Knowing she'll be reeling from embarrassment, I look for Amanda. I find her huddled in a dark corner, shrinking into herself.

Sweat dots her forehead and her lips tremble. "He's made me a laughingstock."

My heart hurts for my friend. I wrap her in my squishy arms, wishing hugs came in stronger doses. But no amount of comfort can mop up Isaac's mess.

10 ~ Ruby

Clarice is a wreck. Ethan is furious. And the gossip is so steamy the air is super-heated. I need to cool things down. All eyes are on Ed and Isaac. As long as the two of them are in the same room, the dynamic will be tense, and Ethan's birthday celebration will be overshadowed by scandal. Since Ed was the aggressor, I'm going to ask him and Connie to leave (just as soon as I figure out a diplomatic way to do it).

Clarice wrings her hands as she surveys the clusters of guests gawking and pointing. "Fix this, Ruby. Please."

I inhale deeply and slide on some false bravado. Distraction is my best option. "Clarice, why don't you offer your birthday toast to Ethan and then we'll open the buffet. I think food will redirect the energy."

"Do you think I should still offer a toast?"

I nod. "I do. It's important to you and it'll reset the evening."

She presses her temples and inhales. "Okay. If you think so."

Clarice and I move to the deejay table. When *A Good Old Fashioned Saturday Night Honky Tonk Barroom Brawl* wraps up (kudos to Jed), I grab the microphone.

"Alright, folks, thank you for your uh, spirited enthusiasm tonight. This party is more on theme than I expected!" Laughter bubbles up. "Now let's give the floor to our wonderful host, Clarice—no masks or getaway cars required, I promise."

After Clarice wraps up her toast and her sons perform the hilarious rap they wrote for their dad, I declare the buffet open for business, hoping the unique deliciousness of Roddy's food squashes any impulses to revisit the drama.

To fulfill Clarice's brief, Roddy has prepared twenty different hors d'oeuvres rather than any entrees. Canapés with fresh cilantro sauce over barramundi, caviar topped blue crab, and horseradish and salmon mousse. Endive wraps with pear and Stilton bleu cheese. Mini pork medallions with smoky blueberry barbecue sauce, and massaged kale bites with apples and roasted carrots, to name a few. His unique flavor profiles are earning him a top-notch reputation. Once word-of-mouth spreads, I'm sure it won't be too long until he can hire some full-time help. That's why the success of every event is so important, to both of us.

As the first bites of food are gobbled, I thank my lucky stars that the talk switches from the altercation (and what may or may not have led to it) to praising the amazing flavors. Well done, brother.

Before the rumor mill starts again, I look for Connie and Ed, planning to ask them to leave. I scan the room but can't find either of them. Apparently, they've slinked away on their own. Whew! Dodged that bullet.

The festive atmosphere returns and Clarice and Ethan relax. Jed plays quieter (but still theme appropriate) music to allow for better conversation. Gail is slinging drinks like a pro. Dad, Roddy—and surprisingly, Felix—are hustling to keep the buffet filled. This party may be salvageable after all.

Before the tension in my shoulders releases, I catch frantic movement out of the corner of my eye. Uh oh, I spoke too soon.

Isaac has turned British white (as Gigi would say) and is coughing. Ugly red hives have popped up on his neck and side of his face. It seems as though he's having difficulty breathing.

"Peanuts," he croaks out between labored breaths.

My eyes fly to meet Roddy's. He shakes his head violently and mouths, "No way!"

I rush to Isaac, loosening his tie and unbuttoning the top few buttons of his shirt.

Amanda, apparently dumbstruck, stands statue-still gawking at Isaac.

"Amanda, does he have an EpiPen?"

She blinks but doesn't answer.

"Amanda!" I yell. "An EpiPen?"

"Yes! Yes!" She grabs his jacket from the back of his chair, searching through his pockets. "It's not here! It's not here!"

Isaac's lips are swelling and he's gasping for air. I slide my phone from my back pocket and dial 911. Roddy and I move him to the floor.

Amanda kneels, shaking Issac. "For God's sake, Isaac! Where is your pen? You always carry your pen." She collapses beside him, muttering. "No. No. No. This is not supposed to happen. He always carries his pen."

Isaac clutches his throat. His eyelids disappear behind his bulging eyes. His terror is obvious.

I kneel down beside him and rest my hand on his shoulder. "Help is on the way, Isaac. You're going to be fine."

"Gail," Roddy yells. "Stand outside to wave down the paramedics."

She nods and runs out the front door. Stephanie and Janelle jump into action, shoving tables and chairs out of the way in preparation for the gurney. Amanda sits on the floor unmoving, clearly in shock.

Isaac slips into unconsciousness and stops breathing. I move to start chest compressions, and Clarice screams. "Get away from him! You did this! I made his peanut allergy very clear. Didn't I? Didn't I? This is all your fault!"

Ethan pulls my shoulder. "I'll handle this." He rolls up his sleeves, bends down, and begins CPR.

Clarice helps Amanda stand, then guides her to a chair.

Roddy and I step back. He grabs my hand and whispers, “It’s going to be okay.”

My eyes zoom to where Isaac was sitting. A few crumbs of food and half of a hundred-dollar-bill cookie are all that’s left on his plate. My mouth dries up and my heart hammers in my chest. All I can see is his chest not rising. All I can hear is Ethan counting compressions. And all I can think about is the terrifying possibility that Isaac might not take another breath.

My brain scrambles through every checklist, every meeting, every conversation we had. Could we have messed up? Could Roddy or Millicent accidentally have added peanuts?

11 ~ Ruby

The wail of sirens echoes through the cavernous bank. Two paramedics rush in, and guests huddle in whispering clusters at the edges of the room. The male medic switches places with a sweat-coated, exhausted Ethan, while the female responder assesses the situation.

"What's his name? Does anyone know any medical history?" she asks the crowd, as a third EMT wheels in a backboard and gurney.

Jed steps forward, pulling his long hair into a ponytail. "His name is Isaac. Isaac Stone. I'm his brother, Jed. He's allergic to peanuts."

Clarice edges Amanda towards the responders. "This is his wife, Amanda."

After a quick conversation with a composed Jed and a barely functioning Amanda, the female medic grabs a syringe and a vial of what I assume is epinephrine from her jump bag, and injects Isaac. As soon as the vial is empty, the three EMTs quickly roll Isaac onto the backboard, while continuing chest compressions, then transfer him to the gurney. All eyes are trained on the unfolding situation. Moments later, when Isaac gasps, my shoulders release and the crowd lets out a collective sigh as the medic stops CPR.

Clarice nudges Amanda towards the gurney. "Amanda, do you want to know where they're taking him?"

Amanda furrows her brows. “Yes, yes. Of course.” She rushes to the gurney. “Is he going to be okay? Why isn’t he talking? Where are you taking him?”

“Ma’am, meet us at the Lancaster General ER,” the EMT says. “We’ll take good care of him.”

Jed grabs Felix’s hand and calls out to me. “I’ll get my equipment later. I’m going to the hospital.”

I nod. “Of course. Of course.”

I’m surprised Jed is as functioning as he is. If it were Roddy lying unconscious, I’m not sure I’d remember how to breathe, let alone move.

The EMTs wheel Isaac out and slide the gurney into the ambulance, tearing out into the night.

Amanda’s body shivers uncontrollably. “Oh my god! What am I going to tell Ian?”

Clarice bends down in front of Amanda. “Just sit for a minute. I’ll get you a drink.”

As Clarice heads to the bar and pours a shot of whisky into a copper cup, Dad slides over to Amanda squeezes her hand and whispers something. Amanda nods, musters a weak smile, and takes a few deep breaths.

I thought Dad said he doesn’t know Amanda.

Before I have time to puzzle it out, Clarice returns to Amanda’s side, handing her the cup of whiskey. Amanda sets it on the table, stands, and straightens her skirt. “What I need is a ride to the hospital. I feel too shaky to drive.”

Millicent swoops in, arms open. “Oh honey, I can take you.”

Amanda twists to avoid contact with her friend. “You and your team have done enough, don’t you think?”

Millicent’s mouth falls open, gobsmacked by her friend’s allegation. “Amanda? What are you saying?”

Clarice steps protectively in front of Amanda, waving an accusing finger at Roddy, Millicent, and me. “I was very clear about the seriousness of Isaac's allergies. This was blatant negligence. Even criminal, I'd say. I'm calling the police."

The police? Worry beats against my throat.

Roddy grabs my hand and squeezes. "It's okay. Having the police come is a good thing. I am one-hundred-percent sure no peanuts or peanut products were used in the food. Isaac's reaction had to be caused by something else. I'm sure their investigation will clear me."

Millicent nods. "And me too. I didn't even use almond flour for my cookies or cake, just in case he could be sensitive to that too. I used rice flour. You risk stodginess, as Paul Hollywood would say, but if you don't overwork rice flour, it should still be light and fluffy." Her hand flies to her mouth and she shakes her head. "Good gravy, here I am prattling on." She pulls her lips in like a reprimanded schoolchild.

I take a step towards Amanda and Clarice and offer a sympathetic smile. "Ladies, emotions are understandably flaring, but can we take a moment to consider other causes? Roddy, Millicent, and I are certain absolutely no peanut products were used in our food. Could Isaac have developed a new allergy? Could he have gotten outside food or drink? There has to be a reasonable explanation."

"You messed up," Clarice snarls at me.

I jerk back, the force of the accusation landing like a punch.

Clarice turns to Amanda. "That's the reasonable explanation. This mistake is completely unacceptable. I hope you plan on suing."

Breath stalls in my lungs, waiting for Amanda to speak.

Her steely silent march out the door is louder than Clarice's rage.

12 ~ Ruby

Liza gives Millicent a supportive hug before rushing out to offer Amanda a ride. Uncomfortable guests dribble out of the bank, murmuring gossipy concern and accusations. At Clarice's insistence, Ethan takes their boys home. She remains, a formidable soldier guarding "the evidence" as we wait for the arrival of the *real* police. Dread drips into my veins, unrelenting as an IV. Ambulance and police aren't the bang-up ending I was hoping for.

My ragtag team sits sullenly at one of the round tables. Roddy's face is flushed salmon, fingers mindlessly massaging his tensed forehead. Gail sits close to him, holding his other hand reassuringly. Millicent stays uncharacteristically quiet, her eyes darting between us. She's probably hurt by her friend's rebuff, and no doubt worried about how the night's events will affect me and Roddy. Every few minutes, Dad's phone pings annoyingly with a text message. His eyes are glued to his phone screen as he taps out rapid replies. He's totally checked out of our current situation.

In the four years since Roddy and I met him, Dad has done his best to make up for lost time, but fathering doesn't always come easy to him. He's often awkward and restrained in his affection, and sometimes his support feels forced—like he's meeting an expectation rather than acting from a genuine place of love.

It hasn't been smooth sailing for me or Roddy either. The truth about our parentage came with a lot of anger and pain. Our emotions have cooled, and I've been mostly able to let go of the hurt. But I know Roddy still feels the sting. Growing pains, I suppose.

Another text pings Dad's phone, increasing my irritation.

Usually, I can give him grace. Becoming a father at age seventy, to thirty-four-year-old twins couldn't have been easy. I know he's doing his best. But at times like this, his withdrawal is very frustrating.

My eyes well with tears. I desperately miss Gigi. She would've taken charge of the situation all while offering unwavering, motherly concern to Roddy and me. But Gigi was one-of-a-kind. We were lucky to have her for as long as we did.

I snap when yet another text comes in. "Dad! Who on earth are you texting with?"

He glances up, face lined with anxiety. "I, uh, sorry." As he types a response, his brows press together.

"Dad?"

He huffs. "Yeah, okay. Sorry." Still looking at his phone, he reaches across the table for my hand. "Hang in there, kiddo."

His distracted platitude irritates me. I stand and push my chair back.

Clarice swoops in. "Where are you going?"

"To the bathroom. Would you care to escort me?" I regret my snarkiness immediately. No need to further antagonize a customer. "My apologies, Clarice. We're all a bit on edge."

"You!" She crosses her arms with a dramatic harrumph. "I paid top dollar for this debacle."

She didn't. As fledgling businesses, Roddy and I keep our prices below competitors'.

I bite back a correction and slather on a sympathetic expression. "It's so unfortunate the party ended this way, but I know we'll be cleared of any culpability."

Once the results of the food testing are in, I am certain Clarice will change her tune and give us good word-of-mouth.

I hitch my thumb towards the restroom. "I'm just going to pop into the bathroom. I'll be back in a jiffy."

Once in the ladies' room, I hear a keyed-up voice—I think it's Janelle's—coming from the far stall. She's on the phone, so I only hear one side of the conversation.

Her tone is almost chatty. "Well, the cops are on the way." She shuffles her feet on the floor. "No, no. It'll be fine. I'm good." A long silence, followed by an exhale. "What can I say?" Her tone sharpens. "Karma's a bitch."

The toilet flushes. She exits the stall, phone tucked in the crook of her shoulder. She startles when she sees me. "Oh hey. I didn't know anyone was in here," she says to me, before returning to her call. "Listen babe, gotta run. I'll get home as soon as I can."

She slides her phone into the deep pocket of her deputy's uniform and washes her hands. "Crazy night, right?"

I stare at her. Seems awfully breezy to describe a man's near death.

"Tragic," I say, pushing open the door to the middle stall.

"See ya out there," she calls as she leaves the bathroom.

My hunch strengthens: Janelle's earlier behavior wasn't just about Isaac's rude drink request. There's something else.

As I rejoin the group, one hawk-nosed police officer arrives and thoughts of Janelle's odd reactions leave my mind. At Clarice's behest, the officer slips the half-eaten cookie and the crumbs from Isaac's plate into a plastic baggie, then boxes up all the remaining food. Though the officer is going through the motions of due diligence, it's clear he's unconcerned. His nonchalance is reassuring.

After loading the "evidence" into his cruiser, the officer returns to the room. "Okay folks. You can go ahead and get cleaned up. I'm sure it's been a long night for you all."

"Wait one minute," Clarice screeches. "What about statements from everyone? I want it on record that I was crystal clear Isaac suffered from a severe allergy to peanuts. These, these incompetents," she sputters, pointing at Roddy and me, "have nearly killed a man. They need to be held accountable."

Annoyance flickers across the officer's angled face, before his expression settles into an appropriate look of concern. "I can assure you, Ms. Hall—"

"Mrs.," she interrupts.

"Pardon me, Mrs. Hall." His voice is tinged with a sharp edge. "I am taking the situation quite seriously, but it's rather cut-and-dried. Either the food is tainted with peanuts, or it's not. Until we have those findings, there is not much more to be done."

Clarice's nostrils are so flared she looks like a raging bull. "Well, don't you at least think you should get a copy of the guest and employee list, so you know who witnessed it and who is responsible?"

Still hoping to salvage my relationship with a client, I slide in. "Officer Cojant," I say after reading the nametag on his uniform. "We all want to understand what happened to Isaac. I'd be glad to give you a complete guest list as well as the names and contact info for all my team members."

"I'll give you my and Janelle's info, as well." Stephanie chimes in.

His nod is decisive, like the chop of a knife. "Excellent." He pulls a business card from his trouser pocket and hands it to Clarice. "After I receive the lists, I'm going to head out. My contact information is on the card if you have any additional questions."

"Fine," she snaps, clearly unhappy with his handling of the situation. She turns on her heel and storms towards the door. "I'm heading to the hospital. Poor Amanda must be a wreck."

Though tension lingers in the air, the angry indictment exited with Clarice.

"Listen," Stephanie says. "Like Officer Cojant said, it's been a looong night. We'll help you get the catering stuff and deejay equipment loaded up, but leave the tables and chairs. We'll deal with them on Monday. Let's get out of here as quick as we can."

I nod. "Thanks. I think we all appreciate that."

As I'm wheeling a cooler out to the van, I hear Janelle yell, "Here it is!"

I run back inside to see her holding Isaac's EpiPen in the air.

"It was under the deejay's table," she says.

"It must've rolled out of Isaac's jacket pocket during the scuffle with Ed," Stephanie says.

Roddy shakes his head. "I guess when Donald and I were trying to break up the fight, it must've gotten kicked under the deejay's booth."

Dad nods in agreement. "Must have."

I take the rescue pen from Janelle. "I'll get it back to them."

A lump lodges in my throat as I think about Isaac's ashen face as they wheeled him out. I stick it in my bag, desperately hoping to return it to him when he's recovered.

13 ~ Millicent

What a night. I slide my swollen feet under the down comforter and prop over-stuffed pillows behind my aching back. The usually calming scent of the lavender sachets tucked in my pillowcases itches my nose. Flipping to chapter one of Nelson Mandela's autobiography, *Long Walk to Freedom,* I hope to quiet the merry-go-round of thoughts spinning in my head.

I've gone over and over every ingredient I used in the cookies and cake and am absolutely certain I used no peanut products. And Roddy is such a stickler for details, I can't believe he did either. But if neither of us made a mistake, what happened?

Maybe it wasn't an actual allergic reaction. Maybe it was some kind of stress-induced attack. Isaac was already in a pickle over Amanda discovering his tryst with Connie (as he should be, the heel). Add in the "Ed incident" and that could've pushed him over the edge. That's got to be it. Stress can be dangerous. I remember Myrtle telling me about her best friend suffering a panic attack when they were driving across the Chesapeake Bay Bridge. She couldn't breathe and thought she was having a heart attack. Myrtle said even after they got to the other side her friend had chest pains and was sweating like an Alaskan in Florida for summer. Yes siree, Bob, a panic attack. That's got to be it.

But what if it isn't?

Acid burns my belly. I crawl out of bed and head to the kitchen for a handful of gingersnaps. Ginger is good for an unsettled stomach—in fact, during Myrtle's third, no fourth, no, it was the third pregnancy, she continuously sucked ginger lollipops for her nausea—and the sweet molasses and warm cinnamon is good for my soul. I pop one into my mouth as I pad bare-footed back to bed.

The cold tile floor sends achiness through my feet. Should've worn my slippers. After putting the remaining cookies on my bedside table, I wiggle my bunioned feet into a pair of alpaca-wool socks and snuggle back into bed. Crumbs sprinkle on the pages of my book as I nibble and try to read. The words float on the pages as my brain marches right back to the party.

If Isaac's attack was stress-induced, would the epinephrine shot have roused him? Hmm. Probably not. I think it would actually have sped up his heart rate, making it worse.

If it wasn't a panic attack, maybe he had some kind of infection, or a reaction to a new medicine. Or maybe like Ruby said, Isaac acquired a new allergy. Yes. I'm sure that's it. As we age, all kinds of things change. Up until my forties, I never drank anything with sugar in it. No soda, no fruit juice, no sweetener in my coffee or tea. It wasn't just that I didn't like the cloying sweetness, it actually caused me digestive issues. But now … oh boy! To paraphrase Patrick Henry, give me sugar or give me death! I love root beer and cola, apple and pineapple juice, and the sweetest of sweet teas. Plus, cakes and cookies and pies, oh my! And none of it upsets my stomach. So, it's likely Isaac developed a new allergy. I'd bet my bottom dollar that's what happened.

After shaking the bits of cookie and my worries away, I reread the first page. Pizelle, my furry feline, struts across my bed and plops down on top of my book, demanding immediate attention. I bury my fingers into her light tan fur, rubbing right behind her ears, just like she likes it.

This delicate little cookie showed up on my doorstop, wet and shivering. She was a tiny thing, only weeks old, with mangy hair and crusty eyes. It's hard to believe the pleasingly plump (just like me) spoiled rotten cat is the same creature. Pizelle's low purr soothingly vibrates my stomach, and I lean my head back into the pillow.

I'm dozing off when my phone rings. It's Liza. She took Amanda to the hospital.

"Hi Liza. What's the good news?"

Pizelle leaps off my lap, tail flicking, and vanishes down the hall.

Liza's voice is constricted. "There isn't any. Isaac went into anaphylactic shock. Now, he's in a coma and the medical staff is struggling to stabilize his blood pressure. It's touch and go."

Ginger and cinnamon come back up, burning the back of my throat. I think of Amanda and Ian. Ruby and Roddy. Worry settles in, low and persistent, like an irritating bout of tinnitus.

"Millicent," Liza adds, barely above a whisper, "This time, I'm really afraid the death card might've been literal."

Icy fingers trail down my spine, the kind that belong in late-night thrillers, not under my cozy down comforter. I flip on my bedside lamp, pull the blanket around my shoulders, and shiver with dread. The anxiety ramps up, whining at high volume, like a crescendo of a horror movie soundtrack.

I won't be closing my eyes tonight.

14 ~ Ruby

My hands are shaking and my legs are rubbery, as I pull Sally, my yellow VW convertible bug, into the parking lot of the Lancaster County Prison. The daisy bloom in her built-in vase is wilted, just like my spirits. After the endive wraps, the pork medallions, and the barramundi all tested positive for the presence of peanut powder, Roddy was arrested for criminal negligence.

Mr. Davenport, Gigi's longtime business lawyer, enlisted Angela Whittle, a criminal defense lawyer who was able to get Roddy released on recognizance. She told me if Isaac doesn't rally (God forbid) the charges would likely be changed to negligent homicide and, if convicted, Roddy would be sentenced to jail time. I'm using all my coping skills not to spiral, but panic is nipping at my heels like a cranky Pomeranian.

Sucking in a deep breath, I head into the prison. The odor of disinfectant doesn't hide the scent of sorrow. Roddy hunkers on a backless bench in the drab lobby area, face resting in his hands. I move in front of him and touch his shoulder. He looks up with red-rimmed eyes. His normally tidy stubble is splotchy, and his hair is greasy. He looks haggard after only a few hours in a holding cell. I can't imagine—NO! I'm not going there. Isaac will recover. Roddy will be cleared of all charges. And this whole disaster will be a tiny speck in our rearview mirror.

Determined to lift Roddy's spirits, I wrap myself in flashing, neon optimism. "Let's bust you outta this joint," I say with my best mobster impersonation.

His voice is flat. "I'm not in the mood, Ruby."

I swallow and nod, my sunshine energy flickering to gray. When he trudges out of the prison, I follow quietly behind, subdued, but stubbornly holding onto the last spark of optimism.

After climbing into Sally and strapping on his seatbelt, he rubs his hands over his face. "This is unbelievable, Ruby. I am absolutely certain I did not use anything with peanuts, let alone peanut powder. What chef in their right mind would sprinkle peanut powder on endive, pork, and barramundi? It makes no sense."

I'm far—okay, galaxies away—from being a chef, but even I know you wouldn't add peanut powder to those dishes.

I pull onto King Street and head towards home. "No, it doesn't."

Construction work clogs Route 272 with traffic. Roddy stares out the window, shoulders hiked to his ears, as we inch down the road. Exhaust fumes funnel through Sally's air-conditioning vents, nauseating me. The snail's pace tries my patience. And I'm struggling to hold onto that last little bit of positivity.

"Want to stop at Roland Park and take a walk before we head home. Clear our heads?"

Though I'm not outdoorsy like Gail, I'm hoping the scent of pine trees might soothe my jangled nerves.

Roddy keeps looking out the window when he answers. "Yeah. Okay."

Fifteen silent minutes later, I wheel into a parking spot in front of Akron Pines wooden playground. Toddlers giggle as they chase each other over and under tire obstacles and through planked tunnels. A twinge of guilt zings through me when I notice a few dog owners throwing balls or sticks for their romping mutts. I haven't had Lucy out for an adventure in days. Teams of frisbee golf players take turns winging their discs toward the chained baskets.

Roddy eases himself out of my car like an arthritic old man.

I jut my chin towards the hill. "Wanna take the paved path through the pines?"

"Sure."

I hike up the steep hill to the start of the path. Roddy plods behind me. At the top, I bend, hands on knees, to catch my breath, sucking in the fresh scent of pine. A squirrel dashes across the path and scurries up one of the towering trees.

Roddy looks down the tree-lined walkway. "This could be the last time I take this walk for a long while."

His voice chokes on unshed tears, and it feels like barbed wire is wrapping around my heart. Roddy has always looked out for me. Been my protector. How do I protect him from this?

My heart stutters, dread threatening to overwhelm me. I revert to my usual buoyancy, not knowing any other way to cope. "Don't say that! Isaac will be fine and you'll be cleared of all charges. I know it."

"Your rose-colored glasses are clouding your vision. I'm in deep trouble, Ruby. Even if I don't end up in jail, my business will never survive this." He drops his chin to his chest and shakes his head. "I'm not sure yours will either."

He's not wrong, and the truth of it lands hard. Even my rose-colored glasses can't pinken this situation, but I stay silent. Coach Isaac Stone is a big deal in Lancaster County. News of his hospitalization and Roddy's arrest was already on the front page of the *Intelligencer Journal*. Three out of five of my upcoming events cancelled this morning. And Tabitha left a message telling me not to bother sending her a proposal for the Revolutionary themed party.

I shove thoughts of Make A Splash! folding out of my mind. That's tomorrow's problem. To quote one of Dad's AA slogans, *first things first*. Keeping Roddy out of jail is the priority. Then we can worry about resurrecting our businesses.

"Roddy, if we can prove it was an accident—like maybe the spice manufacturer added peanut powder to the pepper—you wouldn't be negligent, right?"

He kicks a pebble off the path into the thick pine needles covering the ground. "I guess not. Then the manufacturer would be negligent. But that's not what happened. I taste my spices before adding them to my food."

I stop and put my hands on my hips. "Well, it has to be something like that. *You* didn't do it. So how else could it happen?"

Roddy keeps walking, broad shoulders hunched. "I can only come up with one explanation."

I jog to catch up to him. "Well? Care to share?"

He stops walking and huffs out a breath. "It's going to sound nuts."

I wince at his choice of words. "Let's ban that word from our vocabulary."

His laugh is dry and broken. "Agreed."

"So, spit it out. Five years ago, if you had told me our grandparents robbed a bank I would've thought you'd gone around the bend. Your explanation can't be any crazier than that."

His eyes lock with mine. "This wasn't an accident."

My mouth dries up and falls open. "What?"

"I'm not sure if the objective was to punish Isaac or me—maybe both—but I'm sure it was intentional."

I shiver despite the warm air. The pine trees that minutes ago stood majestic and serene, now loom threateningly.

What if he's right?

15 ~ Millicent

Liza sails into my saltbox house, bohemian, ankle-length skirt swirling around her legs, Shammie snuggled in the crook of one arm, a bottle of wine in the other. "You're going to need this when I fill you in on everything."

My stomach flip-flops with unease. Can it get much worse than Roddy being arrested? I'm still reeling over the results of the food testing. Roddy is so detail-oriented and cautious. It's hard to fathom he would've made such a devastating mistake.

I take the wine into the kitchen and scrounge two mismatched wine glasses from the back of the highest cabinet. Luckily, the chilled bottle has a screw top. I fill Liza's to the top, but add an ice cube to my glass, pouring only enough wine to cover it.

As I return to the living room, Liza settles her lithe frame onto my colonial-style couch, Shammie beside her. The bold floral print of Liza's skirt clashes with the plaid upholstery fabric.

Myrtle nags me to update my 70s décor, but the living room furniture with rounded armrests and fabric skirting, my overly-Pledged wooden cupboards and coffee table, and the lovingly-worn braided rug all are perfectly functional. Liza appreciates the kitschiness, assuming it's deliberate. But really, I'm just frugal.

Liza slips off her metallic-gold Birkenstocks. Despite being in her late fifties, she bends her legs under her like a nimble teenager. Maybe there's something to all the yoga she does.

I hand her the glass of wine. "Do you want a sweet treat?"

She throws me a did-you-really-have-to-ask look.

I baked strawberry-topped cheesecake cookies, limoncello cupcakes, snickerdoodles, and blueberry muffins. Baking calms me, and as sure as my muffins rise, I needed a little of that. After fixing a tray with a few of each kind, I set it on the coffee table.

Pizelle leaps onto the arm of the couch, batting a furry paw at Shampoodles. Shammie's growl is a low rumble.

"Hush Shammie." Liza scoops Pizelle into her arms. "Helloooo little lioness," she coos.

Pizelle snuggles her head into Liza's armpit. With anyone else, Pizelle would engage her claws and twist away, but Liza and Pizelle share a special bond. After receiving the appropriate amount of attention, Pizelle wanders away.

I plop into the mustard side chair across from Liza as she nibbles her cookie.

"Delicious," she says.

I take a timid sip of wine and grimace at the sourness.

"Ice?" Liza says, flabbergasted. "You put ice in wine?"

I crinkle my nose and glare at the offensive liquid. "I'm thinking about adding sugar to it."

She rolls her expressive brown eyes, and lifts her glass to her full lips. Her myriad rings tinkle when they hit the side of the wine glass. "Just slug it back because you're not going to like what I have to tell you."

I shove the wine to the side of the end table and brace myself with a cupcake instead. "Okay. Let me have it."

"I was at the hospital this morning, with Amanda."

I curl my toes and hold my breath, preparing for bad news. "Okay."

Liza sweeps her tresses from her face. "She was there with Ian."

The sip of sour wine turns to acid in my stomach. "To say their goodbyes to Isaac?"

"No, no, no." Her armful of bangles clinks together as she shakes her hand. "Isaac is still in a coma, but his blood pressure has stabilized."

My shoulders drop with relief. "Thank God."

Liza nods. "Yes. That tidbit is heartening, but Ian was in the hospital because he had an episode. With his dad, ah … indisposed, Ian was trying to help around the house. He was up on a ladder changing a light in the great room and fell, landing on his arm. Apparently, the force caused a bleed deep in his muscle. His arm swelled to twice its size and went numb."

I finish the cupcake and bite into a snickerdoodle. "Oh no! Poor Amanda. Is Ian going to be all right?"

"Yes, they got the bleed under control with some kind of infusion."

"Well, at least there's some good news."

Liza presses her lips together. "Unfortunately, that's not all. Clarice was also there to support Amanda. I offered to get coffees from the cafeteria, and when I returned to the waiting room, I overheard Clarice urging Amanda to file a suit for civil negligence against Ruby."

"Ruby?" Worry floods my system upping my body temperature. Sweat beads on my lip. Roddy is facing criminal charges. Isn't that enough? Why is Clarice demanding a pound of flesh from Ruby? Isaac is not even her husband. "Did Amanda agree?"

"She told Clarice she's considering all her options." Liza untucks her legs, leans forward, and reaches her hand out for mine. "Brace yourself, Millicent, because it gets worse. Much worse."

I swallow loudly and steel myself for dire news. "Tell me."

"After I left the hospital, I did a tarot reading to gain some insight on the whole situation. I pulled the Justice card and the Knight of Cups. *Both reversed.* Ruby and Roddy need a good lawyer."

I have no idea what that means and I'm not sure I believe in it anyway. But I do believe in disasters, and this one's shaping up to be a five-layer, fondant-covered fiasco with trick candles on top.

16 ~ Ruby

Wowsa! For a few minutes, the idea that Isaac's allergic reaction was caused intentionally threw me off kilter. You see that kind of stuff on TV, but here? In Lancaster County? Hard to fathom. But as we finished the path through the pine trees and I mulled it over, I became convinced his theory has teeth. Three dishes had peanut powder. That's no accident. This mishap was orchestrated.

My mind is racing well over Akron's 35 mph speed limit as I drive to Mirabella. I review every guest, every interaction, every overheard snippet of conversation. My fingertips are literally itching to write down my thoughts.

I pull Sally into Mirabella's driveway and see Gail leaning against her SUV, hands in the pockets of her jeans, cowboy hat riding high on her head. Her bow-shaped lips spread into an ear-to-ear smile, and her straight brown hair sways with her frantic arm waving. She squeals as she runs towards us and hugs Roddy before he's fully out of the car. Her hat falls to the gravel as she peppers his stubbled face with kisses.

"Whoa there," Roddy says, pushing her to arm's length. "I was only gone a few hours."

Gail collects her hat and links her arm with his. "I know. I know. But I missed you."

Gloom weighs down his shoulders and voice. "You better get used to it. I might end up in jail."

Gail blinks her long eyelashes. A single tear drips down her cheek. "Please don't say that."

I backhand my brother's shoulder. "Rodderick Finch! Your pessimism isn't going to help the situation."

He huffs at me. "Neither is your rainbow-and-unicorn positivity."

Gail's eyes leak and she sniffles. "Worst case, won't they just give you a fine or community service?"

Roddy shoots me a quick look, giving his head the slightest shake—a silent warning to keep my mouth shut. "Yeah, of course. Nothing to worry about."

Typical Roddy. Shouldering the worry alone to protect those he loves.

I press my lips tight and cross my arms. I think he should be upfront with Gail. There *is* something to worry about. The lawyer said if Isaac dies, a conviction would likely land Roddy in jail. But given my relationship track record, I suppose I'll defer to his judgment.

She gives him the side eye. "Really?"

I catch the skepticism in her tone, but Roddy just wraps his arm around her. "Really," he says. "I'm just being—"

"Eeyore," I interrupt, trying to break the tension by using my favorite nickname for him.

Roddy rolls his eyes at me. "I was going to say cynical. I have a great lawyer and I'm sure everything is going to work out fine."

I hear his words, but the heart isn't there.

Whether Gail truly believes him or just chooses to, I can't tell. I stuff my voice with optimism. "See, brother, it's not so bad living sunny-side up. Besides, I've got a lot more than unicorns up my sleeve."

"Oh yeah? Like what?" he asks, as he punches the security code into Mirabella's lock.

I tap my temple, eager to share the thoughts buzzing in my brain, as I follow him into the house. "Like a list of suspects for starters."

Gail swivels to face me. Her cheeks blanch of all color. "Suspects?"

I nod. "We think Isaac's attack was intentional."

Roddy shoots me a look—a silent thank-you for jumping onboard with his theory. Twins don't need words; we've got our own frequency.

Her slender fingers fly to her mouth. "Roddy, are you serious?"

Roddy opens the custom blinds, letting sunlight spill through three enormous arched windows that mirror the arches on the front porch. "Very." He kicks off his sneakers, then plops onto the leather couch and rubs his face with both hands.

Gail hugs herself. "Ooh. That gives me goosebumps." Her boots click on the terra-cotta tiled floor as she walks across the room to join him on the couch, sitting close enough that their shoulders touch.

I settle into the matching couch across from them, sinking into the soft leather and a memory of Gigi claiming she had bought one couch for each of us. I'm glad Roddy hasn't changed much in Mirabella. Gigi lives in the custom-made Moorish rug, the hand-thrown pottery, and the reclaimed wood. I know he feels her here too, woven into every piece.

I prop one of the many earth-colored throw pillows behind my back. "Yeah. It's surreal to think someone else would actually add peanut powder to the food, but it's the only logical explanation. I know Roddy didn't make a mistake, especially not in three different dishes. The cookies and cakes tested peanut-free too, so it wasn't Millicent."

Gail snuggles closer to Roddy, resting her hand on his upper leg. "Why would anyone do that to you?"

Roddy leans his head back, staring at the ceiling. "I don't know. I've been racking my brain to figure it out. Other than all of you, the only people I knew at the party were Hank and his wife Iris."

Roddy doesn't have enemies. He's the guy you call when your car conks out on the turnpike. Or when your dog-sitter backs out last minute. Everyone likes Roddy.

"Hank's a guy you shoot hoops with, right?" Gail asks.

Roddy nods. "Yeah, we're buddies. He's got no motive to set me up. I've also met Liza a few times when she was with Millicent and I met Jed here the night we were planning the party. But again, where's the motive?"

Gail nibbles her thumbnail. "Could it be a business rival? Someone trying to sabotage Chef's Secret?"

Roddy crosses his arms. "Hmm. That's a thought. If that was the plan, it's working."

I slip off my sandals, pulling my legs under me. "Or, maybe it's not about you at all. My guess is Isaac was the target and you were just a convenient scapegoat."

Gail's swallow is audible. "Oh my god. If someone deliberately spread peanut powder on the food and Isaac dies, that means it's …"

Roddy finishes her sentence. "Murder."

The word sucks the air from the room. The silence is heavy, oppressive. My chest tightens as the horror sinks in. If Isaac dies, Roddy will undoubtedly be blamed and the real murderer will walk free. I picture my brother behind bars for a crime he didn't commit, and my stomach clenches.

I can't let that happen. I won't.

Leaping off the couch, I run into the library and grab a tablet and pencils from Gigi's massive desk. Back in the living room, I drop to the floor in front of the coffee table, knees cushioned by the plush rug Gigi loved. "Enough wallowing. We're smart people. Smarter than whoever thought peanut powder was a clever murder weapon. Let's figure this out." The scratch of the pencil against the tablet is comforting, as I write: *Guest List.*

Roddy sighs, his mouth sagging with doubt. “Okay, Jessica Fletcher, do you really think we’re going to solve this thing?”

“I think we have to try. I’m not willing to let you take the blame for something you didn’t do.”

Gail grips Roddy’s upper arm, her fingers digging in. “Please, Roddy.” Tears shimmer in her eyes. “If Isaac dies, you could … they might charge you with …” She bows her head, unable to say the words. Her shoulders buck with her sobs. It’s clear Gail knows the stakes.

Roddy turns and wraps his arms around her. She hides her face into his chest and he kisses the top of her head. “It’s going to be okay. I promise.”

Her voice is muffled. “You can’t make that promise. You don’t know.”

He gently pushes her away, lifting her chin with his fingers so he can see her eyes. “I do know one thing—when my sister sets her sights on something, she’s like a balloon in a windstorm. There’s no stopping her.”

I clap my hands together and slap on a confident face. “He’s right! I am. And if anyone can solve a mystery, we can. Gigi made sure of that.”

Gail wipes her eyes with the back of her hand, sucks in a deep breath, and nods. “Then let’s get started.”

Roddy, attempting to cheer up the room, flips his stinky feet onto the iron and wood tabletop directly beside my face and wriggles his toes.

I crinkle my nose and shove his feet off the edge. “Man, I just got a whiff of the apocalypse.”

He laughs, then twists his palms up and puffs up his lips, offering a craptacular mob-boss impersonation. “Give me a break, I just got outta the pen.”

Gail smacks his chest. "Too early. Way too early to joke about it." Her brows stay furrowed, but hope sneaks into the hint of a smile.

Thankfully, Roddy swings his feet to the floor, leans forward, and rubs his hands together like a cartoon detective. "Let's crack this case wide open."

Our ragtag team is not exactly Scotland Yard, but I have enough rainbow-and-unicorn positivity to believe we might actually pull this off.

I write the names of all the guests and employees. "For now, let's assumed Isaac was the target. We can cross off the trio of Powerpuff Girls and the three men in the Bank Robbing Gang. They never met Isaac. Nor had the two pirate queens." I draw a line through each of their names.

Gail leans forward, resting her elbows on her knees. "We can also eliminate Millicent, Liza, and your Dad."

I scratch them off the list. "Ethan is out. The party was a surprise for him, so there's no way he could have planned ahead. And Clarice was mortified by the events. I doubt she'd pay for a party and then ruin it."

"Mark them with a question mark," Roddy says. "Same for Amanda, Jed, and Felix. You'd think they'd be unlikely since they're family, but a good detective never assumes."

"Okay Columbo," I tease as I add the question marks. "Now we're officially good detectives."

He rubs his scruffy chin. "We have to be, Ruby. No one else is going to save me."

The lightheartedness evaporates. He's right. If we can't prove Roddy didn't make a mistake, the consequences could be devastating.

Roddy points to the tablet. "Write down Ed as suspect numero uno. From the gossip blazing through the party, it's clear Connie and Isaac were having an affair."

I bite the tip of the pencil.

"What?" Roddy asks.

"Kinda obvious, isn't it? I mean, if Ed really was going to try to harm Isaac with peanut powder, wouldn't he have reined in his anger? I mean punching Isaac clearly drew lots of attention. Would he have wanted that?"

Gail slips off her cowboy boots and leans back on the couch. "He was slinging back the cocktails. I think he was pretty drunk. Maybe he wasn't thinking straight."

Roddy clasps his hands behind his head. "Or maybe that's what he wanted us to assume. Did you actually see him consume the cocktails?"

Gail's thick eyebrows furrow. "No. I guess not. I just know he kept coming back for refills."

Roddy hops off the couch and paces the room. His voice becomes animated. "So, hear me out. What if drunkenness was just Ed's excuse for starting the fight? Isaac's EpiPen *supposedly* fell out of his pocket and got kicked under the deejay's booth during the scuffle. What if the real reason Ed went after Isaac was to make sure Isaac wouldn't have access to his rescue medication?"

The air turns arctic.

I shiver. "Now *that* gives me goosebumps."

I write Ed's name beside a circled number 1.

Roddy's jaw tightens and all traces of levity disappear. "That's good, Ruby. Listen. I want both of you to really hear me. Anyone who is willing to hurt Isaac and frame me is callous and calculating. We have to be careful. This isn't like Gigi's funerary puzzles. This is life and death."

17 ~ Millicent

After a baked oatmeal breakfast shared with my finicky Pizelle, I throw on a flowy, beige shirt I picked up on sale at Chico's the other day, attempt to tame my gray curls, give up, slide on my bright red glasses, and head to Amanda's house.

Myrtle calls me a meddler. I prefer to think of my myself as grandmotherly. Roddy and Ruby—as close to grandkids as I'm going to get—are being threatened with professional and financial ruin. No self-respecting granny would sit by and let it happen.

The roads are clogged with apparently late-for-work drivers deeply frustrated by my loyalty to the speed limit. Three honking horns, two fist shakes, and one middle-finger later, I wheel into Amanda's circular driveway. Rubbing my aching hip, I waddle to her front door and ring the bell. I shift my weight side-to-side, trying to ease the pressure on my joint. When Amanda finally opens the door, her tired eyes widen in surprise.

"Millicent? What are you doing here?"

I'm surprised too. Amanda's an early riser. It's almost ten and she's still in her robe. Her hair is tangled, and she's clutching a tissue.

"Liza told me Ian had an accident. I came to see how you're holding up."

"I'm, uh … I'm okay." Her bloodshot eyes dart from side to side and she seems hesitant to let me in.

When I wrap my jiggly arms around her, I smell vodka on her breath. "Oh, you poor dear. You've got to be completely overwhelmed."

She doesn't pull away, but she doesn't hug me back. After a few awkward seconds, I drop my arms.

Smoothing her knotty hair, she shrugs. "This too shall pass."

I squeeze her forearm and offer a sympathetic smile. "How about I come in for a chat?"

Her expression is somewhere between welcoming and hesitant. Her throat tightens with a visible gulp. "I suppose…yes, okay. Come in."

As I follow her through the rooms, I notice her normally immaculate house is looking a bit topsy-turvy. A stack of past-due bills is collecting dust on the entry table, used plates and cups litter the coffee table in the living room, and various articles of clothing are strewn on the furniture.

I step over a pair of gardening shoes as we enter her spacious kitchen, and hoist myself onto a stool. A vanilla chai candle flickers on the marble kitchen island, infusing the air with its warm spicy scent. Beside it, sits her phone, and an open pint of vodka.

Amanda catches my glance and her cheeks flush. "I know it's early for a cocktail. I just …" She sighs. "Between Ian's accident—"

"How is he?" I ask.

"He'll need clotting factor infusions, but he'll be okay. But frankly, this has all been too much."

I pat her hand, noticing chipping peach polish. "What can I do to help?"

Her laugh is brittle. "I'm afraid it's beyond help."

She collects two tumblers from her steel-gray kitchen cabinets and pours us each a glass of lemonade. We sit on the stools at the island. Amanda runs her fingers over the cap on the vodka, but resists the urge to add it to her lemonade. I resist the urge to add sugar.

I stick a bunioned toe in to test the waters. "And how is Isaac?"

Her nostrils flare and her eyes flash with an unreadable emotion. "Still in a coma." Her tone holds anger, but I can't tell who it's for. She swipes her unbrushed hair behind her ear and takes another sip of her drink. "That was such an awful night." She continually rubs her thumb over the side of glass. "Isaac made an utter fool out of me. I was so angry I could barely see straight."

Her tone says she's still upset and I can't blame her. A medical emergency doesn't absolve Isaac of his sins. Finding out he was canoodling Connie seemed to have pushed her over the edge.

I offer a sympathetic smile. "Understandable."

She presses her fingertips into her temples. "And now the guilt is eating me up."

My brows pinch together. "Guilt? What do you have to feel guilty about?"

Red colors her neck and cheeks. "I, uh …I," Her eyes avoid mine.

I plop my flabby elbows on the countertop. "He's the one who cheated."

She glues her gaze to her chipped fingernails. "I know, I know, and, I uh, I just feel like a fraud playing the concerned wife."

"It's okay to be mad at him—even if he is in a coma. And there's no need to feel guilty. The anaphylaxis wasn't your fault, and there's nothing you could have done to prevent it."

The red drains from her face and neck, and she pales to ghostly white. She unscrews the cap on the vodka bottle and pours a splash into her lemonade. Holding the glass with two hands, she stares into it.

"Really, Amanda, you are blameless in this situation."

She shoves the drink away from her and drops her face into her hands, "Oh, Millicent, I was talking to *him* right before Isaac's reaction started. Maybe if I hadn't been preoccupied …"

My forehead creases. "Him who?"

She picks at her nail polish. "You know, the man I told you about."

"He was at the party?" My mind flies to Donald and Amanda talking. They definitely looked like more than passing acquaintances.

She shakes her head, eyes still avoiding mine. "Um, no, no. He was on the phone."

Amanda's tone seems less than certain. Is she telling me the whole truth?

I pat her hand again. "Without his EpiPen, even if you had been sitting beside him there was nothing you could have done differently."

She pulls her hand away and stands up, dumping the alcohol-laced lemonade down the drain. She rests a hand on the counter, posture tense. "Millicent, I know how much you care for Ruby and Roddy, but how could they make such a terrible mistake? Clarice swears she conveyed the seriousness of Isaac's allergy to them."

Here's the opportunity I've been waiting for—a chance to do damage control. "That's true. She did. And Ruby stressed the importance to the entire team. She made it perfectly clear no one was to even bring peanuts anywhere near the event. There must've been mislabeled ingredients or something like that. Roddy would not have made such a grievous error. I'm sure once it's investigated more thoroughly, the truth will come out. Please give them the benefit of the doubt." I hold my breath to see how she receives my theory.

Her jaw tightens and her lips press into a thin line. "I'm just taking one day—really, one minute—at a time. I'm too emotionally wrought to make any big decisions."

Her phone rings and the name *Donald* pops onto the screen.

Donald? The hairs on the back of my neck raise.

Amanda snatches the phone from the counter, silences the ringer, and shoves it into her the pocket of her robe.

"Why did you lie to me?" The question tumbles out before I can stop it.

Amanda's swallow is audible. "I, uh, I didn't." Sweat blooms on her upper lip.

"Why is Donald calling you? I thought you said you only know him in passing."

She crosses her arms. Her eyes dart away from mine. "Millicent, there *is* more than one Donald in the world."

She's right about that, but would any old Donald fluster her like this?

Her jaw tightens and she glares at me. "And frankly, your accusatory tone is quite rude."

Her phone vibrates again. She pretends not to hear, but her eyes skip sideways with a telltale twitch. She lifts her chin, trying mighty hard to look unruffled, and that's the giveaway. This isn't about *a* Donald. It's about Ruby and Roddy's Donald.

She's lying. But why?

18 ~ Millicent

My house smells like the Sunday afternoons of my childhood—the scent of savory roasted chicken mingling with sweet carrots, onions, and butter-coated mashed potatoes. I'm by no means a gourmet chef like Roddy, but I can cook good old comfort food. With what Roddy is facing, we can all use a little of that.

I invited the whole gang: Ruby, Roddy, Gail, and even Donald. After my visit with Amanda, I'm itching to get a read on him. Something is rotten in Denmark, and I aim to find out what.

Gail's cowboy boots click on the linoleum as she enters my kitchen. "What can I help you with?" Pizelle rubs against her faded jeans. Gail scoops her up, cradling her like a baby.

"You can grab the ambrosia salad from the fridge."

Gail's full lips pull into a circle. "Ooh, I haven't had that in forever. My mom said it was one of my grandma Bess's favorites."

"I guess it's kind of old-fashioned, but I can't resist that marshmallow gooeyness. When Myrtle and I were around five or six, we were the Ambrosia Queens for our after-church dinners. As we added the ingredients, she'd always steal a few mandarin slices, I'd swipe a few marshmallows, and we'd squabble over the maraschino cherries."

Gail lifts the Pyrex bowl from the refrigerator. After pulling off the plastic wrap she plucks two cherries from the top of the fruity salad and hands me one. "Sounds like a tradition worth reviving."

Laughing, we click our maraschinos together like the finest champagne, then pop them into our mouths.

I crinkle my nose, enjoying the sugary burst of flavor. “Mmm. As good as I remember.”

Gail collects a serving spoon from my utensil drawer. “Having a sister—especially a twin—must’ve been so much fun. I’m kind of jealous of you, and Ruby and Roddy.”

I move the chicken from the roasting pan onto a serving platter, ringing it with multi-colored carrots and onions. “You were an only child?”

She nods. “Yep. Apparently, my mom had a real tough time in childbirth, so it was one and done. Unless you count my menagerie of pets as siblings—dogs, cats, bunnies, hamsters, guinea pigs, goats, a horse, and even a snake—it was just me and the zoo.”

“No wonder you’re a vet tech.”

Her smile pokes a dimple in her sun-kissed cheek. “Kinda my dream job.”

I carry the chicken into my cozy dining room, and Gail follows bringing the bowl of mashed potatoes and the dessert salad. Ruby shifts the fresh sunflowers she’d brought—golden, and bright, just like her—to make room for the food.

“Speaking of my job,” Gail says as she sets the two bowls beside the chicken and vegetables. “I overheard a very interesting conversation today.”

I situate myself on the double-cushioned wooden chair, directly across from Donald. Gail sits across from Ruby and beside Roddy.

“Oh? Tell us.” Roddy ladles a dollop of potatoes onto his plate, passes the bowl to Gail, then moves onto the chicken platter.

“I was at the Laurel Hills Stables changing the bandage on an injured horse and two women were chatting in the aisle outside the stall as they tacked up their horses—”

Roddy lifts one finger up to Gail. “Holy cow, I gotta interrupt you, babe. This chicken is just so good. Melts in your mouth.” He turns to me. “And is that nutty flavor fenugreek?”

Ruby giggles at Roddy. “You’re a fenu-geek.”

Gail's laugh is full throttled. "It is delicious, Millicent, but Roddy is so nerding out right now."

I'm tickled that Roddy noticed. I'm usually a plain Jane when it comes to spicing my food—salt, pepper, maybe a little sage or thyme if I'm feeling daring—but since the king of spice was coming to dinner, I thought I'd be bold.

I nod, pleased as punch that my dish is a hit. "It is fenugreek, and a dash of coriander."

Roddy smacks his lips. "Clever. I might have to steal the recipe."

"Mm mm good!" Ruby agrees. "But Roddy's still a geek."

Roddy huffs dramatically at his sister, crossing his arms and arching his eyebrows into a snooty expression. "Cheffy. Not geeky."

Ruby rolls her eyes. "Tomato, tomahto."

Their ribbing is about as harmless and entertaining as two kittens batting at the same ribbon. Watching them carry on makes me feel warm and fuzzy, like I've been folded right into the heart of their family.

Across the table, Donald clears his throat. "It really is marvelous," Donald adds, after swallowing his first bite. "It reminds me of an entrée I order at the Stockyard Inn."

That's the most Donald's said since he got here. He's been distant and distracted all afternoon, and I can't help but wonder if it has something to do with Amanda.

"I've never been there," Ruby says.

"Me neither," Roddy says.

Donald dabs the corner of his mouth with his napkin. "We should go. I took your mother there once."

Roddy's jaw tightens. From what Ruby has told me, I know her parents' relationship was drug and booze fueled, and it's clear Roddy still has sour feelings about it.

Roddy clears his throat, “Yeah, maybe sometime.” He turns towards Gail. “So, back to what you were saying about the ladies saddling their horses.”

She nods and rests her fork on her plate. “So, these two women were talking and I heard the bottle blonde one say, ‘Poor Amanda. She’s already run ragged with Ian’s medical issues, and now this.’ That’s when I really locked in to eavesdropping on their conversation.”

Ruby pipes up. “Did you recognize the women? Were they at the bank party?”

When Gail shakes her head, her chestnut brown ponytail shines in the light. “Nope. Definitely not.” She sips her drink before continuing, “So, anyway, the redhead said, ‘It’s horrible Amanda has so much on her plate, but I don’t feel bad for Isaac at all. He’s a world-class louse. He deserves whatever hardships come his way.’

I keep my grumbles to myself, but the redhead landed her dart dead-center in the bullseye. Isaac truly is a world-class louse.

“The blonde answered with, ‘Oh Isaac deserves it all right. I’ll tell you one thing, if my husband cheats on me, I will take matters into my own hands and poison him myself.’”

Gail leans back crossing her arms. “Well, by this point in the conversation, I’m all in. I stand and stretch, sneaking glances at the duo. The redhead, hand cupped around her mouth, dropped her voice to a gossipy whisper, but I could still hear her loud and clear. ‘Maybe that’s exactly what Amanda did.’”

My eyes fly wide open at such a vicious rumor. Mercy me, people will say anything when they think no one’s listening. The very notion that she’d poison her husband is just outrageous.

Then again, she did give me a jolt when she admitted she’d been seeing another man…

But no. She’s too decent a woman to hurt Isaac. For all his serial cheating, she’s stayed true to her marital vows. The suggestion she’d intentionally poison him is pure nonsense.

Ruby's question pulls me back to the table. Her mouth hangs open and her fork is frozen halfway to her mouth. "Do you think Amanda really could have done it?"

Gail holds up her hand. "Hold on. I'm not done. Here's the kicker. The redhead continued with, 'Amanda has been seen around town with a sophisticated, white-haired man. If she's stepping out too …' The redhead shrugged her shoulders, and paused for a beat before adding, 'I'm just saying, it warrants consideration.'"

I snap my head towards Donald. His face blanches as white as his hair. A truck that looked an awfully lot like his at Amanda's, their tête-á-tête at the party, his name on her caller ID, and now this. It all adds up to one thing, Donald and Amanda are much more than "passing acquaintances."

Roddy throws his napkin on his dinner plate. "Wow, it does indeed warrant consideration. I mean, we kept Amanda on the suspect list, but I never truly thought it was her. And what about this white-haired guy? Could he be involved too?"

Suspect list? Involved? Wait a darn minute. It sounds like Ruby, Roddy, and Gail believe Isaac's accident was anything but. My mouth goes dry. *Could* it have been deliberate?

I mean, it does make sense. There *was* peanut powder sprinkled on the food—that's a fact. And unless a seasoning was mislabeled, which doesn't seem to be the case, Roddy didn't put it there. That means someone else did. Intentionally.

Could those tongue-wagging busybodies at the stables actually be onto something?

I glance back at Donald. Beads of sweat dot his hairline. He gulps down a swallow of water. If guilty has a look, he's wearing it right now.

Ruby twists a red curl around her finger. "That's pretty vague. That could describe a million men. Even you, Dad. But I definitely think we need to erase the question mark beside Amanda's name on our suspect list."

Green edges into Donald's cheeks, like he might be ill. "Suspect list? What am I missing?"

Ruby leans her elbows on the table. "Oh, I guess we need to catch you and Millicent up to speed. We're pretty sure someone at the party intentionally hurt Isaac. And to save Roddy's skin—and both our businesses—we need to prove it. Are you in?"

Donald dabs his hairline with his napkin, then clears his throat. "Of course, I'd love the heat to be off you, Roddy, but I think we need to think rationally. A man who is deathly allergic to peanuts would never leave home without his EpiPen. No one could have known a scuffle would send his rescue medicine under the deejay's table. A deliberate poisoning is just not a logical theory."

"And me making a possibly lethal mistake is?" Roddy growls, pushing his chair back.

Uh oh. Ruby bristles like a terrier defending her favorite person. Getting between her and Roddy is like breaking up a dogfight—pure foolishness. She squares her shoulders and holds her jaw tight.

"Dad, you were at the pre-party meeting. You know how clear Roddy and I were about no peanuts. He absolutely did not spread peanut powder on the food. *That's* not logical."

Roddy's jaw is tight. Gail reaches over squeezing his arm. "We've thought about the EpiPen, Donald. And we think Ed might have started the fight as a way to make sure the EpiPen went missing."

Donald rubs his tightly trimmed beard. "I still think the most prudent course of action is to let your lawyer handle things."

Ruby crosses her arms with a huff, irritation written all over her face. "It's not either or, Dad. The lawyer is handling things, but we can still try to figure out who really did this."

Donald shrugs and keeps his tone even-keeled. "Or you could focus on growing your businesses and let the wheels of justice run their course."

Ruby's posture stiffens, and her sigh comes out hard and loud. "Clearly, we're going to have to agree to disagree."

Ruby, Roddy, and Gail are not happy with Donald's thoughts on this very sore subject. And truth be told, I would've thought he'd be gung-ho to help them prove Roddy's innocence.

Wait. My stomach drops to my knees, and sweat trickles down my side. Mercy me. I *saw* Donald sprinkle something on the food *after* Roddy had prepared it. And Amanda? A wife could make an EpiPen disappear faster than a sock in a dryer. Could they be in cahoots?

For a split second, I consider telling Ruby and Roddy what I remembered, but I can't. Not unless I'm one-hundred-percent certain, and maybe not even then. If Donald is involved, it will destroy them.

Bile stings my throat, threatening to be more. I shove back my chair and rush to the bathroom. The twins will get to the bottom of this disaster, I have no doubt, but Heaven help me… what will they find?

Ruby may seem perky and bubbly, but I know that hides her soft underbelly. And Roddy's practicality and cynicism do the same for him. The last thing they need is another bombshell concerning their father.

I splash cold water on my face and think about Donald. Would he really be involved in something that would hurt his kids? It makes no sense. From what the twins told me, Donald spent over two decades trying to be their father. Unbeknownst to them, he attended plays and games and special events. He mailed cards and letters. He begged their grandmother to let him back in their lives. Why now, after all that time and effort, would he deliberately hurt them?

It just can't be true. There has to be another explanation. There just has to be.

But what if there isn't?

19 ~ Ruby

Lucy and I are cuddled on my couch. The lavender polka-dot throw pillow her long snout is snuggled under, muffles her snores. On my shabby chic end table, a cup of ginger peach tea steeps in one of the four green Fiestaware mugs Dad added to the set of plates Gigi gifted me.

I chew on a pencil as I look over the guest list willing it to spill its secrets. The Peanut Posse—the name I've dubbed our mystery-solving trio—has been able to narrow the list to thirteen. *Lucky* number thirteen.

We've agreed Ed is still at the top of the list, but after what Gail shared last night, Amanda has moved to a close second. Not only did Isaac cheat on her, if the rumors are true, she has a secret lover.

I absentmindedly knead Lucy's loose furry skin and try to place myself in Amanda's head. Does having a lover give her more or less motive to poison her husband? If she's cheating too, wouldn't she be less likely to care if he is? Thoughts ping-pong as my fingers stroke Lucy's oversized, velvety ears. Maybe Amanda wants Isaac out of the way. Maybe she decided death is easier than divorce.

A shiver skitters up my spine. Reaching for my tea cup, I hope the warmth of the mug between my hands will ease my chill. I startle when my cordless phone rings, splashing scalding tea onto my hand. I hop up, wiping the hot liquid on my sundress, and grab the phone out of the charging station. Thunderstruck, I gape at the caller ID.

It's Marty.

The chills scoot away replaced by millions of migrating monarchs. I haven't talked to him in eleven months and three days (but who's counting). Not since the day I backed out of moving in together. Not since the day he broke it off.

My teeth chatter with nerves as I punch the talk button. I've thought about calling him so many times, but always chickened out. He made it pretty clear he was done with my wishy-washiness.

"Hello."

"Ahoy there, Ruby. It's your friendly neighborhood journalist."

My breath catches at his voice. I hold onto the kitchen counter to steady myself.

"Ruby? Are you there? Hello?"

I force a casual breeziness into my words, and chuckle. "And here I thought you were the neighborhood ghost." I cringe at my lame comeback. "Not that I'm saying you should have called. I just mean … it's been ages since we talked."

"It has."

Do I detect sadness in his voice? My heart flutters as if it's blinking in the sunlight after a long hibernation.

I move back to the couch, claiming a tiny corner of it from my stretched-out Basset Hound. "Well, to what do I owe this honor?"

"I'm checking on you. Are you okay? I mean with everything happening to Roddy."

I wilt. Of course, he's calling for work. Roddy's arrest made the front page of the *Intelligencer Journal,* and Marty's one of their lead reporters.

I flatten my voice so he doesn't hear my disappointment. "I have no comment."

"Ruby, I'm not calling for work—oh, I see. When I said 'neighborhood journalist' … sorry. That was me trying to be clever. Gadzooks! This is awkward."

He sounds as tongue-tied as I feel.

I perk up a little. "So, if not work …"

"Almost a year since we've talked and I've flubbed it up." I picture him running his hand over his balding head.

It almost seems like he's thought of calling me, too. The little flutter turns into a full-blown drum solo. It's allegro in my chest, but I aim for smooth jazz on the outside. "Let me guess, you need a deal on a caterer and figured a criminal negligence charge would get you a good rate?"

He chuckles. "Well, it's good to see you still have your sense of humor. Really, Ruby, I know you and Roddy have to be reeling. What can I do to help?"

For Roddy's sake, I've been plucky and positive, but Marty's kindness makes it impossible to maintain even a shred of cool. Tears press against my eyes and my voice quivers as I fill Marty in on everything, including the Peanut Posse's certainty it was deliberate.

"Then we've got some investigating to do. I helped you solve your grandmother's funerary puzzle, I'm sure I can help you with this."

The knots in my body loosen. Marty has a lot of resources. He'll be an invaluable addition to our team. And maybe … if there are still sparks … No. I'm afraid to even think it.

"Do you want to come over tomorrow? Around six? I'll cook dinner. We could go over the details from that night, and I could give you a copy of the guest and employee list?" I squeeze my eyes shut like that'll somehow shield me from rejection.

"Well, um …"

I barrel in before he can finish. "Or, I could write it all down and fax it to you, if that's easier. No dinner required."

"The dinner part is fine, it's the who's cooking it part I worry about."

Relief fills my laugh with more exuberance than necessary. "I'll have you know I've added a few dishes to my repertoire."

"Well then, I'll be like fresh-baked bread and rise to the occasion."

Happiness hijacks my face, stretching my lips from ear to ear. "I see your jokes haven't improved with age."

His snicker curls my toes. "We'll see if your cooking has. I'll bring the wine. See you at six."

The call ends with a soft click, but the conversation lingers—teasing, familiar, and absolutely nerve-wracking. Until I heard his voice, I convinced myself I had moved on. But my brain can't fool my heart.

I miss him.

I miss his periwinkle blue eyes, his John-Lennon glasses, his pleasingly plump belly, and that perpetual smile that made everything feel less serious. I miss his corny jokes, bad impersonations, and out-of-tune karaoke.

Why did I let my fears ruin things?

I stare at the phone, half smiling, half panicking. In less than twenty-four hours, Marty will walk through my front door. Am I brave enough to quiet the doubts? To stop protecting myself against some imagined, inevitable heartbreak? Am I daring enough to ask for a do-over?

And if I muster up the courage to speak the words, will he say yes?

20 ~ Millicent

The MoonGloss slathered on my tresses smells like citrus, and promises a sleek, glass-like shine. Liza swears it works. I'll believe it when I see it. I still have a drawer full of beauty products from when Myrtle decided to sell Lila Mae Skincare. I hosted her very first makeover party and loaded up on skin firmers, wrinkle reducers, dark spot lighteners, and beauty enhancers. I tried the whole kit and kaboodle for one full month—thirty minutes each morning and night to get through the whole regimen—thirty wasted hours of my life. By the end of the month, Myrtle had quit sales and the only difference in my skin was an allergic reaction that took a steroid and two weeks to clear up.

After wrapping my head in plastic to activate the glossing serum, Liza hands me a glass of sweet tea. "Connie will be here in a few minutes. Do we have a game plan?"

Connie is the only reason I subjected my scalp to MoonGloss. At my dinner, Ruby asked me to investigate Connie and Ed—specifically, how furious Ed was when he found out about Isaac, and whether he could've added peanut powder to the menu.

With every aching bone, I hope Donald has nothing to do with Isaac's attack. I don't think the twins could recover from that. So, I jumped at the chance to prove he's in the clear.

Since Ruby gave me her blessing to loop Liza in on our theory about Isaac's allergy attack, I asked her to help me set up a chance to question Connie.

I take a sip of the tea. "Let's just get her talking about that night."

"Okay. Just go with the flow. That's definitely my modus operandi." Liza pops a CD into her player. A gentle piano melody, laced with birdsong drifts from the speakers. She adds a few drops of essential oil to the diffuser. "Neroli," she explains. "Promotes feelings of trust and openness."

Shampoodles lazily lifts her head and sniffs as the floral sweetness fills the air. She yawns and flops onto her back, legs up in the air.

I hitch my head toward the poodle. "It's working on Shammie."

Liza laughs as she wipes the salon chair down with an all-natural sanitizing spray.

A gust of hot, humid air follows Connie as she flounces into Mystic Mane. She slides a cobalt Kate Spade bag off her shoulder and hangs it on a hook beside the door. After untying a matching blue sweater from around her neck, she slides into it. "I get so chilly in the air conditioning."

The bangles covering Liza's forearm clink when she motions to the chair. "I'm ready for you, Connie."

Connie bustles towards the chair, then stops moving when she sees me nestled in the recliner in the cozy back corner of the salon. "Millicent?" She blinks. "I didn't know you visited salons."

Well, that's a passive-aggressive little jab if I ever heard one. But maybe Myrtle's right. If my look screams "never visits hair salons," it might be time to spruce up a little.

I shrug my shoulders. "Time for something new, I guess. Liza tells me the MoonGloss currently tingling my scalp will have my gray hair shining like glass."

Connie settles into the chair. "Is that so? Maybe I should try it? Liza, will it work on my hair?"

Liza's flowing locks tumble across her eye when she shakes her head. "Nope. Only for gray hair. I can give you a Copperlight treatment. It adds luminosity to auburn tones."

Connie primps in front of the mirror, fluffing her textured waves. "Yes, let's add that in. I deserve luminosity."

"We all deserve luminosity," Liza chuckles as she drapes a black cape over Connie.

I stifle an eyeroll.

Connie preens at her reflection. "Yes. I need to look my best. Lately, I'm always in the public eye. I suppose that comes with serving on so many boards. It seems like I have an event or speech every other day."

Heavens to Betsy! If she toots her own horn any louder, we'll need ear protection.

Liza responds diplomatically. "Good to hear you're so productive. So, what are we doing with your hair?"

Connie pulls her hair away from her part. "Getting rid of these detestable roots, and then a light trim."

Liza grabs a mixing bowl, adds a bit of this and that, and stirs.

Connie rests her hand on her cheek. A huge diamond sparkles on her finger. "And I've got this award banquet coming up. You might have heard I'm receiving a bronze plaque on the donor wall of the hospital."

As Liza paints a henna-based dye onto Connie's gray roots, she shoots me a this-is-it look. "Yes, you mentioned the banquet at Ethan's surprise party. Wasn't that quite the eventful night?"

Connie arches her sculpted eyebrows. "I'm certainly glad Ed and I left before the buffet opened. If the caterer was too incompetent to avoid peanuts, you can bet the meal wouldn't have been gluten-free."

I bite my tongue. Now is the time to dig, not call out her rude remarks.

"You didn't even get to taste the food?" I ask.

Her sigh is audible. “No. After Ed’s embarrassing behavior, I thought it best to slip out as quickly as possible.”

Ed’s behavior? What about her cheating?

Shammie wanders over to me and I lift her onto my lap. “I didn’t know Ed and Isaac aren’t friendly.”

“Ed was in his cups. He heard a snide remark about Isaac and me, and it set him off.”

Liza winces. “Sorry to say, I heard it too.”

Connie flicks her hand dismissively. “It’s no secret. Ed has had a mistress set up in an apartment in downtown Lancaster for years. And I’ve had my own share of romantic trysts. What bruised his ego was the gossip painting him as a cuckold.”

I sink my fingers in Shammie’s gray curls, taking a beat to remove the judgment from my voice. “Oh, so you have an open marriage?”

She pauses, then shakes her head. “No. I wouldn’t define it as open. It’s more… flexible. Honestly, I think a lot of couples have their own arrangements. Like Isaac and Amanda for example. Clearly, she knows he’s been cheating for years and doesn’t care.” She shrugs. “I mean, let’s be real. Monogamy sounds lovely in theory, but real life’s a bit more complicated.”

Anger bubbles up as I think about the pain in Amanda’s eyes when she told me about Connie and Isaac. How can Connie be so blasé about her adultery? Does she really think no one gets hurt?

I open my mouth to give her a piece of my mind, but Liza gives me a warning glare. I clamp my mouth shut as Liza moves Connie under the dryer hood.

When Liza situates me at the sink to rinse out the MoonGloss, she leans in and whispers, “Not exactly a ringing endorsement for marriage.”

I snort, “Hardly.”

“But it does seem like we can cross Connie and Ed off the list of suspects since they left before gaining access to the food.”

I huff with disappointment. “True.”

After rinsing off the goop, Liza adds a curl enhancer, then dries my hair using a diffuser. Ten minutes later, she spins my chair around so I can see myself in the mirror.

Well, I’ll be.

My curls gleam like the moon on a black sky night. My salon appointment didn’t clear Donald’s name, but it might’ve earned me a spot in a MoonGloss commercial.

21 ~ Ruby

The seasoned beef is warming on the stove. The lettuce is shredded. Olives, tomatoes, and onions are cut, cheddar cheese is grated, and the taco sauce is in the gravy boat. All I need to do is bake the taco shells and get dressed.

I dash up the stairs taking them two at a time, and careen into my bedroom. I root through my closet until I unearth the kelly-green leggings and the daisy-print A-line tunic I wore on my first official date with Marty. (Yes, I kept it all these years.) I consider playing the soundtrack to Saturday Night Fever—the movie we saw—but decide that's way too obvious. With any luck, my outfit will be enough to send a subtle signal: I'm open to a sequel.

After wrangling my unruly red curls into a bright yellow scrunchie, I dab some color onto my freckled cheeks, swipe on lip gloss, and mist myself with Citruslicious body spray. Then slide into my newest thrift shop score—a pair of bright yellow Chuck Taylors—and give myself the once-over in my full-length mirror.

Passable.

Since the breakup, my shelves groan with self-help relationship books. Thanks to the learned professionals, I've realized I don't just fear vulnerability, I run from it like it's a flying monkey and I'm Dorothy Gale.

Turns out believing both my parents died before I hit a month old, can lead to "avoidant attachment styles." Add in the bombshell of Dad popping back into our lives, turbo boosting my abandonment issues … No wonder I chased Marty away.

After eleven months of spelunking through the deep, dark caves of my psyche (armed with only a journal, a slobbery Basset Hound, and Millicent's chocolate chip cookies), I think I'm finally ready to give love the old college try. Let's hope Marty is—before I buy another book.

The doorbell rings as I'm halfway down the stairs. Lucy offers one measly bark before resuming snoring. I take a deep breath, square my shoulders, and open the front door.

Marty's pink polo shirt is partially untucked, and has a ketchup stain. His khaki pants are wrinkled and the wisps of his remaining hair are plastered to his head from the high humidity. He's totally adorable.

A bottle of wine is wedged under his arm. He brandishes his messenger bag like a badge. "Investigative reporter at your service."

Guilt and disappointment creep in. I've been flitting around like a schoolgirl on prom night, while Roddy's facing possible jail time. The giddiness escapes from my hot air balloon and I land back in reality. This isn't a date. Marty—kind man that he is—is here to offer his professional help.

I salute him, then blush at my ridiculousness. "Come in. Come in."

"Righto!"

As he steps inside the cottage, Lucy jumps off the couch, tail wagging, and jogs over to greet him (that's high-level enthusiasm for her).

He bends down, allowing her to lick his face. "Well, who is this lovely creature?"

"Lucy."

He plops on the floor, setting the wine and work to the side, and uses both hands to pet her. "As in Ball, or van Pelt?"

"As in Queen Lucy the Valiant."

He holds her head and touches his nose to hers. "Aah! Brave, kind, and the first to discover Narnia. Well, Lucy, it's just ducky to meet you."

Lucy pushes forward, trying to climb on Marty's lap. Her enormous snout clearly can sniff out good character.

He laughs, letting her climb over him. "How do you ever get any work done? I'd roll around on the floor with her all day."

I lift my chin and don a haughty tone. "Her desipience is a delightful distraction on tough days."

Lucy's wagging tail whacks him in the face. "Ooh, that's got to be a ten-pointer. Plus, bonus points for alliteration."

I'm touched he remembered Gigi's favored word game.

"Twenty-five, it is," I say, laughing. "It basically means buffoonery, by the way. I just learned it. From Leacock's *Nonsense Novels*. If you haven't read them, I think you'd like them."

"I'll give them a read." He hauls himself up from the floor, dusting off the dog hair. "What delectable smell is in the air? Chiles. Garlic. Onions. Tamales? Mole Poblano?"

I put my hands on my hips. "Dial it back to beginner level, bub. *Old El Paso* taco kit."

He collects his messenger bag and wine from the floor. "A perfect meal for the vintage Yellow Tail Shiraz I brought."

"Yepper. We are channeling the *Dynasty* life."

We move into my kitchen. I arrange the taco shells on a baking tray while Marty cracks open the wine. Remembering where I keep them, he opens one of the mint green kitchen cabinets and pulls out two wine glasses, pouring us each a glass. Being together feels so natural and easy, it's hard to keep my hope in check.

He pulls out a lilac ladderback chair, and settles into his usual spot at the kitchen table. "Let's eat first—give your undoubtedly incredible meal the respect it deserves—and then crack on with our investigation. Sound good?"

The mention of the real reason for his visit throws cold water on the romantic prospects for the evening. I hide my disappointment in a swirl of spicy steam. “Sounds like a plan.”

*****

I stack the dinner dishes in the sink, refusing Marty’s offer to help clean up, and we move into the living room. Shoving Lucy’s rump towards one side of my white slip-covered couch gives me just enough room to squeeze in beside her.

Marty sits in the aqua-blue chair across from me and digs a tablet from his messenger bag. “Okay. Off we trot!”

I hand Marty a copy of the guest and employee list. “I crossed off anyone we ruled out and circled the likely suspects. Ed Baker is top on our list. He accosted Isaac during the party. Millicent is meeting with his wife Connie—actually, she probably already has—to see if she can uncover anything useful.”

“Righto!” he says, scanning the list. “I ran into Millicent outside the office a few months ago. It was lovely to see her.”

I am so lucky to have Millicent in my life. The gaping hole Gigi’s death left feels smaller because of her. She doesn’t try to replace Gigi—no one could—but she seems to know exactly when to listen, when to fuss, or when I just need a cookie and a hug. Even now, there are still moments I wobble with grief, and Millicent’s there to steady me.

“She’s one-of-a-kind,” I say, pulling my focus back to PeanutGate. “She’s also tight with Amanda. Gail overheard a rumor that Amanda may be cheating on Isaac. If we don’t come up with any other leads, I plan to ask Millicent to get a read on her.” Marty skims the list. “So, we’ll wait for updates on Ed, Connie, and Amanda. Let’s start with Oscar and Tabitha Reed. What can you remember about them?”

I pinch my bottom lip, as I try to recall the details of our interaction. "Hmm. Tabitha is planning a 60th anniversary party for her parents. And before PeanutGate I thought Roddy and I had the job."

Marty frowns and cleans his round glasses. "Did you lose a lot of business?"

"Oh yeah! My job prospects dried up faster than a puddle in the Mojave Desert at noon."

"Making it even more critical to clear your names." He scribbles a note on his yellow, lined tablet paper. "Anything else about Tabitha?"

"She's in a wheelchair. Not sure that has any relevance." I pause rifling through my memory of that night. "Oh," I say, snapping my fingers. "She said Oscar has lost a small fortune playing poker with Ethan, Isaac, and Bob."

"Did she seem bitter about it?"

I shake my head. "Not at all. In fact, she joked about it and claimed diamonds are her hobby."

He taps his finger on his chin. "Gambling and expensive jewelry. Maybe they've gotten in over their heads."

"But why hurt Isaac?"

He shrugs. "Easier to blame someone than take responsibility? Or maybe Oscar caught Isaac cheating at poker?" Marty adds a note beside their names. "Doesn't hurt to look into them. I'll see if there are any bankruptcy filings, foreclosure actions, civil judgments, or tax liens."

It feels so reassuring to have Marty on our side, I get a little choked up. "This whole thing has been super stressful. I really do appreciate your help. Especially since I, uh, messed things up between us."

He holds up his hand like a stop sign and offers a sympathetic smile. "You know I'm always game to solve a good mystery. Just fetch me my deerstalker and pipe and I'll be on the case."

I clear the lump in my throat. "Oh, I wish I still had the hats and pipes Gigi left for Roddy and me."

"What? No cap? I didn't realize PeanutGate was BYOC."

I laugh. "You'll just have to solve without it."

"Elementary, my dear Ruby! So, who's next? How about Bob and Betty?"

"They're country club members and seemed very friendly with Amanda and Isaac. Apparently, Bob plays golf with Isaac frequently. That's about all I know about them." I move down the list. "As for Hank and Iris, Gail overheard Hank saying something along the lines of 'it'd be a cold day in hell before he'd sit with Isaac and Amanda,' so clearly, there's no love lost between them. I'm pretty sure Hank has played basketball with Roddy, maybe he can get the scoop on him."

Marty makes a star beside Hank's name. "I'll check into him, too. If Hank's got a beef with Isaac, I'd like to know if it's rare, medium, or well done."

"Ba-dum tss," I say, pretending to hit a drum.

Marty rolls his hand and bows, taking full credit for his groan-worthy one-liner. "Okay, moving on to the hired help. Tell me about Stephanie."

"Professional. Cool under pressure. As was her—" I pause, recalling the incident with Janelle and Isaac.

Marty cocks his head. "As was her?"

"I was going to say as was her assistant, but I just remembered something. Janelle snapped at Isaac when he waved an empty glass at her, and asked for a drink. Granted, it was a smug move on Isaac's part, but it didn't warrant her level of hostility. And then right after that, I found her in the bathroom, clearly upset."

"More upset than a rude customer would justify?"

"Absolutely." Another memory hits and my hand flies to my mouth. "Oh my! I just remembered her reaction after the ambulance left. She was in the bathroom, talking on her phone, and I heard her say, 'Karma's a bitch.' Plus, she was oddly upbeat after such a tense situation. There's definitely more to her behavior towards Isaac than just dealing with a difficult customer."

Marty underlines Janelle's name on his list. "I'll see what I can dig up."

"I'm sure Roddy's lawyer will appreciate anything that creates reasonable doubt. Especially if Isaac …" I gulp, unable to finish my sentence. Despite my best efforts, a tear rolls down my cheek.

Marty leaps from his chair, gallantly grabs a tissue, and scooches Lucy over so he can sit next to me. "Is it okay if I hug you?"

I nod and dab my leaking eyes. His embrace stirs a kaleidoscope of emotions—comfort, longing, hope, worry. I lean into his side, and block myself from reading anything into his hug. Oh, how I wish I could rewrite the three years we shared. He deserved better than what I had to give. And having him as my partner now would make this disaster much easier to bear. But at least I have his friendship.

He gives me a gentle squeeze. "Ruby, don't lose hope. Now's the perfect time to slide on your rose-colored glasses. Isaac *will* rally. And we *will* find out what really happened."

I suck in a deep breath and slap on a smile (fake it till you make it). He's right. And so are Mulder and Scully. The truth is out there. With our brains and grit, a bottomless kettle of tea, and a hefty dose of luck, the expanded Peanut Posse just might uncover it.

22 ~ Millicent

I park on the street in front of Penelope. No, Persephone. No, that's not right either. Heavens to Betsy, I can't recall Ruby's name for her cottage. I know it starts with a P. Myrtle claims her memory loss came from raising a baseball team full of kids. I don't know what I should chalk mine up to. Maybe too many sweets?

I would've parked in the driveway, but a white Prius already sits behind Ruby's VW bug. I wonder who's visiting her? Maybe I shouldn't interrupt in case it's a date. Though, I highly doubt she'd be dating right now with all that's hanging over her and Roddy's heads. But you never know. Stress does peculiar things to people.

My mother used to throw a rip-roaring party when she felt overwhelmed. It sounds a bit backwards—adding more chaos to the chaos—but somehow, it calmed her. And I know when Myrtle's husband, Rick, is on his last nerve, he'll laugh like a cackling hyena. That's my nieces' and nephews' cue to head for the hills.

I tap my fingers against my chin, deciding whether I should risk intruding. When I glance at myself in the rearview mirror, the decision is made. My hair looks entirely too good to waste on Pizelle. And though Liza gifted me with the curl enhancer and a tutorial on how to recreate this miracle, my frizzy curls have a mind of their own. I'm not betting on a repeat performance.

I lumber between the boxwoods lining the walkway and rap on the bright yellow front door.

Ruby looks almost bubbly as she claps her hands together when she sees me. "Hey, Millicent. What a nice surprise."

"Is it?" I whisper conspiratorially. "I noticed the Prius in the driveway. Do you have a gentleman caller?"

Her lips twist into a crooked smile. "In a manner of speaking." She winks. "Marty volunteered to help us find out what really happened at the bank. Come on in."

Marty? Well, I'll be jiggered! This is the happiest little surprise I've had all week—even better than my frizz-free hairdo. And Ruby looks tickled, too.

I would love nothing more than to see those two find their way back to each other. But as I step into Ruby's shabby chic living room, full of pinks and blues and polka dots, a bubble-bursting memory flickers: Marty's arm around that young woman in front of his office. Oh, dear! I hope Ruby isn't setting herself up for disappointment.

Marty greets me with a big hug. "Millicent, you look so good, even the obits would crack a smile."

I pat his shoulder. "Still clever as ever, I see."

"Don't you mean corny as ever?" Ruby chimes in. "But he's right. You do look amazing. Did you get a haircut?"

"MoonGloss magic." I say, as I spin around in a circle to give them a panoramic view. "Liza gave me the full how-do-you-do."

Ruby's eyebrows lift in surprise. "You went to Mystic Mane?"

I nod as I plop my wide bottom into an overstuffed side chair. "Connie was coming in for an appointment. It gave me a reason to be there."

Marty takes the other blue chair. After pouring me a cup of fresh-brewed meadow tea, and adding a heaping tablespoon of sugar per my instructions (I soundly reject the idea sugar could be affecting anything but the size of my rump), Ruby settles herself crossed-legged on the couch.

"This tea tastes like childhood. My mother would send me and Myrtle out to collect a six-quart pot full of apple mint leaves and she'd simmer them the whole day, filling the house with the sweet mint scent. Or sometimes, I'd put the leaves and water in a Mason jar on the windowsill and make sun tea."

Ruby hitches her thumb towards her backyard. "Feel free to grab yourself a few bags full of tea leaves. They've basically commandeered the back corner of my garden."

Marty's eyebrows raise onto his shiny forehead. "I thought you didn't like gardening."

Ruby laughs. "Growing meadow tea is not gardening. I don't weed or water it. I just pick it. I swear I could pave over it and it'd still grow through the cracks."

When I nod my head, my curls—usually frizzed within an inch of their life—bounce a surprising little jig. "It would! Meadow tea survives on stubbornness and sunshine."

Ruby takes a sip of her own tea. "Okay, Millicent. Fill us in. What did you find out about Connie and Ed?"

"Well, their marriage was no stranger to, shall we say, romantic detours. Connie thinks Ed only threw a hissy fit because he drank too much and was embarrassed by the snickers flying around. Take that or leave it. What crosses them off the list is access. They left before the buffet opened, so they couldn't have doctored the dishes."

Ruby sighs. "The timeline fits. When I went to ask them to leave, they had already gone." Her face falls for a second before she slaps on her usual spunkiness. "Oh well. Crossing people off is still progress."

Lucy clambers onto Marty's lap, rutching around until her big ol' butt is comfortable. Maybe Ruby will take a page from her playbook. Mercy me, this hairdo is making me a little spicy.

Marty ignores the dog drool dampening his khaki pants and strokes her velvety ears. "Not to worry. I've got plenty of other leads to chase down."

I wonder if Donald is on that list. I consider pulling Marty aside and telling him my concerns. It would be a huge relief to share my horrible suspicions with someone else. But if his and Ruby's relationship is budding (again) I don't want to burden him with a secret.

As usual, I stuff a throw pillow under my hip to ease the ache. "We might want to look at Hank."

"Why's that?" Marty asks.

"At the party, he made it pretty clear, much to Iris's embarrassment, that he doesn't care for Isaac."

Ruby nods her head. "Roddy overheard Hank's comment about Isaac, too. I filled Marty in right before you got here."

I shift around in the chair, struggling to get comfortable. "I know Isaac and Hank work together at the university. Maybe that's the source of the bad blood between them. And … his aura is dark orange."

Ruby almost spits out her tea. "His aura? I mean, not to be judgy, but since when are you reading auras?"

I cross my arms. "I don't. But Liza does. I wasn't buying her woo-woo stuff at first, but lately her tarot readings have been dead on."

Ruby winces, Isaac's life still hangs in the balance, and I regret my word choice.

Her shoulders sag as if weighted down by worry. "Okay then. What does a dark orange aura mean."

"Jealousy, bitterness, or a bruised ego."

"Hmm," Marty says. "Exactly what you'd feel if you've been cheated on."

Ruby's mouth drops open. "So, you think Iris and Isaac?"

I shrug my shoulders. "I think it's worth considering. Isaac's philandering is a well-known secret. It would explain Hank's hostility towards Isaac."

I consider reminding them that Amanda also has an extracurricular interest, but I'm not ready to lead Ruby down that road. If it does turn out to be Donald …

Ruby flips her palms over and raises her eyebrows. “Looks like we’ve got a new top suspect.”

23 ~ Millicent

After delivering a fresh-baked box of chocolate chip cookies to room 609 where my neighbor is recovering from a broken hip, I swing by Isaac's room. There are only a few minutes left until hospital visiting hours end and I'm not entirely sure I'm one-hundred percent welcome, but I want to show my support.

Jed is walking out of the room as I arrive. "Oh, hey, Millie. How's it hanging?"

He's got pep in his step and his face is the opposite of somber. I'm hoping that means good news.

"I'm fine. Fine. How's your brother?"

A stringy lock of hair falls across his face when he shakes his head. "No change. The nurses just kicked me out. They want to give him a sponge bath. Heh, heh. He'll be pissed he wasn't conscious to enjoy the perks of a hospital stay."

His joking hits me wrong, but I guess everyone has their own way of handling stress.

"Hey, Millie," he says as we walk to the bank of elevators. "I'm glad I ran into you. Do you need a band, or even just a deejay at the Violet House bash? Or any other gigs? I could really use the extra cash. Me and Felix need to scrape up a hefty deposit to lock down the surrogate. I already asked Isaac for a loan, but he shut me down. I guess I'd be a real tool if I tried to sweet talk Amanda into it while Isaac's in the hospital. Right?"

Tool, with a capital T.

The elevator doors slide open and we step inside.

"Um," I stutter. "It does seem like awfully bad timing."

He pulls his stringy hair into a ponytail, fastening with a band he slides off his wrist. "Yeah, yeah. Just spitballing. Felix is up my keister to get this done."

The elevator stops on the ground floor. I exit and Jed slinks out behind me. He points to the cafeteria sign on the wall in front of us. "I'm going to grab some chow. Let me know about the Violet House thing. It was good seeing ya."

He's around the corner before I have a chance to reply. I head out the main entrance and nearly run smack into Donald on the sidewalk in front of the hospital.

His eyes widen with surprise and he checks his watch. "Millicent, what are you doing here? Aren't visiting hours over?"

"They just ended. How about you?"

His eyes scan the street, as if he's looking for someone. "I, uh, have an appointment."

An appointment or a secret rendezvous? I'll stall him a little and see who shows up.

"Have you talked to Ruby today? Marty stepped up—"

His peppered brows furrow. "Marty?"

My chin waddle flaps with my zippy nod. "Yes siree, Bob! He was at Ruby's last night. To help solve the mystery of the peanut powder."

"He was at Ruby's cottage? Was she okay?"

"She was as giddy as a squirrel in a peanut factory. Only thing is, I'm not sure Marty was feeling the same way. I mean he was friendly, but not flirty. Though goodness knows I'm no expert on flirting. It's been a long while since—well, actually I never was the flirtatious type. Now my sister Myrtle on the other hand. The boys were drawn to her like bees to clover. She loved their buzzing about her. That is until Rick came into the picture."

Donald checks his watch again, then shifts from foot to foot. His forehead lines deepen. He's definitely getting antsy.

I lay my hand on my heart and chuckle. "Mercy me, here I am holding you up with my rambling. I've been known to veer off course." I take an exaggerated glance up and down the street. "Are they late?"

"Who?"

"The person you've been looking for. Didn't you say you have an appointment?"

His swallow is visible. "I never said I … I mean, I'm not waiting for … My appointment is inside, I uh, just don't want to be late."

Something's got him tongue-tied.

"Oh. I didn't know doctors held late hours. I hope it's nothing serious."

His eyes dart up and down the street with increased urgency. He holds up a finger. "Excuse me for one second."

He pulls his flip-phone from his pocket and types a text message. I try to see what he's typing or the recipient's name, but I can't get a good look. Once he hits send, his shoulders relax and mine tighten. I'd bet my bottom dollar he warned Amanda to steer clear, not wanting me to see them together.

Donald holds out his elbow. "Let me walk you to your car so you can fill me in on Ruby and Marty."

I link my arm with his, noticing the scent of amber, softened with a touch of vanilla. "But what about your appointment? I don't want you to be late."

"And I don't want to let an opportunity to escort a lovely woman to her car slip away. Shall we?" he says, giving me a gentle tug.

He's got charm. I'll give him that.

It's easy to understand why Ruby—with her usual sunny style—has embraced Donald wholeheartedly. Roddy, on the other hand, has not. Maybe he senses something the rest of us missed.

As we walk to my Ford, my belly rolls with the thought of what Donald's involvement would do to the twins. And it flips again thinking of Roddy behind bars for a mistake he didn't make. Neither possibility lets me breathe easy.

I wish I wasn't in this predicament. I wish the clues weren't leading to Donald. From where I'm sitting, he's been nothing but kind—to me, to Gail and Marty, and especially to the twins. And that only makes this whole business murkier.

But if he's involved, the twins need to know.

Acid bites into my stomach. If this doesn't get settled soon, I'll have an ulcer the size of a frisbee. The worry is chewing holes in my insides, and the worst part is knowing I can't do a darn thing about it—yet.

Once in my car, I dig a Tums from the bottom of my purse and force myself to breathe. Right now, I only have suspicions. Circumstantial evidence. I'm not ready to speak up. No reason to blow up their world.

Not until I have proof.

24 ~ Ruby

Taco night with Marty wasn't nearly spicy as I had hoped. He didn't turn up the heat as much as I would have liked, but it wasn't plain-yogurt bland either. We're planning to meet again, albeit for PeanutGate matters, but I'm keeping my fingers crossed.

Despite my disappointment in the romance department, Marty delivered on his promise to help. Spurred by Millicent's comment about Isaac's philandering, Marty waded through months of Myerstown University's Athletics Oversight Committee's meeting minutes and hit paydirt! Buried in the March notes was a reference to a complaint filed by an assistant coach (presumably Hank) against a senior athletics staff member (almost certainly Isaac), citing "alleged inappropriate conduct involving interactions with undergraduate students."

After that bombshell, Roddy arranged a pick-up game with Hank, and—thanks to Millicent's handiwork—I'm here at Violet House to work a volunteer shift pulling weeds with Iris. By this evening, maybe we'll be closer to clearing Roddy.

Violet House's large backyard has a swing set and slide, a sandbox, three picnic tables, and a few hammocks surrounded by beds of flowers and vegetables. Iris and I have been parked in front of the flower bed for the last hour. She's focused on digging out the dandelions—the kingpin of the backyard underworld—while I eliminate the rest of the garden thugs.

The sweet herbal smell of blooming lavender mingling with the minty scent of bee balm, tickles my nose. The humidity is at rainforest level and sweat dribbles down my neck, puddling in my bra. My knees ache and my hands are cramping, yet another reason meadow tea will indeed be the only crop in my garden. And so far, I've had no luck getting any information that will help prove Roddy's innocence.

I run my hands through my frizzed curls, pulling them back into a messy ponytail, and give it another try. "Why are we battling green invaders, while Roddy and Hank are *hooping* it up?"

Iris's mud-smeared cheeks round with her smile, but she doesn't answer. She dribbles cold water in the palm of her hand and dabs it on her face. "Sheesh. The water got hot before it hit my face."

I take a few swallows of water. "Yeah, it's brutal."

Plunging the two-pronged fork into the roots of a dandelion, she says, "It's not the heat, it's the humidity. I'm originally from New Mexico. Our summer temps get high, but we don't have this kind of swampiness. It makes it hard to breathe."

"That it does." I wipe my forehead with the back of my gloved hand and suck in the soupy air. Here we go. Attempt number three-hundred-and-four. "What brought you to PA? Hank?"

She shakes her head as she guzzles from her water bottle. "Nope, college. I went to Villanova."

"Did you meet Hank there?"

Her hair, plastered to her scalp by sweat, doesn't budge when she shakes her head. "No."

It's been like this all day. Every question I ask hits a wall. This is what people mean by pulling teeth. I can't get the conversation to move in the right—really, any—direction.

She stands and stretches. "This is back-breaking."

I twist long green leaves around my hand and yank, falling back when the ground gives way. A round bulb comes up with the leaves. "Oops. I think this one was a flower." I shrug. "Horticulture clearly wasn't my major."

Her laugh is robust. "Clearly. Where'd you go to college?" Using her foot, she scoots the pad to the next section of garden, then kneels on it.

"Penn State."

"Oh, yeah?" She jabs another dandelion root. "That's Hank's dream university. He'd love to be head coach for the Nittany Lions."

Ooh! Here's my chance!

I take another swallow of water to douse my enthusiasm before it leaks into my voice. "He's interim head coach now, right? Since Isaac's in the hospital?"

Her lips press tight together and her nostrils flare. She impales the next dandelion in a full-out assault. Evidently, I'm onto something.

"I'm sorry. Did I say something to upset you? Hank did get the interim position, didn't he?"

"Finally." The bitterness is evident in her tone.

Red creeps up her neck, and I suspect it's from more than the summer heat. Normally, I wouldn't push, but I need info.

"What do you mean, finally?"

"He should have been made head coach a year ago."

Her stabbing is so savage I feel bad for the dandelion.

"Really? I thought Isaac's held that position for a long time."

"Too long." With one forceful plunge, the fork sinks deep into the soil. Iris sits back onto the walkway and takes a long swallow of water. "Last year, when Isaac's contract came up for renewal, the university asked Hank to apply for the position. They told Hank the team needed new blood."

I swivel to sit on my butt, stretching my legs in front of me to give my knees a break. How anyone can think gardening is relaxing is beyond me. "So, Hank and Isaac were up for the same position?"

She nods. "Hank's prospects looked good until Isaac 'let it slip' to the hiring committee that Hank's father was dying from Alzheimer's. Said he was simply concerned Hank might not be able to give the job his full attention."

How despicable to use someone else's tragedy as leverage. That must've been a real gut punch. And I hate to admit it, but a tiny part of me isn't sorry Isaac's in a coma. If *I'm* feeling that, could Iris or Hank be carrying enough resentment to want revenge?

"That's just wrong," I commiserate. "I don't even know how you can stand being around Isaac."

She drops her face into her hands and shakes her head. "That's not the worst part." Her hands slide down her face and rest, clasped, on top of her chest. "I didn't even know about it. I've had countless drinks and dinners with Isaac and Amanda over the past year. I played mixed doubles with Isaac as a partner. I've attended parties at their house. Hank kept me in the dark because he didn't want to ruin my friendship with Amanda."

My hand flies to my mouth. "Oh, my stars! How'd you find out?"

"After the night of the bank party, I was nagging him because he refused to sit with Amanda and Isaac. I just wouldn't let up. I guess too many Safecrackers had me feeling feisty."

Hmph. Apparently, a lot of folks had too many Safecrackers that night.

She presses her lips together. "That's when Hank told me."

Looks like I can cross Iris off the list.

Dirt smudges on her temple when she presses her fingers against it. "I feel like such an idiot."

I scooch across the walkway and pat her shoulder. "You shouldn't. There was no way for you to know. Hank was so sweet to try to preserve your friendship, but how was he able to work with Isaac after what he did? I think I would've been too angry."

"I truly don't know. It had to be torture. Especially, to have Isaac as his boss."

Violet House's volunteer wrangler gives Iris and me a pointed look. We both move back into weed-pulling positions. Will this job never end?

Iris slides her hands back into her gloves and attacks a few more dandelions. "I can tell you, even though Hank's busier now, he's coming home a lot less stressed. And the athletic director is full of praise for the job he's doing pre-season."

I wrestle a few more weeds out of the dirt. "Who knows? Maybe, now that they see how well Hank's doing, he'll get to keep the job."

Iris holds up her hands and crosses her fingers. "That's what we're hoping. I know this will sound terrible, but I'm not sad Isaac is in the hospital. It gave Hank the shot he rightfully deserved, and Isaac had it coming."

If Hank feels that way too, it's beyond resentment. It's motive.

25 ~ Millicent

After another day of stress-baking, I've realized there isn't enough flour in the world for me to handle this alone. My suspicions about Donald have me in a full-blown tizzy. If I don't share the burden soon, I'll be shopping for a house with a double oven just to survive the week.

With a tin of freshly-baked snickerdoodles in hand, I plod down the sidewalk. Mystic Mane's black glass exterior gleams in the sunlight. The bell tinkles as I push open the door.

A teeny-bopper sits in Liza's salon chair; hot pink hair being gelled into jagged spikes.

"Sorry to barge in on you, but I brought cookies," I say, leaning against her reclaimed wood desk. "Do you have any time to talk?"

Liza rests her hand on the teens shoulder. "She's my last client, and I'm just finishing up."

I crack open the tin and offer Liza and her client a treat. I almost call her Pinky Tuscadero—though honestly, Pinky never had pink hair. It was red. Or reddish. Something in the red family. Anyway, this one's definitely pink, and she grabs two cookies without a second thought while Liza waves me off, too busy pulling and twisting and lifting and scrunching. Five minutes later, the fuchsia grenade—yes, that fits her much better than Pinky Tuscadero—struts out of the salon, ready to take on the world as only the young can. My once-again frizzy, limp curls yawn with exhaustion. Like me, they only had the stamina to bounce for a day. Liza flips the closed sign on the door, then bustles about cleaning up. "You have my *divided* attention. What's going on?"

I nibble a cookie as I share my suspicions about Donald and Amanda. Liza does less sweeping, more listening as the circumstantial evidence piles up.

"There's only one thing to be done." She motions me to a deep-purple velvet chair positioned in front of a small, hand-hewn pine table.

The rounded arms envelop me within the seat like a swaddled baby. Liza pulls a tarot deck from a wall shelf, then sits across from me in a matching chair.

"We're going to solve the attack on Isaac with a tarot reading?" I say, with unmasked irritation. Maybe Marty would've been a better confidante, because this is certainly not the kind of help I had in mind.

She shuffles the cards "If you want me to be involved, I need the universe's guidance. My first inquiry will be why. I know Ruby and Roddy's well-being is your main concern, but I do need you to be prepared to hear that it was just an unfortunate accident."

"Hmph." I cross my arms and pout, frustrated with my friend. "After everything I told you, you don't think there's something shady going on?"

"Millicent, I think it's likely Donald and Amanda are hiding a relationship, but deliberate poisoning …" She sets the deck in front of her and waits for my answer.

I know in my heart, Roddy did not make a mistake, and no crystal-ball logic is going to convince me otherwise, but I could use a fresh set of eyes. A friend to confide in. I wave my hand across the table. "Let the cards lay where they will."

She lays three cards face up on the wooden table. "Intention leaves fingerprints in the energy. These cards indicate the motivation behind the misdeed." Her many chunky, silver and gold rings twinkle under the salon lights as she taps each card with her fingertips. "The Page of Cups. The Five of Pentacles. Aah, the Seven of Swords. It was not an accident."

Even though I don't really believe in this stuff, the tension drains from my muscles at the confirmation. "What else do the cards tell you?"

She rests an elegant, manicured finger on her lips, and cups her chin as she contemplates. "The Page of Cups typically symbolizes the love for a child, reflecting emotional bonds that are pure and nurturing."

I crinkle my already wrinkly forehead. "This has to do with a child?"

Her flowing mane of gunmetal-gray hair shimmers with the tiny shake of her head. (Clearly, the MoonGloss works for her).

"Not necessarily," she says. "It could also indicate the wonder of a new, tender, romantic love."

I slap my hands on the little table, shifting the cards with my force. "Donald and Amanda!"

"Possibly, but let's not twist the meaning to fit our narrative. Let the cards speak fully."

I sit back in my chair, bouncing my knee as I wait for more.

She slides a card with two decrepit people walking in the snow towards me. "The Five of Pentacles signals loss, poverty, insecurity and struggle. It can indicate a period of financial strain or material setbacks. Or even emotional isolation but usually tied to money worries."

I think about the past due bills I noticed on Amanda's kitchen island. I assumed with all the trauma surrounding Isaac and Ian's medical issues, paying bills simply got shoved to the wayside. Could they be having financial difficulties? And then I remember Jed telling me Isaac refused to give him a loan. Maybe—despite the big house and fancy cars—he doesn't have it to give?

I point to the card with the guy holding five swords trying to sneak away. "What's this one mean."

She leans back, a resigned smile planted on her lips. "That's the kicker. It's the classic card of stealth and deception. It's safe to assume someone is hiding something."

I feel vindicated. "So, now what. Do we confront Donald and Amanda?"

"I'll pull one card for insight on what direction we should take." She flips another card. A confident young man holding a sword.

"What does it mean?"

She shakes her head. "It's a strong suggestion to put confrontation on hold. We need to be curious, watchful, and truth seeking."

I huff out my disappointment. "So, we wait."

Her resigned smile curls into something sly—almost Cheshire. "Not necessarily. It can also mean surveillance."

My heart skips, stumbling into a jittery beat. "You mean … a stakeout?"

Liza nods. "A stakeout."

26 ~ Ruby

Our debrief on the outcome of the Iris/Hank meetings is at Sugar & Spice Café. Gail, Roddy, Marty, and I have claimed a bistro table on the front porch. The drop in humidity and slight breeze make it the perfect late-summer afternoon for dining alfresco.

Roddy was surprised (pleasantly, I think) to learn Marty and I had reconnected, and was more than eager to have him on the Peanut Posse. Already, Marty's fishing has caught a whale.

I sip my watermelon basil lemonade (my summer fav), as I wrap up my retelling of Operation Root Out with Iris. "Isaac did Hank dirty. Strong motive for payback, I'd say."

Gail tsks. "Isaac's a real jerk. Way to kick a guy when he's down. What a loser."

Marty nods his adorable balding head in agreement. "Looks like Isaac got a taste of his own medicine—too bad it came with a side of peanuts."

Gail's eye roll is big enough to count as exercise. She slips off the jean jacket covering her sleeveless prairie-style dress. "So, Iris and Hank are definitely in the running."

I shake my head. "No, not Iris. She had no idea Isaac had sabotaged Hank until *after* the party. He kept it quiet so as not to ruin her friendship with Amanda."

"Aww," Gail says. "That's sweet of him. Do we really think a guy that thoughtful would deliberately hurt someone?"

I savor a bite of the delicate squash blossom, its petals wrapped around lemon-infused ricotta. "Hank tolerated a year of working under Isaac. That had to take a toll. Everyone has their limits."

Roddy holds a finger in front of his lips as he munches a bite of his peach and pulled pork sandwich. "Wait till you hear what I found out." He swallows, and dabs a dribble of the rosemary-mustard glaze from the corner of his mouth. "First off, Hank definitely knew about Isaac's peanut allergy. Nuts of all kinds are banned from the university locker rooms and gym because of the seriousness of it."

Marty sings his out of tune version of the Mounds/Almond Joy jingle. "Sometimes you feel like a nut, sometimes you don't."

I groan (with delight).

"You still got it," Roddy says, clearly amused. "Glad you're here. We needed a little lightheartedness—before things get nutty."

We all crack up (peanutty pun intended). It feels so right for the four of us to be together again. I *really* missed this. I hope Marty did too.

"Anyway," Roddy continues. "Hank also confirmed what Marty found in the Oversight Committee's minutes did refer to him and Isaac. But the school declined to wield any disciplinary action claiming the relationships were between two consenting adults."

I frown. "Consenting or not, there's definitely an imbalance of power in that situation. Isaac is a sleaze bucket."

Roddy lifts his hands, palms facing me. "I'm already in your corner on that, Sister."

Gail munches on her blood orange and jalapeño salad. "Roddy, do you think Hank filed the report to get back at Isaac for derailing his job prospects?"

Roddy's bangs fall across his forehead when he shakes his head. "Not at all. I think he truly believes Isaac was taking advantage of female coeds."

"I repeat, sleaze bucket."

Gail raises her glass of blackberry iced tea. "I'll toast to that."

Marty chimes in. "It's obviously been well established; Isaac's character is less than sterling. But what about Hank? Would he file a report—or worse—to be vindictive?"

Roddy polishes off the last of his sandwich. "I mean, Hank was definitely ticked that he lost the job to Isaac—though he never mentioned Isaac's part in it—but I didn't get the vibe that the report was retributive. Ruby, you think Gigi would give me any points for that one?"

I shake my head. "Nah. Not obscure enough."

Roddy shrugs dramatically. "C'est la vie."

I roll my eyes. "Still no points."

"But," Roddy says, flipping his palms up. "Even if—maybe especially if—the report was filed with good intention, when no disciplinary action was issued, Hank might've felt it necessary to take things into his own hands."

The mood turns heavy.

Gail pushes her plate away. "So, you think that's Hank's justification? Saving coeds?"

Roddy rubs the back of his neck. "Maybe. Or maybe he just wants revenge. Either way, I think Hank is a strong suspect."

I press my lips together. "Hmm. Did you get any inkling that he might have felt guilty that you were arrested?"

"Not really," he answers, shaking his head. "But I was pumping *him* for info. We didn't talk about me or, uh, my situation."

At the mention of Roddy's situation, Gail busses her half-eaten salad like she can no longer bear the thought of food. I understand, the uncertainty is brutal.

As if he read my mind, Marty reaches out and pats my hand. My heart hopscotches at our connection. Why did I ever let him slip away?

"Righto," Marty says, sighing. "Let's recapitulate."

I shoot him an anemic smile and give a half-hearted attempt to lighten the mood. "Five points for that."

"Oh," he says. "I didn't know the competition is open to non-twins.

Roddy wags his finger. "It's not."

Coming up behind him, Gail rests her hands on Roddy's shoulder. "Nice effort, Ruby, but the fun's fizzled out." She slumps in her chair beside Roddy. "Might as well focus on why we're here. Is Hank to blame?"

Marty pulls a pencil and tablet from his messenger bag. "Number one," he says, writing notes. "Isaac sabotaged Hank, snagging the head coaching position out from under him. Number two. Hank knew—well in advance of the party—that Isaac is deathly allergic to peanuts. Number three. Hank filed a complaint against Isaac and no official action was taken, possibly allowing Hank to rationalize drastic action as a moral duty to save vulnerable coeds from Isaac's lust. Motive, opportunity, moral justification." His expression hardens. "The trifecta of crime."

I lay my napkin over my last squash blossom, my appetite totally gone. "Even if we all agree Hank was responsible, how do we prove it?"

27 ~ Millicent

By six the next morning, I'm packed and ready for the stakeout. Liza picks me up in a seen-better-days silver Chevy Suburban she borrowed from her neighbor, so we're not easily recognized. I stuff my cooler in the back seat, my spy toolkit on the floor in front, and hitch my aching hip into the Suburban. Shampoodles sits on a round doggie bed wedged on the console between the bucket seats, and yips when I snap my seatbelt.

Liza twirls her black polished fingernails into Shammie's gray fur. "Hush now. She's excited for her first stakeout."

My ticker is doing the two-step but I wouldn't call what I'm feeling excitement. Maybe closer to dread. This is a no-win venture. If I can't tie Donald to this mess, then Roddy's still on the hook. But if I *can* prove it, Roddy and Ruby will be faced with the truth that their own father threw them under the bus. Rock, meet hard place.

I breathe deep, girding myself for whatever comes next. "Ready."

Liza eases the Chevy onto the empty street and heads towards Amanda's house. Less than five miles in, Shammie whines.

"Oh, she's got to pee." Liza pulls over, snaps a leash on Shammie's collar, and lifts her out of the car.

Liza's long patchwork skirt flutters in the morning breeze. Shammie sniffs every blade of grass but never squats. I click my short fingernails on the armrest, waiting to get this show on the road. After Shammie thoroughly investigates the first yard and rejects it, she trots to the next tract of land. She sniffs. She circles. She nibbles something she finds in the grass. But no whizzy. My sigh is long and frustrated. For goodness' sake, Shammie, you're not picking a plot for a summer home. Do. Your. Business.

A few minutes later, when still no tinkling has transpired, I toot the horn. Liza scoops the poodle into her arms and returns to the car. "I guess she was just tired of being in the car."

"She's been in less time than she's been out." I flop my head back on the seat. It's going to be a long day.

Liza pulls a treat from the deep pocket of her skirt and feeds it to Shammie. "Millicent, your nervous energy isn't helping. It's making me feel antsy, too."

I exhale, long and slow. "You're right. You're right. I'm definitely on edge."

"What will be, will be," Liza says, patting my arm reassuringly.

She buckles up and drives a few more miles to Amanda's house. We park across the street, cattycorner from Amanda's circular driveway so we're able to see it and the front door. The driveway is empty and the house is still asleep.

I open the duffle bag and dig out the binoculars, using them to zoom in on the windows. "Can't see a thing. All the blinds are closed."

Liza holds out her hand. "Let me see." After she uses them to scan the house, she agrees.

"Can you tell anything from its aura?" I ask.

"Only living things have auras. Houses have vibes, and this one is trying very hard to impress."

"But we already knew Amanda—love her to bits—is climbing that social ladder."

Twisting the oversized ring on her slender finger, Liza says, "I'd suggest her rise might be easier without a tomcatting husband, but if Connie is to be believed, monogamy in the country-club set is more of a suggestion than a standard."

"So, you don't think Isaac's infidelity is enough motive for Amanda to put him into anaphylaxis?"

Liza's shoulder grazes her large dangly earrings when she shrugs. "Do you? I mean she has tolerated it all these years. She was definitely miffed to find out about Connie, but …"

"More than miffed, I'd say. She told me she was done. Right before she told me she met a new man."

"True. Add the new man to the mix and who knows. Oh look!" Liza points to the front door.

It opens and we hold our breath. A robed Amanda bends to retrieve the newspaper, then turns and shuts the door.

Liza and I look at each other. Shammie yips.

"Now what do we do?" she says.

Raising my eyebrows, I tilt my head. "Beats me. It's my first stakeout."

Liza scoots her seat back as far as it will go and snuggles Shammie on her lap. "I guess we wait."

Using the binoculars, I scan up and down the street. I pull out my disposable Kodak camera and snap a photo of Amanda's house.

"Why are you taking a picture? Nothing has changed."

"Establishing the 'before' so I'm ready for the 'after.'" I tuck the camera into the drink holder under Shammie's bed.

I hope something—other than a bursitis flare—happens soon.

*****

Two hours have passed and the sun has risen in the sky, making the interior of the Surburban stuffy. I roll down the window. Shammie leaps from Liza's lap onto mine and pokes her head out the open window.

"She might have to pee," Liza says.

"Not on me, I hope."

Liza's laugh ends with her usual snort. "No promises."

I collect the leash from the bed and snap it on her collar. "I'll walk her. My hip needs a change of position. And maybe I'll have better luck."

Liza slides her seat forward. "You can't walk her here. What if Amanda spots you. I'll drive around the block."

After we're parked out of sight, I lift Shampoodles down. She flounces to the closest patch of grass and pees.

"It's all in the leash angle," I smugly say to Liza, as I climb back into the Chevy.

Within minutes we're back to our lookout spot, watching the non-activity at the Stone household.

I twist sideways in my seat to face Liza. "I'm hungry."

"It's only eight. Didn't you eat breakfast?"

"I did, but I get hungry when I'm bored. Can you reach my cooler?"

After shoving her seat back, she moves the dog bed, with Shammie in it, to the driver's side floor. Then she flips around, knees on the seat, and grabs my cooler. Her yoga is really paying off. "This weighs more than the world's unresolved karmic debt. What on earth did you bring?"

"Enough for a couple meals. I didn't know how long we'd be out here."

She flips my cooler onto the seat beside me, then grabs her own—much smaller—lunch box. "If you're going to snack, I suppose I will, too."

I swing the cooler off the seat beside me and onto the floor between my legs. Holding hers in her lap, she unzips it and pulls out a plastic bag of celery sticks and a Tupperware container of something tan and mushy.

I wrinkle my nose. "What is that?"

"Hummus."

I look at her like she's sprouted horns. "Hummus? Who brings hummus to a stakeout?"

She feeds a bite of celery to Shammie. "What did you bring?"

"Stakeout food. Donuts, soda, chips, jerky. A fast-food burger would be ideal, but I settled for a ham and cheese sandwich."

She roots around in her lunch box. "I also have some chia pudding and an avocado."

"That is the worst stakeout food in the history of stakeouts. Don't you watch TV?"

She stuffs her hummus back in the bag and sits up tall in her seat. "Look," she says, pointing to the driveway of Amanda's house. "Movement."

A shaggy-haired Ian walks across the circular driveway, long, loose limbs swaying with his stride. The garage door opens. He jumps into Amanda's Mercedes and tears off down the street, not bothering to close the garage door.

Liza's brown eyes widen. "Amanda lets him drive her car? He only got his license a few months ago."

"She wanted to buy him a used Honda. Had it all picked out. But Isaac kiboshed it. Said Ian had to buy his own. Which I don't necessarily disagree with, but with Ian's hemophilia they don't let the poor kid have a job. So, I guess he's stuck borrowing hers."

"More of a hardship for Amanda than Ian, I'd say." She pulls an avocado and spoon from her bag and settles in her seat.

"I know my nieces and nephews—all nine of them—wouldn't have wanted to be caught dead in their parents' cars. They all started saving money as soon as they could work and ended up sharing four cars between them. Myrtle and Rick would kick in on the bigger repair bills. And some of them were doozies. I remember one incident with Delilah. Myrtle's fourth—no, fifth—wait, nope, definitely the fourth. Anyhow, Delilah had a temperamental Ford Pinto—of course, before the explosion risk was known. Mercy me, I shudder every time I think of that sweet girl driving in a death trap."

I crack open a soda, take a big gulp, and continue the story. "She was out on the country backroads headed to Farmersville to hang out at a friend's pool—you know, one of those above-ground jobbies—wearing a bathing suit and not much else. She hadn't even brought shoes, just a towel and a book. She rounded a corner and the Pinto died beside a cornfield."

My bag of chips pops when I open it. I offer Liza a few but she declines, sticking to her celery and mush. "It was fry-an-egg-on-the-sidewalk hot and the road was sizzling her bare feet. She's hobbling along the edge of the field. Twenty minutes passed and she hadn't seen a car. Finally, she heard the clop of horse hooves and spotted an Amish buggy rolling up the road. Now, Delilah, practically naked by Amish standards, knew it was going to be a mighty awkward ride, but she didn't have a choice. She waved them down and crammed herself between the four children in the back—learning real quick why Amish kids press their faces out that tiny back window: it's the only breeze they get. An hour later—buggies move slowly in the heat—they dropped her off at her friend's house, parboiled and grateful for chlorinated water and indoor plumbing. Sadly, even after hundreds of dollars in garage fees, the Pinto could not be revived."

Liza stuffs the empty skin of the avocado into a baggie and sticks it in her lunch bag. "Considering the explosion risk, I'd call the whole thing divine providence. Even the Amish won't trust a Pinto."

I adjust my Sally-Jessy-Raphael glasses. "Yes, well, the Amish also know better than to buy a car from Earl 'Trust Me' Zook. That sweaty, doughy handshake of his—and those dirt-cheap prices—have talked more than one of Myrtle's kids into a lemon."

As I finish the snibbles of my potato chips, a black truck wheels into Amanda's driveway and parks in front of the open garage door, backend facing Isaac's Mercedes.

Liza's burgundy-lined lips fall open as she points to the driveway. "That's a repo truck."

I zero in on the scene with my binoculars. The back of the black truck extends, sliding under the car. A bearded man in coveralls hops out. As he's making some adjustments near the wheels of the Mercedes, Amanda rushes from the house, bathrobe flying behind her like wings. We can't hear what she's saying, but her hands are gesturing wildly. The man continues his task with little interaction and minutes later he's driving away with Isaac's Mercedes.

Amanda crumples to the ground in front of the garage, face covered by her hands. Her shoulders buck with sobs. The pull to comfort her is strong, but then we'd have to explain what we were doing at her house so early. We sit quietly, helplessly, and watch our friend weep.

After a few minutes, Amanda stands, wiping her face and tying the sash of her robe. Even from a distance, we can feel the weight of each of her steps as she trudges inside.

Liza's tone is solemn. "Financial strain. Loss. The cards never lie."

A horrifying thought takes root, turning my stomach. And, despite the heat, a cold chill shivers through me. "What if she poisoned Isaac for the life insurance?"

28 ~ Ruby

The sidewalks of downtown Lancaster are filling with business-suited crowds hurrying toward their lunch spots. The concrete radiates the heat of the noon sun, and exhaust fumes mingle with hot tar to create that familiar baked-city scent. I pop on my newest thrift-store find—a pair of lime-green sunglasses—and enjoy the hustle and bustle of the city as I amble toward the *Intelligencer Journal* building.

Marty had mentioned getting together to brainstorm how to prove Hank's behind PeanutGate, so I decided to surprise him and take him to lunch at Dip Co. They have a new pancetta mac and cheese on the menu that I've been wanting to try.

I window shop as I stroll down King Street. Éclairs and macarons tempt from a display case in the newest pâtisserie. Hand-blown glass sculptures shimmer in the sunlight. A sunny yellow dress on a mannequin in front of a quirky boutique catches my eye. The price tag, however, turns my head—the other way.

Half a block from Marty's building, I spot him coming out the double front doors, a perky brunette by his side. My heart hiccups at their wide smiles, before they turn and make their way down the block ahead of me. The disappointment is only a niggle until he lays his hand on her shoulder and pulls her in for a hug. Now it's a full-body blow. The sides of their heads touch and then she throws her head back in laughter. My stomach twists. I turn away, crestfallen.

It was silly of me to think there wouldn't be someone new in his life. He's a catch. Of course he has a girlfriend.

I head back to my parking spot, depression seeping into my muscles and joints, making every step a chore. By the time I reach Sally, the waterworks have started. I slide inside, unconsoled by the cheery daisy bloom stuck in her bud vase.

Resting my forehead on the steering wheel, I let the tears flow, crying out my heartache. Our break up—ironically caused by a subconscious irrational urge to protect myself from heartbreak (or at least that's what all the self-help books say)—was devastating. I couldn't, and still can't, imagine dating anyone else. I guess I assumed, or maybe just desperately hoped, Marty felt the same. It's painfully clear he does not.

My wallowing is interrupted by my ringing phone. I flip it open, seeing it's Dad.

"Hi, Dad," I answer, unable to disguise my misery.

"Ruby, what's wrong?"

I break down, sobbing. "Oh, Dad. Marty has a girlfriend."

"Where are you?"

"In my car in Lancaster. Near his office."

"Don't drive. You're too upset. I'll come to you. Can you meet me at Isaac's Deli?"

I sniff and nod. "Okay."

"See you in twenty minutes."

I let myself cry for another ten minutes, ignoring the stares of passersby. Then I slide on my sunglasses to hide my puffy eyes, feed the meter more quarters, and head towards the deli. The walk does me good and by the time I arrive, the crying has stopped. I sit on the brick knee-wall and wait.

Dad rushes down the street a few minutes later. He wraps me in a hug, patting my back. "Oh, honey. It's okay."

I nod against his chest. "I think it was just the shock of seeing him with someone else." I don't share my ridiculous hopes that we would reconcile. I already feel stupid enough.

"Nothing a Gooney Bird sandwich and red potato salad can't fix."

I give Dad a weak smile. "And maybe a warm ice-cream topped brownie."

He kisses the top of my head as he escorts me into the restaurant. "Anything my girl needs."

The hostess seats us in a bright orange booth in the middle of the restaurant. I order the Gooney Bird sandwich and potato salad (as Dad predicted), and he chooses a Scarlet Ibis.

"So," Dad says sipping his lemonade. "Do you want to talk about it?"

The tears bubble up in my throat. I swallow them down with a huge gulp of iced tea. "No. But I'm glad you're here."

He smiles and pats my hand. "No place I'd rather be."

Though Gigi's secret rocked me to my core, it's nice to have a dad in my life. Don't get me wrong, Pop was amazing. As was Gigi. But no matter how wonderful they were, I—and I think I can speak for Roddy, too—felt the loss of our parents. And according to my shelf full of life-coaching tomes, their absence shaped us in ways we're still uncovering.

Roddy and I leaned on each other. It was a gift to have a twin (still is), but with Gail in the picture—which I am unreservedly ecstatic about—Roddy doesn't have as much time for me. He doesn't just pop in for spaghetti dinners, or lazy Sunday afternoons playing games. In fact, unless we're working together—or lately, trying to crack our case—I barely see him.

My heart skips a beat as reality crashes down. If we don't solve PeanutGate will either of us have a business? Will Roddy be a free man?

Here I am bemoaning thwarted romantic dreams, while the possibility of jail time looms over my brother's head. I screw my head on straight and put my priorities in order.

Our waitress brings our meals. Melty muenster cheese topping spinach, mushrooms, and oven-roasted turkey soothes my tattered heart and I pivot to the bigger problem.

"We've come up with some good leads regarding PeanutGate—that's what we're calling the bank party fiasco."

Dad frowns. "What kind of leads?"

I fill him in on everything we learned about Hank.

He pushes his sandwich aside, as if he's lost his appetite. "Ruby, you and Roddy are adults and I'm late to the party, so I try to keep my meddling to a minimum, but I really think the idea of PeanutGate, as you call it, being deliberate is far off base."

I drop my fork on the table. "What are you saying, Dad? You think Roddy made a mistake?"

"Everyone makes mistakes. I'm a walking billboard for that. Making a mistake does not mean you are one. But a person needs to admit their missteps and accept the consequences."

I can hardly believe what he's saying. "So, you think we should just let Roddy rot in jail? For a *mistake* I know he didn't commit?"

"No, I think you should let the lawyer do her job."

My volume increases along with my anger. "We've been telling her our theories and she told us to keep 'em coming."

Dad clasps his hands in front of him. "Then, by all means, do so. But you both should be open to the possibility that Roddy inadvertently added peanut powder to the dishes." His gaze turns pained, and his tight lips signal regret. "I've spent nearly a lifetime running from responsibility and it led me nowhere good. I don't want that same thing to happen to Roddy. Or to you. You can recover from this setback. Both of you. I am a walking example. After the despicable things I did, you and Roddy still allow me in your lives. If I can bounce back from my mistakes. I know you two can."

My insides are boiling. I want to swipe the dishes off the table and storm out of the restaurant, but I don't. Healthy adults don't run from disagreements; they work through them. (At least that's what Dr. Lauter says in her *Relationship Repair Manual*).

I bite the side of my mouth and take a slow inhale to cool my jets. "Clearly, we're going to have to agree to disagree."

The waitress brings the check. I reach for it, but Dad grabs it.

He digs cash from his pocket, and clips it to the bill. "I'm on your side, you know."

I do know. He came running when he realized I was in distress, didn't he? But I just can't believe he doesn't see how out of the question it is that Roddy made that huge of a mistake. And if Roddy learns of his lack of faith, the slow progress they've made in their relationship will switch to a fast track in the wrong direction.

I modulate my voice, ridding it of any anger. "Based on your life experiences, I can understand your concern for what you see as deflecting blame, but your doubts would crush Roddy. You and he have made such strides in your relationship over the past four years, I'd hate to see it damaged. Maybe, if you can't be supportive of our investigation, it would be best to limit contact until the dust has settled, and we can prove to you we were right."

His shoulders slump, and his face sags. "I understand."

The waitress takes the money, and we slide out of the booth. On King Street, before we part ways, he grabs my hand, giving it a loving squeeze. "Ruby, I need you to hear this. With every fiber of my being, I hope Roddy is proved blameless. But if he's not, I'll be here—emotionally, financially, physically—to help you both pick up the pieces. Restart your businesses. And if need be, your lives. You know as well as I do, I'm a master at that. I love you, kiddo."

I give him a hug. "I love you, too, Dad."

We step apart, and head in opposite directions. Horns beep, pedestrians laugh, music drifts from chic bistros. The city is oblivious to the ache in my chest.

I don't want to imagine picking up pieces or starting over. I want Roddy cleared. I want our lives back.

29 ~ Millicent

The car repo really rattled me and Liza. It's painful to think a dear friend could have a murderous heart, but the evidence keeps piling up. It all makes perfect sense. Amanda admitted she can see spending the rest of her life with her new man, which unfortunately is most likely Donald. When I asked if she was thinking of divorce, her response was cryptic. And now, after watching Isaac's car be repossessed, I know why. Half of nothing, is nothing. Amanda would abhor being poor. Not only would Isaac's accidental death clear the way for her and Donald, it would unlock a windfall from his life insurance.

Liza, Shammie, my hip, and I hung in there for another painful four hours after the car was towed away, hoping Amanda would call Donald for support. We really need a photo of them together. Since they both claim not to know each other, we need proof of their connection. But we went home, dejected and empty-handed.

We decided an evening stakeout might get us better results. Liza will be picking me up at five, fifteen minutes from now. I finish packing three dozen fresh-baked cookies into four tins (it felt like a thirty-six-cookie day), but only toss one tin into the cooler I'm filling for the stakeout. I add a few sodas, another ham sandwich, a bag of Tom Sturgis pretzels, and some homemade sweet-and-spicy Amish mustard I picked up at a farmstand—because any self-respecting Lancastrian will tell you: pretzels without mustard is sacrilege.

When I'm finished gathering my food, I jog upstairs (at least that's what I'm claiming since I'm huffing and puffing when I get to my bedroom). I change out of my flour-dusted T-shirt into a cream-colored sweater set from Chico's, and slip into gray elastic-waist pants. The khaki pants I wore for our last stakeout were a bad choice. After six hours in the car, the tight waistband (and maybe the sodas, chips, and jerky) gave me indigestion that four Tums and a swig of Pepto couldn't touch. I run a brush through my curls, making them frizzier. Much to Liza's dismay, I still can't get the hang of the curl enhancer and diffuser.

I'm shoving my bunioned feet into my Clarks when I hear the toot of Liza's horn. Pizelle gives her tail an annoyed flick as I scratch between her ears, and I promise catnip when I return.

Tonight, Liza is in a borrowed pick-up truck. The bench seat offers plenty of space for Shammie's bed. I hoist my cooler inside, sliding it beside Liza's lunch bag in the middle of the truck's floor.

"Hi." Her flat tone echoes my gloominess.

I nod and we drive in wary silence to Amanda's house. Using the binoculars, I confirm her Mercedes is parked in the garage. I scan the windows. The blind in one living room window is half open. I glue the binoculars to that spot, waiting for a glimpse of Amanda—and maybe Donald.

My arms tired from holding still and my vision gets fuzzy. I hand the binoculars to Liza and she takes up the surveillance.

As I'm dipping a pretzel into the mustard, Liza says, "I see her."

"Is anyone with her?"

She shakes her head. "No. She just sat down on the couch, facing the window."

I plunge another pretzel knuckle dip in the mustard, then pop it in my mouth. "Now what is she doing?"

"Just staring."

Three pretzels later, a car pulls into the circular driveway. "Incoming," I say.

Liza swivels the binoculars to the car. "It's Ian. Some kid is dropping him off." She turns the lens back to Amanda. "She hasn't moved."

I watch Ian fling open the door and stroll into the house. "Now what is she doing?"

"Still staring. Wait, oh, she startles when Ian touches her shoulder. He gives her a hug. Oh, now he's gone and she's just sitting there again. Staring at the wall."

"Guilty conscience?"

Shrugging, Liza lays the binoculars on her lap. "Maybe."

Acid burns in my stomach, whether from the spicy mustard or my friend's sins, I can't tell.

*****

Almost three long hours later, Amanda emerges from her house. I use the binoculars to get a close-up look. Her normally perfectly coiffed bob is pulled back with a headband, she's wearing a blue track suit (out of character for Amanda unless she's on the tennis courts), and no make-up. She is obviously out of sorts.

She opens the garage door, slides into her Mercedes, and cruises out of her driveway. Liza and I follow at a respectable distance. Once in downtown Lancaster, we get delayed at a stoplight. Luckily, we see her make the left onto James Street. She must be going to the hospital. I check the time. 8:15. Visiting hours ended fifteen minutes ago.

Our light turns green. We also make the left onto James and wheel into the main parking lot, hoping our assumption is correct. Not only do we spot Amanda crossing the macadam, we see Donald waiting for her at the entrance.

I duck under the dashboard, grab my spy bag, and fumble inside it, feeling for my camera. Finally, I lay my hands on it, whip it out, and snap a photo just as Donald puts his hand on Amanda's waist and guides her inside the front doors.

Fear, like frosty fingers, creeps up my spine. "What are they doing here together after visiting hours?"

Liza's olive complexion has turned sallow. "Nothing good, I'm afraid."

"You don't think … I mean, they wouldn't … Oh, Heaven help us! Do you think they're here to finish the job?"

"I don't know what to think," Liza says, fidgeting with her rings.

The tension is thicker than my thighs after a weeklong cruise. Even Shammie feels it and huddles under the seat.

I grab the door handle. "Should we go to Isaac's room?"

Liza flings her door open. The cuffs of her wide-legged pants flutter when she whips her legs out. She grabs Shammie, settling her in her oversized purse. "Let's go!"

We're stopped in our tracks at the nurses' station at the entrance to Isaac's floor. "Visiting hours are over," a burly nurse says, allowing no room for argument.

We argue anyway.

I offer my most charming smile—maybe I should've let Liza schmooze—and say, "Oh, but our friends—a white-haired man and blonde woman—just went in there. Her husband is Isaac Stone. She forgot her keys. All we need to do is return them and we'll be out of your way."

The nurse crosses his muscled arms and widens his stance. "No one went in there. Like I told you, visiting hours are over."

Liza twirls a lock of her shiny hair and bats her long eyelashes. "Could you at least just check? Poor dear is such a mess with her husband being in a coma. We'd sure hate for her to be locked out of her car on top of everything else."

He gives us a terse nod. "Fine. Stay here. No one went in, but if it'll get you on your way …"

Liza and I breathe a unified sigh of relief. If Donald and Amanda are up to no good, the nurse should be in time to stop it.

Less than a minute later, he's back. "Like I told you. No one went in there. The lost and found is on the main floor. I suggest you leave the keys there." He turns his back on us, picks up a chart.

We have no choice but to leave.

The ride home is again silent, both of us lost in the shadows of dark thoughts.

At my house, Liza helps me carry my cooler inside. I offer tea and cookies but she declines. I walk her to the door.

She hugs me. "At least you got the photo of Donald and Amanda. CVS has one-hour film developing. You could show Ruby and Roddy tomorrow."

Nausea roils my stomach at the thought. "Maybe we're jumping to conclusions. Just because they met doesn't mean they sprinkled the peanut powder."

"No, but it does mean they lied."

"They could still be innocent, right? I mean, she *is* married. They probably just want to keep things quiet."

"Totally possible. But the tarot deck told us the anaphylaxis was no accident and I trust the cards. Someone deliberately sprinkled peanut powder on the food. Someone is out to harm Isaac. I'm gutted to say it, but Amanda and Donald look like the most logical option."

My whole body droops. "I have to show Ruby and Roddy the photos, don't I? It could help clear Roddy's name."

Liza hugs me again. "I'm afraid you do. Do you want me to come with you to show them?"

My sigh is filled with sadness. "No. But it may take me a day or two to work up the nerve."

She offers me a sad smile. "Call me if you need me."

When the door clicks behind her, I sink to the floor. Pizelle climbs on me, licking my hand with her sandpapery tongue. I snuggle her into my arms, and cry into her fur.

How do you choose the right moment to shatter someone's world?

30 ~ Ruby

My pulse is faster than a hummingbird's wings as I pull open the door at Ten Thousand Villages. Marty is seated on a stack of pillows at a chowki-style table in the back corner of the international café.

When he called to invite me to lunch to work on PeanutGate, my first instinct was to decline. After seeing him with the brunette, I feel too pulpy, too raw. But then I realized how much I've enjoyed having him back in my life—even if it can only be as friends. I box up my romantic stirrings, and file them between what-to-do-with-my-inheritance and grief-for-my-imaginary-father, in the deal-with-later center of my brain. Squaring my shoulders, I suck in a deep breath, paste a bright smile on my face, and pull up my big girl panties.

My wave is boisterous as I walk towards him. "Hi! Great choice of café."

"Yeah, Zimbabwe's cuisine is featured this week and I know how much you love dovi. Pull up a pillow."

Warmth radiates through my body and a tender pressure builds behind my eyes. The fact that he remembers is bittersweet.

I slide out of my Chucks, leaving them on a mat beside Marty's Docksiders, then arrange a few crimson, embroidered baithaks to form a comfortable seat. Two glasses of the café's signature orange mint tea already sit on the intricately carved tabletop.

"I assumed you'd want the tea," Marty says.

I take a sip of the refreshing drink. "You assumed correctly. Thanks."

The waitress brings two menus. Marty and I don't bother to look; we both order the dovi.

Marty shifts on his teal cushions. "Ironic to be eating peanut stew while trying to solve a peanut-powder sabotage. Do you think this counts as evidence tampering?"

I almost spit out my tea laughing. "Only if you lick the bowl to destroy the fingerprints."

"If the food is as delicious as the last time I ate here, I most definitely plan to do that."

After a few more minutes of small talk, our meals come. The rich aroma of onion, garlic, and curry mixed with the warm nutty smell, makes my mouth water.

I spread a linen napkin over my lap. "Are we doing traditional-style eating or using spoons?"

"Spoon for sure. Less fingerprints."

I throw him a cheeky wink paired with a *tch*. "Good thinking."

I scoop a spoonful of sadza—a doughy, porridge made from maize—and dip it into the savory sauce. "Aah. Saporous and soothing."

Marty pantomimes shooting a basketball. "She shoots and scores! Five points for saporous. Gigi would be proud. I really wish I could've met her. She sounds like my kind of lady."

"She would have adored you!" Marty's kindness and quick wit, would've won Gigi over instantly. And maybe if she were still alive, still here to cheer me on and bolster my courage, I wouldn't be sitting across from the love of my life, pretending a platonic relationship is enough. Maybe I'd have found the nerve to move in together, instead of giving into my skittishness.

I use a heaping spoonful of sadza and dovi to swallow my regret. "You said you had some more information about the guests?"

Marty pushes his wire-rimmed Lennon glasses up on his nose. "I poked around Oscar's life and I'm fairly certain we can cross him off the list of suspects."

"Why's that?"

"Well, we speculated that if his poker losses caused him financial hardship, he may want payback. I checked all the usual suspects: bankruptcy, liens, court filings and came up with diddly-squat. I changed direction and dove a little deeper. The Coast Guard registry shows he owns a 42' Ocean and, get this, he also owns a VLJ."

My eyebrows squish together. "VLJ. Sounds ominous. What's that?"

"A Very Light Jet."

I snort, and a fine mist of tea launches from my lips.

"No, really. That's what they're called. And they typically cost around a million bucks, used. Between Tabitha's diamond hobby and Oscar's expensive toys, I think we can safely assume he wouldn't get bent out of shape over some piddly weekly poker losses."

"Hmm. What if Isaac cheated? Maybe Oscar did it on principle."

"Possible, but it seems more likely you'd just stop playing with him, rather than risk jail time."

"Fair point," I say, sopping up the rest of my stew with the sadza.

Marty finishes his meal, then rubs his round belly. "Why did the peanut butter stew get promoted?"

I roll my eyes and grab my stomach. "Hold on, let me make room for an influx of cheese. Okay, I'm ready. Why?"

"Because it spreads good vibes and sticks to the plan."

Groaning, I shake my head. "Lame. You can do better than that. Try again."

He taps his fingers on his chin. "Ooh, ooh. I've got it. You'll like this one."

"Okay, hit me with it." Grabbing the sides of the chowki, I brace for impact.

"You must be made of sazda."

I shoot him an amused smirk. "Why's that?"

He reaches across the table and squeezes my fingertips. "Because you are a-maize-ing."

My eyes fly wide open, and my response is more sputter than giggle. My cheeks heat up. I was prepared for cheesiness, not … not whatever that was.

I drop my chin towards my chest and mumble, "You're, uh, not so bad yourself." Talk about lame, Ruby Finch. It doesn't get much more meh than that.

His fingers linger on mine a few awkward moments more. Then he clears his throat and raps his knuckles on the tabletop. "Righto! Is dessert on our horizons? I hear the candy cake is just ducky."

Was he joking, being a supportive friend, or flirting? I'm so flustered, words are beyond my capabilities. The should've-saids are clogging up the network.

Is it too late to tell him how I feel? What about the brunette? They looked more than friendly. But just now I thought I felt a romantic vibe; a spark when our fingers touched. I can't be sure. My swoon sensor is rusty.

My heart patters in my throat. I could still say something. Ask him for a do-over. But what if it makes it weird? What if it screws everything up?

I channel Gigi's wisdom and gumption—she always said opportunity rarely knocks twice. "Marty, I—" My ringing phone interrupts. It's Stephanie, from the bank. I don't know whether I'm relieved or annoyed.

I flip open my phone. "Hi, Stephanie. What's up?"

"Hey, Ruby. I hope you and Roddy are hanging in there."

"We're doing okay."

"The party's end was so helter-skelter, lots got left behind. I packed up everything in a box. Any chance you could pick it up soon? We have a huge event coming up this weekend and I don't want it to get lost in the shuffle."

Thanks to the bad publicity surrounding the party, my schedule is wide open.

"I could come by today."

"Perfect. I'm not at the bank, but Janelle is. I'll let her know you're coming. Thanks, Ruby. Take care of yourself." She ends the call.

I slip the phone back in my purse. "I have to head over to the bank and pick up a box full of items that were left at the party."

"Want company?"

He wants to spend more time with me. My heart somersaults. "Um, sure."

He motions for the waitress and grabs the bill. I protest, but he insists. "I invited you here, so it's only right. Besides, your work is a bit dodgy right now. You can treat after the dust has settled."

He wants to see me *after* PeanutGate. Hope unfurls its delicate petals.

"It's a date," I agree and instantly regret my choice of words.

His eyes lock mine for the briefest second. "With any luck."

My breath catches. Is he saying what I think he's saying?

My thoughts are muddled like the mint in the orange tea as I step off the carpeted platform that houses the traditional eating area.

"Ruby. Shoes?"

I blink, then blush. "Oh yeah."

I slide into my sneakers. When Marty's hand touches the small of my back, my toes tingle (and not just from sitting cross-legged for the past hour and a half).

"Thanks for letting me tag along. I've been wanting to get a look at the crime scene."

Oof. Of course. It's all about the peanuts.

This roller coaster ride is making me nauseous.

*****

The *friendly* chit-chat during the twenty-five-minute car ride was painful. Marty talked about the riveting Amish buggy safety debates story he's working on. His foray into throwing pottery that quickly ended in "clay-tastrophe." And the madcap adventures of Becky and Bart (his sister and brother-in-law) as they deal with a teenage Brad. All while I desperately tried to analyze our luncheon.

I park in front of First National Bank.

Marty lets out a long whistle. "Whoa, doggie! What a spectacular slice of history. And a novel concept in entertainment—breaking into a bank." He twists to face me, eyes twinkling with excitement. "After all the hullabaloo is resolved, we should do it together. With the brainpower between us, I'm sure we'll be in the safe in minutes."

My heart skips a few beats. More plans for the future.

Feeling on shaky ground, I self-consciously titter. "It's harder than you think. Roddy and I failed."

He pops out of the car and runs around to my side to open the door, his old-fashioned gallantry endearing "The dynamic duo? If you two couldn't crack it, it must be super difficult."

I shrug. "We thought so, but Clarice's family solved it in forty-five minutes. I guess Roddy and I didn't inherit the bank-robbing gene."

"Pity. That could be a nice supplemental income," he wisecracks.

I grimace. "Or primary source, if Make A Splash! goes under."

He turns to face me and rubs both my upper arms. “Oh, Ruby! Let me get the clodhopper out of my mouth. How insensitive of me. I’m sorry.”

I brush it off. “You’re fine. You’re fine. Just me being morose. I know everything will work out.” I playfully punch his shoulder to put him at ease. “Especially with Mighty Marty-Man on the case.”

He slaps his palm against his shiny forehead. “Oh jeez! I forgot about your collision with a bike.”

“I didn’t! You were my hero then, and now you’re coming to the rescue again.” I rest my hand on his forearm. “Seriously, thank you.”

His cheeks turn magenta, and beads of sweat dot his forehead. His Adam’s apple bobs as he swallows multiple times. He’s clearly choked up. Have I stirred up happy memories—*amorous* memories—or is he just embarrassed by the compliment?

Lifting his shoulders, he flips his palms open. “That’s just what garden-variety superheroes do.”

I jut my chin towards the bank entrance. “Well then, strap on that cape, and let’s solve a crime.”

I do a double-take when we enter the bank. The space has been transformed. The lobby area is filled with rows of white satin-covered chairs, each topped with an enormous blush-colored bow. White twinkling lights are strung around the perimeter. Thick silk garlands, crafted from baby’s breath, dusty-green ferns, and pink roses, create an aisle from the tellers’ counter to the safe. The safe floor is covered with more delicate rose petals and a crystal chandelier dangles overhead. Clearly, the huge event is a wedding.

“Ruby, hey,” Janelle says as she bustles by us lugging an enormous speaker. “I’ll be right with you.”

As we wait for Janelle, I recap the layout of the bank on the night of Ethan’s party. “The lobby was set up with round tables. The tellers’ counter was the buffet. The bar was here, to the right of the food. And the deejay’s booth was across the room, over there.”

Marty scans the bank. "Where was Isaac sitting when his attack started?"

I point to the area where his table was positioned.

"And where did you say his EpiPen was found?"

I hitch my thumb to the left. "Under the deejay's table. Our working theory is that during the scuffle with Ed, it fell out of Isaac's jacket and scooted across the floor, landing under the table."

"Hmm." Marty puckers his lips, and strokes his chin. "Or maybe the fight provided a perfect cover for the EpiPen to be missing from Isaac's jacket. Where was the jacket when his attack started?

"It was draped on the back of his chair. I rifled through the pockets looking for the rescue pen."

"Anyone who stopped to chat with Isaac during the evening could've easily removed it."

I shiver, still horrified to be so up close and personal to an attempted murder. "Yes. I suppose that's true."

"Who found the EpiPen?" he asks.

"Janelle."

"Did I hear my name?" Janelle says, catching her breath and dusting off her hands.

"I was just telling Marty you found Isaac's EpiPen."

Her smile drops and her face hardens. "I did. Is he dead?"

Her bluntness stuns me, but then I recall her hostility towards him the night of the party.

"As far as I know he's stable, but still in a coma."

Her jaw clenches. "Let me grab the box of stuff. Be right back."

Marty's eyebrows raise. He lowers his voice and leans close to my ear. "Like you said before, she is definitely not a fan of Isaac's. When I get back to the office, I'll see what I can dig up."

I nod. "Good idea."

Janelle retrieves the box and Marty insists on carrying it to the car. I lift Sally's hood for him to slide it inside her front trunk.

The day is warm but the humidity is mild. "Should I put the top down?"

His hand flies to his balding head. "And mess up my hair?" His cheeks round with his smile. "Why not!"

After folding Sally's convertible top, we hop in and head to Ephrata. Highways aren't much fun with the top down—then again, Route 30 isn't great even with the roof up—so I stick to the backroads. The soft warmth of the sun settles on my face, and my red curls dance in the wind. Marty leans his head against the seat, closing his eyes. Ten glorious, sun-drenched miles roll by before Marty pulls his tablet from his messenger bag.

"Back to business," he says.

The cheery lightness is replaced with anxiety.

The corners of the tablet pages flutter in the breeze as he reviews his notes. "You told me Janelle was unnecessarily rude to Isaac, and after their "incident" you found her in the bathroom upset."

"Yep."

"You also said after the ambulance left she was oddly upbeat and you heard her say, 'Karma's a bitch' which you assumed to be directed at Isaac."

I nod. "Correct."

"Okay. Combined with today's curt question about Isaac's condition, Janelle definitely merits investigation." He taps his pencil on the paper. "I'm just not sure where to start. Anything else you can think of regarding Janelle and Isaac?"

Traffic slows, bogged down by a buggy ahead. As we crawl forward, I drum my fingers on the steering wheel, racking my brain. "She definitely heard me tell Stephanie that Isaac is deathly allergic to peanuts."

"Advance knowledge." He scribbles on the tablet. "That's good. When did you tell Stephanie?"

"At our pre-event meeting, after Roddy and I failed to open the safe."

Marty nods encouragingly. "Okay. Focus in on that meeting. What was Janelle's reaction when you mentioned Isaac?"

I suck my bottom lip behind my teeth as I replay the meeting. We were stuck in Stephanie's tiny office. Janelle was in the doorway behind us …

The road finally clears and I ease past the buggy. In Leola, I veer off Route 23. Fields of tasseled sweet corn rustle in the summer breeze. Cows seek the shade of a weeping willow tree and horses graze in the pastures.

At the traffic light in Brownstown, it clicks. "Janelle got really irritated. At the time, I thought it was because Stephanie asked her to drag the wheelchair ramp out of the storage closet, but now I'm thinking it could've been about Isaac. I noticed it shortly after I mentioned him."

He rests the pencil's eraser on his chin. "Interesting. If mentioning Isaac annoyed her, it stands to reason she had interactions with him before the party."

I nod in agreement. "Someone—I can't remember who—even mentioned knowing a lot of the guests since Marietta is a small town."

"It'd be great if we could figure out Janelle and Isaac's connection. That might lead us to motive."

I have that nagging feeling that I'm forgetting something. I mentally rewind the conversation, over and over, hoping to dislodge a memory. Janelle mentioned that Liza is her hairstylist. Think, Ruby, think. What am I missing?

As I'm heading into Ephrata, it hits me. "I've got it! Their connection. Janelle said her son was on the football team at

Myerstown University. Isaac is the head coach. That's how she knows Isaac."

"Ooh! Good work! That gives me a lot to go on. Let's meet up again, as soon as I know something."

Longing gnaws at my belly. I want to see him again, but being with him as friends is like the bottom-of-the-bag chip crumbs and a smear of onion dip—you get enough of a taste to crave more.

"Sounds good," I say with forced joviality, as I slide Sally beside Marty's Prius.

We step out of Sally. I run a hand over the Prius's white hood. "What's her name?"

He laughs. "Still naming things, I see. I love that quirk. Why don't you do the honors?"

"White Knight. Appropriate for a garden-variety superhero, I think."

His blush starts on his chest and blooms across his face. Even his arms pinken. "White Knight, it is."

He takes a step towards me, opening his arms for a hug. I lean in, heat flooding my body.

"I missed this," he says, before releasing me.

"I did, too." My words aren't much more than a whisper.

He pulls away, clears his throat, and unlocks White Knight. "Righto, then. I, uh … Janelle. I'll look into Janelle."

We stand there, close but not touching, tangled emotion thick in the space between us. My hesitation is fear—fear of rejection, fear we'll never again be more than friends. And his hesitation? Is it the Brunette?

I wave as he drives away, wondering if he felt it too—the weight of everything we didn't say.

31 ~ Millicent

My hand reaches out from under the covers, patting the end table in search of my glasses. My head is pounding and my eyes are crusty and stuck shut. I feel hungover. I suppose stress can do that to you. After following Donald and Amanda to the hospital, I considered a hot toddy, but settled for a ginger tea and a slug of Pepto Bismol.

Despite many antacids, my belly burned all night. Heavy thoughts flooded my mind, more relentless than Hurricane Agnes back in the seventies. As much as I hate to jump to a dark conclusion, the crumbs lead me to the same *offal* pie—Donald and Amanda conspired to … to … Heavens to Betsy, it's hard to even think it. They conspired to commit murder.

It's soul-crushing to believe Donald would knowingly allow Ruby and Roddy to be collateral damage, but with his history … I'm a big believer in second chances. I know people can change. But he did basically sell the twins to Evie. His paternal instincts may be warped.

Finally finding my glasses on the floor beside my bed, I slip them on my face, blinking my eyes to focus. Holy Toledo! It's eleven o'clock.

The last time I slept this late was with Myrtle, during an impromptu overnight in Chesapeake City, Maryland. Let's just say engine problems (and Myrtle's need for a breather from Rick—bless his patient heart) turned a lunch outing at the canal-side Bayard House into the two of us sharing the V-berth of a 42-foot yacht. (What can I say? People like to help tipsy old ladies.) Between the gentle roll of the boat, the rhythmic lap of waves, and maybe the two margaritas from our detour to the Hole in the Wall Bar, I slept like Rip Van Winkle. By noon, the yacht's owners were poking me to make sure I hadn't sailed on to meet my maker.

I shove my bunioned feet into slippers and haul my aching body out of the bed. Mornings are the worst. I'm stiffer than a starched collar. As I limp towards the bathroom, I hear a furious knocking on my front door, followed by repeated doorbell ringing.

What on earth?

"Hold your horses," I yell. "I'm coming."

I throw on a robe and move as fast as I can with the hitch in my gitalong. I open the front door to find Liza and Shampoodles. "Millicent, it's not good."

"Come in. Come in. What's not good? Wait, can I have a cup of coffee first?"

Liza sets Shammie on the floor. Pizelle takes a swipe at her. When Shammie yips, Pizelle flicks her tail and strolls away.

Liza follows me into the kitchen, a faint cloud of sandalwood drifting along with her. "Why are you in a robe? It's almost lunchtime. Are you sick?"

"Couldn't sleep."

"Well, what I'm about to tell you won't help with that." She spins one of her many rings.

Worry tenses my already tight muscles. Liza never fidgets.

"I'm still groggy. Give me a minute to wake up." I fiddle with the coffee maker, setting it to brew, then reach for the banana nut bread in the bread bin—stalling. "Banana bread?"

Her sigh lands somewhere between impatience and resignation. She slides off her Birkenstock sandals and sits cross-legged on the dining room chair. My hip hurts looking at her pretzel shape. "Sure. How about a mug of hot water, too. I know I have my special SereniTea blend in here somewhere," she says as she rummages through her oversized, patchwork bag.

I put the kettle on. By the time I've sliced two pieces of banana nut bread from the loaf, and fixed my coffee, adding a teaspoon of sugar, vanilla creamer, and a swirl of whipped cream, the water is boiling. I pour it in a mug and move everything to the table.

Liza dunks her reusable, muslin-cloth tea bag in the hot water, and offers Shammie the first bite of her bread as it steeps. "Good for her potassium levels."

I pat my ample hip. "Good for padding, too."

After two gulps of coffee and half my bread, I cross my arms and rest them on the table. "Okay. I'm ready. Let me have it."

"Clarice had a balayage appointment with me this morning and filled me in on the latest news."

"I am assuming balayage is a hair treatment, not a French patisserie?"

Liza rolls her eyes. "Millicent, be serious."

I take another swallow of coffee. "Sorry. Continue."

"*Last night*, sometime after we followed Donald and Amanda to the hospital, Isaac took a turn for the worse."

I set the mug down, heart thudding.

"His blood pressure tanked and they had trouble stabilizing him." Liza cradles her cup like it's the only warmth left in the room, and breathes in the steam.

My throat constricts with worry. "Mercy me!"

"And that's not all. Right after Clarice left, I pulled a tarot card to get clarity."

I lean in. "And?"

"The Magician showed up." Her voice is low, almost strained. "It's a card of intention. Millicent, I don't think Isaac's downturn was coincidence."

"Good gracious!" The coffee turns bitter as it slides down my throat. "You think Isaac and Amanda …" Acid churns in my stomach. "What do you think they did to him?"

Liza shakes her head sadly. "I don't know."

"Bless my soul! What should we do? What should we do?" I clutch my hands against my chest. "Do we call the police? Or tell Roddy's lawyer?"

Shammie whines, sensing our dismay, and Liza scoops her onto her lap. "I don't think we're ready for that. We're short on actual proof. Circumstantial evidence and intuition won't get us far with the police. But after drawing the Magician card, I did a second reading asking for guidance on how to proceed."

I squirm in the chair. "Not to, uh, disparage the deck, but when up against attempted murder is relying on tarot cards really our best course of action?"

Liza sets Shammie on the floor, then clicks her eggplant-colored nails on the mug. "If you have a better plan, I'm open."

Unfortunately, dealing with murderers is not in my wheelhouse. I huff and shake my head. "I don't. Looks like mystical wisdom for a thousand, Alex."

Liza uncurls her twisted legs and picks at her bread. "The second reading was clear. I pulled the Queen of Swords, the Ace of Swords, and The Tower."

"A lot of swords. Are we going to challenge them to a duel?"

Liza arches her perfectly-shaped eyebrows over unblinking eyes.

I take the hint. "Sorry. My sarcasm runs rampant when I'm anxious. Tell me what the cards mean."

"The Queen embodies direct communication. The Ace indicates the need to cut through lies with honesty. And The Tower suggests confrontation may be necessary to prevent further damage."

"Who do we confront? Donald or Amanda?"

Liza shrugs. "Maybe both. But let's start with Amanda. Get the photos of her and Donald developed. We can show them to her and ask why she lied about knowing him—twice."

My stomach rolls. This cloak and dagger stuff? Not for me. I like my intrigue safely on the pages of historic biographies, with footnotes, not actual danger.

"Okay, but I can't do it today. My nerves need a warm-up. I'll have to bake at least three dozen cookies, possibly a cake, and have a heart-to-heart with a lemon tart before I'll be ready to challenge Amanda."

She snickers and lifts her tea cup. "I have lemon balm and valerian root; you have flour and sugar." After feeding the last bite of her bread to Shammie, Liza rinses her cup and plate in the sink. "Give me the film; I'll get it developed. You get to baking."

I collect the disposable camera from my desk and hand it to Liza.

She drops the camera into her bag, nestles Shampoodles under her arm, and heads for the door. "I'll pick you up at nine tomorrow morning."

The door closes behind her, leaving me with a nervous stomach and the overwhelming urge to preheat the oven. I tie on my apron, gather my ingredients, and get to work stirring up some courage.

32 ~ Ruby

Lucy strains against the belt-leash, eager to reach the streambank that ribbons through the Sawmill parking lot at Nolde Forest. Despite the unseasonably cool day, Marty's impending arrival has me sweating like an English major taking a math final.

"I'm going to let her wade into the water," I tell Gail and Roddy as they stretch their hamstrings.

Gail—the outdoorsy type—suggested a hike to escape the doom and gloom of Roddy's legal battle and our floundering businesses. When Marty (the opposite of outdoorsy) called with new information, we couldn't bear to wait to hear it, so we invited him along.

I was actually surprised he agreed to join us. Unless he's drastically changed in the last four years, he'll be out of breath before we reach the trailhead, just like the day I met him. He'd shown up in Bermuda shorts and a safari hat, cutting quite the figure—much like Indiana Jones, if Indy had swapped his whip for safety goggles and a bottle of sunscreen.

Lucy's ears hit the water at the same time as her feet. She wades upstream, lapping the water as she goes.

Though I can tell Roddy's wondering about the status of my relationship with Marty, he hasn't asked. Which is good, because I have no answers. I *think* Marty was flirting, and *I* felt tingly and gooey inside when we hugged, but did he? And what about the brunette? Is Marty even available?

I'm bracing myself on the bank, trying to keep Lucy's fifty pounds of pure muscle from pulling me into the creek, when I see White Knight turn into the parking lot. My stomach hums with electricity.

When Marty pops out of his car, I can't help but smile. I swear he's wearing the same khaki Bermuda shorts he wore four years ago, but he's added a wide-brimmed hat tied under his chin, and an orange fanny pack around his waist. His nose is slathered in zinc sunscreen. Lucy drags me to him, beating a rapid-fire rhythm with her tail.

"Hey, pretty girl." He kneels and lets Lucy lick his face. "She's quite the droolicious kisser," he says, wiping the slobber from his cheeks.

Roddy extends a hand to Marty. "Hey man, glad you could join us."

Gail has traded her cowboy boots for rugged hiking boots, but her faded desert-scene T-shirt still conveys her western flair. She slides her backpack onto her shoulders. "Yeah, nice seeing you."

"It's a great day for a hike. I just hope my rusty legs don't slow you down."

When Lucy lunges at a squirrel I'm hitched forward.

Marty grabs my shoulder to steady me. "You alright?"

I tighten up the leash, allowing less slack. "Yep. All good. Just let me know if you get tired, I'll strap Lucy's leash around your waist. She's basically a four-paw tow truck."

"I may take you up on that."

The four of us head into the woods led by Lucy. Her need to sniff every bush and log keeps our pace leisurely, leaving Marty only mildly winded by the time we hit the trailhead. We veer off the crushed-stone path onto the Watershed Trail, a one-mile out-and-back hike that follows the stream.

Marty points at Lucy as she happily splashes down the center of the shallow water. "I always thought Basset Hounds were couch potatoes. She's super energetic."

I crinkle my nose. "Eh … I'd call her an enthusiastic explorer. I guarantee this excursion will be followed by a five-hour-nap and a snore that could register on the Richter scale."

Marty laughs. "Oh, just like you. They say dogs take on their owner's traits."

I pout and pretend to be offended. "I do not snore."

He raises one eyebrow and gives his head an are-you-kidding-me tilt. "You do not *not* snore."

"C'mon, Sis," Roddy chimes in. "You know you do. I've shared bunkbeds with you on many an occasion."

Gail backhands Roddy's chest. "You, the human chainsaw, are one to talk."

Again, I'm struck by how effortless it is when the four of us get together. The banter. The camaraderie. It all just clicks.

Roddy grins. "We should do this more often. I missed getting roasted by all of you."

Glad to see I'm not the only one soaking up the joy of being together. I glance at their smiling faces, lit by the lightness of the moment and the late-morning sun, and time rewinds. For a fleeting second, everything is okay. The break-up never happened. Our businesses are thriving. And Roddy is not facing criminal charges.

Gail laughs. "And we love roasting you!"

Roddy smirks. "Yeah, well, be careful. Last time someone roasted peanuts, I got arrested."

The joke lands, but so does the reminder of the stakes. The mood shifts, along with our conversation.

Roddy rakes his fingers through his shaggy blonde hair. "Sorry to crap on the fun. I guess the charges hanging over me are never far from my mind."

Gail wraps her arms around him. "They're never far from *any* of our minds."

Marty finds a rock and sits down for a breather. "I do think I have some good news for you. Give me a minute to replenish my oxygen to normal levels and I'll fill you in."

"I could use a water break," I say, opening my refillable water bottle. Even though the temps are mild for a summer day, it's still hot. The cold liquid sliding down my throat is a welcome refresher.

Gail pulls her bottle from her backpack. "Me too."

Lucy moseys towards Marty, lays at his feet, and promptly falls asleep. Gail and Roddy join me on a fallen tree trunk on the other side of the narrow trail. Goldenrods bloom abundantly and their earthy, musky scent mingles with the crispness of the pine trees.

Marty takes his hat off and mops his sweaty, bald head. "Okay. I think I can talk without hyperventilating. So, I looked into Janelle, and found her connection to Isaac. Two years ago, her son died at football practice. A football practice run by Coach Isaac Stone."

Gail's ponytail whips the back of Roddy's head when she snaps around to face Marty. "Oh, my word! That's horrible."

I feel an ache in my chest. Gigi always said the death of our mom was the hardest trial she ever faced. "Heartbreaking. No wonder she dislikes Isaac."

"Did she sue him?" Roddy asks.

Marty shakes his head. "No. Isaac was charged with involuntary manslaughter. The death occurred during a heatwave, and apparently, despite the extreme temperatures, Isaac pushed the team hard. But when, Tyler's—that's Janelle's son—autopsy revealed a pre-existing heart condition, the charges were dropped."

"Oof," I say, hitting my chest with my fist. "To have the man she believed caused—or at least contributed to—her son's death suffer no consequences had to be unbearable."

"Unbearable enough to spur her to murder?" Roddy asks, rubbing the back of his neck.

I pinch my lower lip. "It's definitely a strong motive."

Roddy swats a mosquito away from his face. "Stronger than Hank's?"

I shrug. "Who knows? I mean, without a doubt, the death of your child ranks much higher on the trauma scale than losing your dream job, but murder isn't exactly a standard coping mechanism. I think the reaction depends more on the person than the trigger."

Gail stands, leans against the trunk of an oak tree, and crosses her arms. "Maybe we need to look into mental health history. Any signs of volatility—bar fights, outbursts at work, that sort of thing."

I lean my elbows on my knees. "Marty, can you do that? Do journalists have access to that type of information?"

His mouth lifts and tightens at one corner. "Mental health history, no. That's protected information. If police were called for a bar fight or some other kind of public altercation, I could find that. Accessing work incidents would be trickier, but not impossible."

Roddy unthinkingly scratches the ground in front of him with a stick. "Does it really matter?"

Gail's brows furrow. "Roddy, please don't be disheartened. This Janelle info is good stuff. I'm sure your lawyer can use it."

He stands and paces. "No, no. I'm not discouraged. All I'm saying is we don't need to prove Hank or Janelle or anyone else did it. We only need to create reasonable doubt. Right?"

Marty rocks his hand side to side. "Well, yes and no. In legal jargon it's called third-party culpability. As you said, the goal is to introduce reasonable doubt by shifting suspicion onto someone else. But—at least from my limited legal understanding—it takes more than speculation. There has to be evidence linking the third party to the crime. So, I'd assume finding a pattern of emotional volatility could help build that case. I think we need to nose around into the lives of Janelle and Hank. I'll handle what I can from my end, but you all should sniff around too."

Right on cue, Lucy lifts her head, her droopy eyes settling on Marty. He chuckles. “Yes, you too, Lucy. That sniffer of yours might come in handy.”

She flaps her ears, then lumbers over to me. I knead her wrinkly neck. “Basset Hounds are the official sleuth dog, after all. Welcome to the Peanut Posse, Lucy girl.”

Roddy rests his hand on a tree trunk. “I’ll talk to the guys I shoot hoops with—see if Hank’s got a temper.”

Marty nods his head. “Good idea. You could also swing by the Locker Room in Myerstown. It’s a college hangout; you might get the scuttlebutt on Coach Hank. And Ruby, you mentioned Liza is Janelle’s hairstylist. She could be a great source. I’d check in with her.”

“What should I do?” Gail asks.

I bite my thumbnail, conflicted by what I’m about to suggest. “Janelle might be attending some kind of grief support group. If so, you could… I don’t know… sit in, maybe. Blend in. Just listen. See what she shares when she thinks no one’s watching. Since you were wearing a wig and costume at the party, she probably won’t recognize you.”

Three pairs of eyebrows rise, and even Lucy’s tail flicks with disapproval. I hold up my hands and sigh. “I know, I know—it’s morally gray. Forget I mentioned it—it’s too icky. I’m just worried. The stakes are high.” I cover my face with my hands.

Roddy plops down beside me and bumps his shoulder into mine. “Hey. It’ll work out.”

“You don’t know that,” I say from behind my hands.

Roddy pulls my hands down, then pretends to slip glasses onto my face. “Put your rose-colored glasses back on. We could all use some of your rainbow-and-unicorn positivity.”

Just then, Lucy whips her head from side-to-side flinging slobber in every direction. She digs in her paws, straining at the leash with such force that I'm yanked off my log perch. My butt hits the ground, kicking up a puff of dust.

Gail snorts. "Lucy's clearly done with this conversation."

Roddy helps me up. "I am too. We've got our game plan. Now, let's not waste this beautiful day. Back to hiking!"

"Righto!" Marty says, jabbing his finger in the air. "But about the hiking. According to my calculations we're only a half mile in, and my legs have filed a formal complaint. They're going on strike unless a shortcut is negotiated."

I crack up and come to his rescue. "Lucy's short legs have probably had enough, too."

Gail nods. "I'm sure. You know Basset Hounds have to take four times as many steps to cover the same distance as a person?"

"And with four legs, do we double that again?" Roddy says with a wink. "Lucy, according to my math, you've darn near completed a marathon."

Marty chuckles. "Trust me, I feel like I have."

Gail turns to head back, but I stop her. "Gail, why don't you and Roddy finish the hike. I know you've been itching to get on the trail. I'll lead Huff and Fluff back to the parking lot, as long as Huff's willing to give me and Fluff a ride home." I climb to my feet.

Marty rolls his hand with a flourish and bows. "White Knight is at your service."

Roddy rolls his eyes. "Don't tell me—Ruby named your car, too."

I shoot him a mock glare. "Obviously I named it. Who rides around in something nameless? That's just sad."

Gail pipes up. "You name boats. Why not cars?"

I flip my palm up and give Gail a vindicated nod. "Thank you."

Roddy holds his hands up in surrender. "You win. Now can we finish this hike?"

Gail wraps her arms around Roddy. "C'mon, Sir Grumbles-A-Lot."

Laughing, they head up the trail.

As I dust myself off, Marty slumps with theatrical relief. "Whew! Now who's the superhero? You just diverted a full-scale rebellion—four limbs and a torso were ready to picket. And my knees were seconds away from unionizing. But now that you've intervened, they'll settle for some BenGay and a nap."

I laugh. "Ranger Ruby at your service. I led you out of the fossil pit, I can lead you and your sore muscles out of here."

Marty pushes himself up from the boulder, with a groan. "I'd boycott hikes on principle, but if *you* keep rescuing me, I'll risk the blisters."

His words land me right back on the emotional rollercoaster. I'm getting whiplash. I need clarity. Is this just friends-zone repartee or let's-give-us-another-try flirting?

I suck my bottom lip behind my teeth, and take a beat to muster up some courage. "Um, I would … I would love to be your trail-side emergency contact." I drop my eyes to the ground and kick at the leaves. "Unless I'm stepping on someone else's hiking boots."

He's quiet for a beat, then shakes his head. "No. No other boots." He lifts his foot. "Just this clearly for-decorative-purposes-only pair." His smile is half-hearted and fades quickly. "I haven't dated anyone since us."

My heart hopscotches.

I step closer, leaving only inches between us. "Neither have I." I raise my hand, cupping his cheek. As I lean in, he presses his palm gently against my chest.

"Ruby, I… I care about you. I really do. But when you backed out of moving in together…" He shakes his head. "I can't go through that again."

My hand drops. My shoulders drop. My heart drops.

We *are* so perfect together. I see that now. I can't just let him walk away—again. This time I have to fight—for us, for me.

"Marty, I was scared. And if you take stock in the dozens of self-help books I've read over the last year, I have abandonment issues. I know my fear created the very thing I was desperate to avoid—losing another person I love."

He presses his lips together and steps out of my reach. "I get it. I do." He pauses and exhales. "But I don't know how to trust that it would be any different now."

I nod, swallowing the lump in my throat. "I understand."

I have no one to blame but myself. I nagged, I picked, I refused to trust Marty's feelings for me. A person can only take so much. I hoped for a second chance, but I know I don't deserve it. If our roles were reversed, I wouldn't risk my heart again either.

Hot pressure builds behind my eyes as we walk to the parking lot in silence. Lucy trudges beside me, tail tucked and ears hanging lower than normal, like she senses my distress. Marty unlocks White Knight, but the name rings hollow now. Paper Moon feels closer to the truth—not meant to last.

After hoisting Lucy into the back, I slide into the passenger seat. Marty throws his hat in the backseat beside Lucy, then puts the key in the ignition but doesn't start the car.

I wish he would just drive. I don't know how much longer I can hold back my tears.

He twists in his seat to face me. "Ruby, I … Can we just …" He rubs his bald head and blows a stream of air through his pursed lips. "I'm flubbing this up worse than my karaoke performance at your friend Kelly's '90s bash."

The memory of Marty in bright-red Hammer Pants, belting out an off-key *U Can't Touch This,* nudges a reluctant smile to my lips. "Nothing could be worse than that."

He takes my hand. "What I'm trying to say is, the door is not locked. Okay? I'm just not ready to open it. And, to be honest, I can't promise I ever will be. What I do know is I want to be friends. I want to watch movies together, and shop at indie bookstores. I want to have lunches and dinners and do bad karaoke. Without expectations. Without plans for the future. Can you live with that?"

I take a breath. Can I? Can I do all the things we love, and accept that friendship might be all there is? Can I suppress the part of me that wants more, and give him the space he's asking for? Give him the space he needs? I think about how much lighter I feel when he's around. Life with some Marty is better than life with none.

Steadying myself, I give the smallest nod.

I allow my usual rosiness to tint the moment and sow the seeds of hope. Maybe this is what starting over really looks like. Not grand gestures or big promises, but quiet understanding and a door left unlocked.

For now, that will have to be enough.

33 ~ Millicent

Liza's torch red Volvo sails into my driveway a few minutes before nine. I slip my feet into my trusty Clarks, toss a sand-colored cardigan over my shoulders—Amanda's house is always an icebox—and waddle out to the Volvo. I open the front passenger door to find the seat taken by Shampoodles lounging in some kind of velvety, indigo car throne.

"Oh, Millicent. I just got Shammie's new custom-made safety seat secured. Strapping it in nearly threw my chakras out of alignment. Would it be too much to ask you to sit in the back so I don't have to undo it?"

My chakras get carsick in the back, but I climb inside keeping my grumbles to myself.

"Did the pictures come out okay?"

Liza nods. "Yep. They're in my bag. Take a look."

A blend of patchouli and eucalyptus wafts from her patchwork purse when I open it. I have to dig past tarot cards, lipstick, bottles of essential oils, a few gold bangles, two teabags, and a handful of loose crystals, before I find the packet of photos.

I flip through them. "Well, there's no way she can deny knowing Donald once we show her these."

Liza glances at me in the rearview mirror. "No, she certainly can't."

"What are we going to say?" My foot jiggles with nervous energy.

Me and confrontation go together like Pizelle and bathwater. Now Myrtle, on the other hand, I swear she'll get in a row now and again just to keep her blood flowing. One time, at Root's Market in Manheim, she and a burly man had a shouting match over the last bunch of radishes. She doesn't even like radishes—they give her gas—but the man had elbowed his way in front of her and she was having none of it. She put her hands on her hips and asked him if he really wanted to go toe to toe with the mother of nine kids. He backed off pretty darn quick. She took her radishes home and fed them to the kids' guinea pigs.

Liza flicks on her blinker and turns left into Amanda's exclusive development. "I think we should be direct. Let's just ask her why she lied to you about knowing Donald."

The sweat dampening my scalp frizzes my hair even more than normal. "And we should ask her what she and Donald were doing at the hospital after visiting hours."

"Absolutely."

I inhale deeply as Liza pulls the Volvo into Amanda's circular driveway behind a silver Mazda. She lifts the bag with the photos onto her shoulder and untethers Shammie from the safety seat.

Her car door swings open. "Away we go."

I'm a lot slower getting out the car. By the time my swollen feet hit the ground, Liza's almost to the front door. Her shiny hair and long skirt are tossed by the light summer breeze as she walks. Noticing I'm not beside her, she stops and waits.

"I'm going to read the energy," she says, as I ring the bell. "I'll know when the time is right to show her the photos."

I nod. "Sounds good to me."

A slightly pale, but otherwise jaunty, Ian opens the door. "What's up?" he says with a lazy grin.

"Is your mom home?" I ask.

He hitches his thumb towards the far back corner of the house. “She’s in Dad’s study with Uncle Felix.” Apparently done with us, he wanders upstairs.

Liza shrugs. “I guess we’ll show ourselves in.”

Felix and Amanda’s muffled voices become clearer as we get closer to Isaac’s study.

“Amanda, I am just overwrought. After all my efforts, we’re at a standstill. We could even lose the surrogate.” His sigh is loud and huffy. “If he would just die already, all our issues would go away.”

There’s a sharp intake of breath—Amanda’s I imagine. “Felix! Hush! Don’t ever say that out loud.”

Liza and I lock eyes, dumbfounded by what we just heard. She tilts her head to the front door and mouths, “Go.”

I nod my agreement. As we turn to hightail it outta there, Shammie yips.

“Hello?” Amanda’s voice rings through the hall. She pokes her head out of the study just as Liza and I paste on bright smiles.

My words are tangled behind my teeth. “Amanda, um, hi. We saw, I mean Ian let us in. We, uh, we wanted to …”

Liza swoops forward, bangles clinking as she wraps her arms around Amanda. “Clarice told me about Isaac’s condition. We just wanted to check in on you and see if there’s anything we can do to help.”

Felix saunters out of the study. “Well, if it isn’t the Golden Girls. Hello ladies. How are we today?”

After what I just heard him say, I can’t even look at him. I open and close my mouth but no sounds come out.

Liza saves me again. “Felix, nice to see you. We just popped in to check on Amanda.”

“How sweet,” he says. He wraps his arms around Amanda, “But no need to worry, she’s in good hands.”

I wince. Sounds more like deadly hands to me.

I pull my cardigan tight, but it's not Amanda's air-conditioning chilling me.

Amanda motions towards the kitchen. "I'll fix us some tea."

Liza lays her hand on Amanda's forearm. "No, no. We don't want you to go to any trouble. Like I said, we just wanted to check in on you. Do you need any groceries? Can we take Ian to any medical appointments?"

She shakes her hand in front of her. "No, no. I'm fine. Really. Ian's doing well and they got Isaac stabilized this morning. I'm heading to the hospital shortly."

Liza lifts her hand to her chest. "That's wonderful news."

I'm thanking my lucky stars Liza's with me. She's serving up an Oscar-worthy performance while I'm still too stunned to form a sentence.

"Well, girls. Must dash." Felix puckers his lips and sends us a flurry of air kisses. "Amanda, give Isaac an extra special hug from me."

My eyes bug out at his sassy wink. Does *extra special hug* mean suffocation?

"Millicent, are you well? Your coloring is a bit … green," Amanda says.

My thoughts are racing, but my body is in slow motion. My mouth needs a minute to catch up. "I um, yes, I'm fine, fine, fine."

Amanda's sculpted brows furrow. "Are you sure?"

Though I suspected it, hearing the words knocked the wind right out of me. My dear friend and her brother-in-law's husband—and maybe Donald—are actually plotting murder. I am so far from fine I couldn't spot it with a telescope.

Liza links her arm in mine. "Bad oyster at dinner the other night. It's just taking its time working out of her system."

I clutch my round belly. "Ooh. Heavens to Betsy, I think the oyster is staging an encore. I hate to run but I think a lie-down is in order."

"Go, go," Amanda says, shooing us to the door. "I'm fine. Really. I appreciate you stopping by, though."

Amanda air kisses Liza's cheeks while giving her one of those society squeezes. I beg off, holding my hand against my mouth as if the oyster might exit any second.

My waddle back to the Volvo is a lot faster. Disbelief, disgust, and dread are making me sicker to my stomach than any spoiled seafood ever could. Liza and I stay silent until we reach my house, as if words might slow our escape.

Once inside, Liza lets Shampoodles duke it out with Pizelle and heads to my kitchen. "I need a drink. Something stronger than SereniTea."

"Me too." I dig a dusty bottle of elderberry wine from the back corner of my cupboard and pour some into two teacups.

We both slug them back in one swallow. Liza pours herself another. I take an antacid and open a tin of cookies.

Bringing the cookies with me, I sit at the table. "Jed told me Felix is desperate to have a baby, but I never thought—"

"He'd kill for it." Liza downs a third shot of wine before joining me at the table.

I'm so glad I brought Liza into this. I can't imagine carrying this on my own.

I slide the tin of cookies towards her. "Want one?"

"No thanks." She roots a clip out of her bag, then scrapes her hair back into a messy bun.

I finish one cookie and grab another. "So, does this mean Donald's in the clear?"

"Hard to say." She shrugs, then rubs her temples. "If you think back to that initial reading, the Page of Cups came up. We took it to mean a new love, but it also symbolizes the love for a child."

I swallow. "Felix's need to have a baby."

"Possibly." Liza stands and paces around the table. "The Five of Pentacles was also in the reading. It indicates financial insecurity.

Amanda and Donald clearly have a new love, and the overdue bills and car repo prove her financial insecurity."

"So, Amanda and Donald?" I ask.

She twists a strand of hair that's fallen from her clip. "Maybe. But Felix's energy is laser-focused on having a child, and the costs associated with surrogacy also point to financial insecurity."

"I'm befuddled. What's it all mean?"

She plunks into the chair, exasperated. "New love, money troubles, a desperate longing for a child—the cards don't point to one person; they point to all three."

My head spins.

I eat another cookie. "The cards also told us to confront Amanda. Do we still do that?"

"I'm not so sure." She twists her lip. "The energy surrounding Amanda and Felix was dark. Maybe even dangerous. And interpreting the cards is not an exact science. We should consider that, rather than confrontation, the cards were nudging us towards telling the truth to someone who can act on it—like the police."

I shiver. I can't say I felt darkness—maybe my chakras are clogged with sugar and butter—but overhearing Felix wish Isaac dead? That sent a chill right through me. But telling the police seems like a nuclear option. Once we set those wheels in motion, there's no going back.

I take my glasses off and wipe my brow. "I mean, are we one-hundred percent sure? Felix did help with the food at the party, so he had access. But it's not like he admitted trying to murder Isaac. All he said was he wished he would die soon."

Liza taps her fingernail on her teacup. "True, but if Amanda wasn't involved, wouldn't she have had a stronger reaction to Felix wishing her husband dead?"

I slip my glasses back on, shoulders slumping with the heaviness of our decision. "What if we tell Ruby and Roddy? Let them decide what to do. After all, it's Roddy's neck on the line."

"Are you ready to cast suspicions on their father?"

My stomach lurches at the thought. I shake my head as I grab another cookie. "No. Not without more proof."

"We can follow Donald—try to rule him in or out."

I brush the crumbs from my shirt. "Hmm. Maybe. Though unless we hear what he and Amanda are saying to each other, will it really prove anything?"

Liza sighs. "I suppose not."

I break a cookie and leave one half in the tin. "Maybe I don't have to mention Donald. I could just tell Ruby and Roddy what we heard Felix say, and that Amanda is having financial and marital difficulties. I wouldn't have to tell them Donald is her secret man."

"I like that. No conjecture, just facts."

Oh, who am I kidding? I grab the other half of the cookie and finish it in two bites. "I think it would still help Roddy's case. If they tell his lawyer it'll stir up more reasonable doubt."

Liza pulls her tarot deck from her purse. "Should I do a reading? Just for clarity?"

I pluck one more cookie from the tin. "If you don't mind, this time I'll go with my gut. It may be full of cookies, but it rarely steers me wrong."

34 ~ Ruby

I shimmy into my bootcut Levi's and slide my feet into the cutest pair of teal platform sandals—only ten bucks at Divine Consign. My curls frizz when I pull my *Vote for Pedro* T-shirt over my head. After a generous spritz of curl tamer, I add a thick, yellow headband. Using my fingers, I pat shimmery gold eyeshadow on my lids, brush on some mascara, swipe a shiny tangerine gloss onto my lips, and head out the door.

I'm meeting Roddy and Gail at Wahtney's, a local tavern that serves casual fare and a mean, boozy ice cream dessert. Roddy also invited Marty—hence the makeup. After the hike, Roddy asked where things stood between me and Marty. I shared my hope and Marty's reluctance and now, apparently, Roddy's decided to play matchmaker. (I'm not complaining.)

Sally bounces into the parking lot, the Gerber daisy in her dashboard bud vase bobbing its bright pink head. I soak in her jauntiness, determined to make tonight feel like a celebration. Though we're not out of the woods yet, the lawyer told Roddy that with all we uncovered about Hank and Janelle, she's confident she has a strong third-party culpability defense. Obviously, there are no guarantees in a trial. And sadly, even if—no, *when*—he's cleared, we'll still have the damage to our businesses to contend with. But for tonight, we're choosing joy. So, Tipsy Turtle Sundaes all around!

Roddy calls my name as I'm stepping onto the front porch of the stone tavern. I turn and wait for them to catch up. Gail looks adorable in her cropped top, jean skirt, and teal cowboy boots. The setting sun casts a coppery glow onto her long chestnut hair. And for the first time since the party, Roddy's green eyes twinkle, and the tight, tough-it-out smile he's been forcing gives way to a genuine grin.

"Hey, Sis," he says draping his arm around my shoulder. "How are ya?"

"Good! I got a new booking to plan a book club Christmas party." I don't mention all the leads that have dried up since Roddy's arrest. Tonight is for good vibes only.

"That's awesome." He pulls open the heavy wood door and we head inside.

We grab a high-top table in the center of the barroom. Roddy orders three minty Grasshoppers. Since Gigi's death, it's become our tradition to start any night out with her favorite drink. I guess it's our way of keeping her spirit alive—one flamboyant cocktail at a time.

He brings the drinks and menus to our table.

"To Gigi," I say, raising my glass.

Marty arrives (cue the belly butterflies) as our glasses clink.

"This is bull puckey!" he says. "You started without me."

Roddy stands and claps Marty on the back. "Oh, man. You said you'd be late."

"Lucky me, I finished ahead of the deadline." Marty hangs his messenger bag on a hook under the table and hops up on the seat beside me, letting out a loud exhale. "So, other than tipping my glass to your grandmother, what'd I miss?"

Gail licks the frothy white foam from her lips. "Not a thing. We haven't even looked at the menus."

"Do you want me to grab you a Grasshopper?" I ask Marty.

"No thanks. I'm feeling rather mammalian tonight. I'm going with a Salty Dog." He slides out of his seat, "Back in a jiffy."

I watch him go, his awkward swagger so familiar it makes my chest ache.

Gail leans close. "His eyes lit up when he saw you."

Roddy joins in the Cupidry. "Don't worry, you two are meant to be together. Now that you're hanging out again, he won't be able to resist your charms for long."

I roll my eyes (but hope they're right). "Okay, okay. Let's not turn this into a rom-com. We're just friends celebrating good news."

Roddy sips his crème de menthe and shoots me a satisfied smirk. "Friends for now."

Marty returns, licking the salt from his lips. "Where are Donald and Millicent?"

"Bars aren't really Millicent's scene." I laugh awkwardly. "Not Dad's either. He, uh, he's been really busy lately. He's on the planning committee for the Eastern Pennsylvania AA Convention." I've shielded Roddy from Dad's reluctance to support our plan to find the real culprit behind PeanutGate.

"Makes sense. He's got a professional event planner in his back pocket." He playfully bumps his elbow into my side.

I twirl my swizzle stick in my cocktail. "Oh, I can't really help. Anonymity, you know. Dad's open about his battle with alcohol but apparently lots of people aren't."

Gail tsks. "So many people battle addictions. It's awful that there's still a stigma attached to it. I mean, alcoholism is a disease. You wouldn't shame people for having cancer. I admire your dad for being so outspoken about his struggles. Honesty takes guts."

I cringe, regretting my last lunch with Dad. I've been avoiding him because he was honest. He wasn't cruel. He wasn't demanding. He just didn't agree with the way Roddy and I are handling PeanutGate. Instead of hearing him out, I shut him out. And that's not fair.

Four years ago, when the *who's-your-daddy* bombshell dropped, I stressed the importance of no more secrets, saying what you feel even if it's uncomfortable, and trusting each other enough to be vulnerable, as the way to create a strong, healthy relationship. I talk the talk, but clearly, I'm not walking the walk. Not when it came to me and Marty. And not with Dad. It's been okay for me to dump my feelings on him, even if it stings, but as soon as he shares something I dislike, I steer clear.

Roddy raises his glass, "Cheers to Donald. And no, the irony of toasting his sobriety is not lost on me."

We chuckle and clink glasses.

Roddy rakes his fingers through his hair. "I've gotta admit, Donald's been a real sounding board for me since my arrest. For what might happen if my case takes a nosedive—"

Gail backhands Roddy's chest. "Don't say that!"

He gives her a side hug. "I'm not saying it will—in fact, that's why we're celebrating tonight, because I've got a good defense—I'm just saying it's helped to talk out the what ifs, man to man. Donald doesn't blow smoke. I'm not stoked that he isn't certain I didn't make a mistake, but I value his honesty."

I'm stunned. Here I am meddling like Lady Catherine in *Pride and Prejudice*, swooping in to "protect" Roddy, when he's actually appreciated Dad's honesty. Apparently, because their relationship has taken longer to find its footing, I decided it was my twin duty to smooth every bump between them. Never mind that they're two grown men perfectly capable of sorting out their own stuff. Okay Dr. Lauter, what do you have to say about me appointing myself as their referee? Does that fall under abandonment issues or conflict avoidance? Either way, I clearly have *more* work to do—starting with an apology to Dad, which I mentally star, highlight, and underline at the top of my to-do list.

Roddy passes out the menus. "No more talk about my case! We're here to unwind and enjoy."

"And pig-out!" Gail adds.

Her appetite is heartier than a lumberjack's.

Her finger slides down the menu. "Everything looks so yummy! Instead of dinners, should we just get a bunch of bar snacks and share?"

"Yes!" we say in unison.

Fifteen minutes later, an outrageous amount of food covers our table. Shrimp Jammers, wings, crab dip, and of course Wahtney's—ridiculously decadent—fries, topped with ham, bacon, peppers, mushrooms and cheese.

Marty rubs his round belly. "Aah, a feast for reckless appetites."

I grab a fry, melty cheese dripping from it, and pop it in my mouth. Bliss.

Roddy chomps into a wing. "It's basically, pure gulosity on a plate."

"Okay, brother. I'm giving you big points for that one," I say raising my hand for a high-five.

He smacks my palm with his. "Fifty points?"

I roll my eyes. "Pff. Get real. For fifty points the word needs at least seven syllables. But I'll award you a cool twenty-five for rarity."

Gail dips a Shrimp Jammer in cocktail sauce. "Do seven syllable words even exist?"

Laughing, Marty smacks his forehead and shakes his head. "Oh ho! Now you've done it Gail! The next twin challenge is on the table. Who will win the first-ever Nerdy Wordy award?"

"Easy," I say, shrugging. "Supercalifragilisticexpialidocious."

Roddy turns his thumb down. "*ERRRP!* Real words, Ruby." He finishes the last sip of his Grasshopper. "I think I need a beer for this. Anyone else?"

Mouth stuffed full of crab dib, Gail raises her hand.

I lean in conspiratorially, "Quick guys, help me out."

Gail taps her short fingernails on the table top. "Most of the super big words I know are animal medicines."

I nod my head at warp speed. "I'll take it! Give me one, quick!"

"Oxytetracycline hydrochloride." She lifts a finger in front of her lips. "Oh, wait. I think its technically two words."

"I'll fudge it. What's it for?"

"It's an antibiotic used for livestock."

Roddy hands Gail a bottle of Budweiser, then leans forward so his face is inches from mine. "Disproportionately."

"Nope!" I hold up my hand and count out the syllables. "Only six." I lean back in my stool, cross my arms, and add a smug, confident smile to my face (fake it 'til you make it). "Oxytetracycline hydrochloride."

Roddy forms an X with his arms. "Foul! Words. Not medicines." He points a finger at Gail and gives her the hairy eyeball. "Did you help her?"

Gail crinkles her perky, little nose. "Guilty."

Roddy sticks his tongue out at her. "Traitor."

I lift my hands in surrender. "Okay. Medicines don't count. But guess what. I don't need it. I have a real humdinger: disproportionableness."

Roddy slams his hands on the table in mock outrage. "Cheater! That's my word. Come on judges, there's got to be rules against this!"

I raise my eyebrows and shake my head. "No. Your word was disproportionately, six syllables. My word is the clear winner. Victory is mine!"

Marty snickers. "Shall the judges confer?"

Gail hops off her seat and moves around the table to Marty. After a dramatic, hushed whisper conversation, the judges are ready to announce their verdict.

Marty grabs my hand and lifts it in the air. "Congratulations to Ruby Finch! The winner of the first—and hopefully last—Nerdy Wordy contest!"

"Oh, it won't be the last," Gail says. "I can guarantee many more contests."

I bow my head and wave like the Queen of England. "I am humbled to accept this high honor." I lower my voice and add a scratchy quality a la Jim Carrey's Grinch. "I was told there would be some kind of award."

Marty's smile is snarky. "Of course." He grabs a pen from his messenger bag and writes *Sesquipedalian Crown* onto a napkin and places it on my head. "By the power vested in me by the Council of Pretentious Words, I crown you queen of the Sesquipedalians."

I snort and Gail groans.

"Okay brainiacs," she says. "Tell me what that one means."

Roddy's forehead furrows. "Oh man, Marty, you've stumped me, too."

Holding the edges of the napkin with my fingertips, I shift it side to side on top of my head. "It means user of long words."

Gail giggles. "A long word to describe long words. Figures."

Marty wraps his arm around me. His warm hug sends happiness skipping through my body. "Gigi would be so proud."

Roddy takes a swallow of his Bud and bows his head to me. "I bow to your superior *pretention,* and challenge you to a rematch."

"I accept," I say, shaking Roddy's hand.

Gail crosses her arms and lifts her chin in a mock-smug pose. "Told you."

Marty smiles. "You know the twins well."

She grips the side of the table. "Brace yourself, Marty. It's *Nerds Gone Wild.*"

When I throw my head back laughing, my napkin crown slips sideways.

"The fallen queen—" Roddy's quip dies on his lips as the tavern door bangs open.

Jed and his band stride in, with Felix and friends trailing behind. The reminder of what's at stake for us is an ice-cold shower.

"What just happened?" Marty asks, sensing the obvious shift in mood.

I jut my chin towards the men. "Jed and Felix were at *the* party."

"Righto. They certainly flattened our fizz."

Roddy shakes his head like a wet dog and flicks his hand. "Nope! Add some carbonation back into this night! Nothing has changed. My defense is strong and everything is going to work out."

"Pip-pip," Marty says raising his glass.

My glass is empty so I clink with a gooeylicious fry.

Felix spots us and hurries over, blowing air kisses to each of us. "Hey kids! Fancy seeing you here." He bumps his shoulder against Gail's. "I bet you're glad not to be behind the bar tonight."

"Absolutely! I'm much happier working with animals than people."

"Girl, preach!" He switches his gaze to Marty. "And who is this distinguished professor?"

I love Felix's characterization of Marty.

Marty extends his hand. "Marty Metzger. Nice to meet you."

Felix grins. "Felix Choi. Trophy husband to the fabulous lead singer."

Laughter ripples across the table.

Jed joins us. "Hey all. Thanks so much for coming out to support me and my band."

We don't correct his assumption.

"Sure! Glad to," I say brightly. After a moment of hesitation, I ask the question. "How's your brother?"

Jed rubs his scruffy chin. His long hair sways as he nods. "Hanging in there."

Felix gives Jed a loving squeeze. "Please, that scrappy tomcat's got nine lives."

Jed clears his throat, clearly uncomfortable with the conversation. "I, uh, better get the band set up. Felix, grab me a brew. Will ya?"

Felix pecks him on the cheek. "Coming right up."

"Enjoy the sets," Jed says, before heading into the adjoining room to set up.

Felix sighs theatrically. "Duty calls. See you, gang." He blows more air kisses before drifting to the bar.

The flare of drama drains from the table, leaving a thick, uneasy quiet behind. Jed's less-than-optimistic description of Isaac's condition is sobering, because if Isaac dies, Roddy will likely face homicide charges.

The mounds of food spread across our table lose their appeal. Gail throws her napkin on top of her plate. I shove mine to the side.

"Should we get the check?" Roddy asks.

Clearly, the balloons have deflated and the party is over.

I throw in money to cover my portion. "Might as well. I'm going to use the restroom before we head out."

The wood floor creaks under my feet as I walk to the bathroom. Another woman is waiting for the single bathroom, so I lean against the stone wall. The room only holds eight tables and the makeshift stage, so I can easily hear conversations. I focus on Felix's.

"Jed's fine with our egg donor being Korean. He told me he hopes our child inherits my beauty—because, well, look at me."

His friend rolls her eyes and laughs. "Jed's so sweet, but only you could turn genetics into a beauty contest."

Felix flicks his hair and offers a hundred-watt grin. "And girl, if it is, I'm taking home the crown."

The friend laughs. "I admit, your cheekbones could cut glass."

Felix smiles. "Now who's sweet?" He sips his drink and sighs. "Jed needs some steel underneath all that sugar. I'd like to be able to count on him to get things done but it always seems to fall to me."

The friend shrugs. "Opposites attract. You've got the steel and he's got the sugar."

"I suppose." Felix sips his drink. "Jed would kill me if he heard me say this, but with any luck, it won't be too much longer. And then we'll have the funds to lockdown our surrogate."

"Your turn," the lady ahead of me in line says.

I want to linger longer, in case Felix reveals anything useful, but the lady is holding the restroom door open for me, so I peel myself away from eavesdropping.

After using the restroom, I meet everyone outside, in the parking lot. The mood is somber, lips and shoulders drooping as much as Lucy's Basset-Hound eyes. Channeling some rainbow positivity, I paste on a bright smile. "Isaac will recover. I'm sure of it."

Roddy runs his hand through his shaggy hair and nods. "Yep. You're right. He will. And let's not forget, my defense is strong."

Gail links her arm in Roddy's. "Nothing to worry about."

After subdued hugs all around, Gail and Roddy hit the road. Marty walks me to Sally and opens my door.

I lean against the side of my car. "Thanks for joining us tonight. It was fun … while it lasted."

He sighs. "Yeah. Not exactly the ending any of us hoped for. But I know you're right. I know everything will work out in the end."

"That's what I keep telling myself."

He swirls one of my wandering curls around his finger. The whisper of his finger on my cheek curls my toes. I want him to come home with me. I want to snuggle in the crook of his arm and, for a little while, feel like everything is okay. But I don't move. I don't push. Opening the romance door has to be at his pace. His timeline.

He lingers close for a second or two more, before stepping away. He clears his throat. "I've been craving the eggrolls from Oriental Kitchen. Would you be up for lunch sometime this week?"

A spark flares low in my chest—small but bright. The night's been far from perfect, but his invitation nudges the ending closer to what I'd hoped for.

I think his hand may finally be resting on the doorknob.

35 ~ Millicent

My wrinkled hands are shaking as I finish whisking the white milk gravy, and it's not from old-age tremors.

"Millicent, are you okay?" Ruby asks.

"Fine. Fine. Just not sleeping the best." I'm not lying about that. I've been more restless than the week I made myself sick waiting for the results of Myrtle's breast biopsy. Cancer doesn't run in our family. Well, I say that, but we did have a cousin who died of lung cancer. He was a lifelong two-pack-a-day smoker, so it probably doesn't count. Anyhow, the worry is taking a toll on me.

I point my chin towards my avocado green refrigerator, rattling with its last breath. "How about you and Roddy take the Cobb Salad and cantaloupe to the patio table?"

"Sure." Ruby grabs the salad and Roddy carries the platter of fruit.

I take a big breath, puffing my chest with a confidence I don't feel, then pour the hot gravy into a chipped gravy boat. During my midnight roaming, I had decided it serves no purpose for me to share Donald and Amanda's secret rendezvous. But the twins are sharp, and I'm not good at hiding things. If I start tripping over my tongue, they may figure it out.

Gravy boat in one hand, pitcher of fresh-squeezed lemonade in the other, I lumber out to my backyard. The August sun is high in the sky, but my umbrella casts just the right amount of shade. The broad leaves of my giant elephant ear plant sway in the breeze, while the showy white gardenias in my container garden release their citrus-jasmine scent. The setting for a relaxing picnic, if not for the tangle knotting in my belly.

"Looks delicious, Millicent," Ruby says.

I scoop a hefty portion of salad onto Roddy's plate. "Nothing fancy, but you can't go wrong with bacon and bleu cheese."

Ruby chuckles to herself.

"What's so funny?" Roddy asks, as he coats his cantaloupe in warm gravy.

"Oh, the bacon made me think of a Marty joke."

The detour to—fingers crossed—this little second-hand-rose romance loosens the tension in my stomach. "You're seeing Marty again?"

She flips her hand from side to side. "Seeing, not dating. Not yet anyway."

"It felt like old times, last night," Roddy says. "I really hope you guys can make it work."

I add salad to Ruby's plate. "Me, too. You two are like peas in a pod."

Ruby holds her hands up. "Preaching to the choir. The ball's in Marty's court, now."

After serving myself, I ease into my double-cushioned chair. "Well, let's hear the joke."

"It's corny," Ruby says.

Roddy pours himself some lemonade. "Does Marty tell any other type?"

Ruby's laugh tinkles with joy. "Uh, no! Here goes. What do you call a pig that does karate?"

"Jackie Ham?" I venture.

Ruby's mouth forms an O. "Good one, Millicent! I'll have to share that with Marty. But no, the answer is Pork-chop."

"Ugh," Roddy says. "More groan-worthy than normal."

Forgoing the gravy, Ruby salts her cantaloupe. "I warned you."

"So, Millicent," Roddy says, between bites of salad. "You said you found something that will help my case?"

Here goes. I steady my nerves with a slice of bacon and a swallow of lemonade before spilling what I know. "So, ever since Gail told us what she overheard at Laurel Hills Stables, I've been conducting my own little investigation into Amanda."

Ruby dabs the corners of her mouth with the napkin. "Did you find out who the white-haired man is? Is he involved?"

My stomach drops to my knees. I barely started my story and already the worst possible question is on the table. I don't want to outright lie, but I really don't want to bring Donald into this. If they figure it out on their own, so be it. But I don't want to be the one to break their hearts.

"Well, I, uh …" Stalling, I stuff a huge bite of gravy-topped cantaloupe in my mouth. Should I just blurt out my suspicions? Let the chips fall where they will? No, I just can't do it. I can't bring Donald into this without solid proof. Best thing I can do is skirt the truth.

I use the lemonade to wash down my food, then dive in. "Amanda did tell me she is seeing someone, but more importantly I learned she is having major financial difficulties. There are stacks of unpaid bills at her house and Isaac's Mercedes was repossessed."

Roddy spoons another serving of melon onto his plate. "Okay. Sad, but how does that play into my case?"

I nibble a piece of bacon like a timid little mouse, carefully choosing my words. One misstep could spill more than I mean to about Donald. "Life insurance. I mean, it's only a guess," I add in a rush, "but it could be a motive."

Ruby drops her fork on her plate, and her eyes widen. "Wow. So, you think … Wow."

"And I'm also pretty darn sure she's not acting alone." My lips curl in, tight with stress.

Roddy shivers. "The white-haired guy. Get Isaac out of the picture and collect on the insurance policy."

"I'm not talking about …" Sakes alive! I catch myself just before I blurt out Donald's name. My insides wobble with jitters. I'm not built for this sneaky business. I fake a little cough and take a sip of lemonade to give myself time to collect my thoughts. "The white-haired man may or may not be involved. I honestly don't know." It's not a lie. Suspecting is not knowing. I lean in. "But I do know Felix is."

Ruby's head juts towards me. "Felix? Jed's husband, Felix?"

"Yes. I overheard him and Amanda talking. Felix said, 'If he would just die already, all our issues would go away.'"

Ruby's hands fly to her face covering her nose and mouth. "Oh my god! I overheard Felix talking to his friends at Wahtney's. He said something like, 'with any luck it won't be too much longer and then we'll have the funds for our surrogate.' He must be splitting the insurance money with Amanda." She shakes her head with disgust. "That is so heartless. They're just counting the minutes until Isaac dies."

"Man," Roddy says, pushing his plate away. "It's hard to believe something like this happened here. At our event. A cold and calculated attempted—and let's hope it stays that way—murder. How could Jed do that to his brother? His own brother?"

Ruby swats a bug away from her face. "From what Felix said, I don't think Jed knows."

"Well, that's something, I guess." Roddy hangs his head, giving it a slow shake.

If I'm right about Donald, Ruby and Roddy don't have the foggiest idea how bad it really is. I push back my chair, steadying myself with a hand on the table as I stand up.

My friend. Their dad. It's all too horrible. I blink back tears.

Ruby jumps up, flying to my side. "Oh, Millicent. How insensitive of us. This has to be so hard on you. I know you and Amanda are good friends. To think her capable of something so … ruthless. That must be so upsetting. What can we do?"

Isn't that the million-dollar question. What can any of us do? If the whole truth is rooted out and Donald is involved, it will devastate their world. If the truth stays hidden and Roddy goes to jail, it will devastate their world. Where is the win in all this?

I pat Ruby's arm. "I'm okay. Don't worry about me, I'm just so sorry if my friend is to blame for all this hoogery-boogery."

Roddy wags his finger at me. "Millicent, there is absolutely nothing for you to be sorry for. All through this, you've been nothing but helpful. In fact …" His voice cracks. "After Gigi died, I kind of spiraled. She was just so loving, so nurturing … I felt really empty without her. And insecure."

Roddy's not prone to mushiness or tears, so when he sniffles, it sets off my own.

A few tears slide down his cheek and he chuckles. "Sorry about the waterworks, it's just … Millicent, you filled that hole. I can never thank you enough. I am so grateful to have you as part of my family."

Now I'm the one leaking.

Roddy stands, joining Ruby and me in a group hug.

"Okay, okay," I say. "Enough tugging on my heartstrings—though I hope you both know I count you as family, too."

"We do," they say in unison.

Our hug breaks apart, and the sad reason for our picnic settles back in like a draft under the door.

I grab a napkin from the table and dab at my eyes. "Would it help if I told the police what I heard?"

Roddy shakes his head. "No. My lawyer was adamant—do not talk to the police. But I'll tell her, of course. We can use all the fodder we can get for the third-party defense."

Despite the lingering warmth of our hug, a chill slices through me. Lies and betrayals, stakeouts and lawsuits, arrests and defenses, poison and attempted murder. When did my plain Jane life get so wild?

36 ~ Ruby

As much as my heart aches for Millicent over the whole Amanda situation, I can't help but ooze glitter-and-sunshine optimism. How much more reasonable doubt can we need? I feel it in my confetti-filled bones, Roddy's case is in the bag.

I'll be so glad when his trial is over, finally clearing us. Then we can move full force into getting our businesses back on track.

I turn in to the parking area of Dad's townhouse development to find my normal guest parking spot taken by a Mercedes. Hmm. Wonder who's visiting Dad?

Sliding into a new spot, I snag the frozen Gene Wenger's ham loaf from the passenger seat—a peace offering—and head to his front door, knocking out "shave and a haircut" before pushing it open.

My mouth falls open to find Amanda and Dad in an embrace. "Wha … I … uh."

They pull apart. Dad's face reddens. Amanda twists her pearl necklace, the epitome of cliché.

"Ruby," he says. "I, uh, wasn't expecting you."

My mind flashes to Dad's denial that he knows Amanda and what Gail overheard about a "sophisticated white-haired man."

"Clearly." My tone is sharp.

Dad ignores it, trying to finesse the moment. "To what do I owe this honor?"

All I can think about is Amanda purposely poisoning her husband to get him out of the way for her new love. A new love that disturbingly appears to be my dad. My breath hitches, and despite clutching a frozen ham loaf, my palms get clammy.

Setting the ham loaf on the entry table, I cross my arms. "What is going on here? You told me you didn't know Amanda. Why did you lie to me, Dad? What are you hiding?"

His eyes blink in rapid succession, and then he averts his gaze. Why is he acting so sketchy?

My gut clenches as a horrendous thought lodges in my brain.

He knew. He knew Amanda added the peanut powder to Roddy's dishes.

I grab my stomach, doubling over. A blast of heat flashes through my body.

No! No! No! It can't be! He wouldn't allow someone to hurt us like that. It's not possible.

Desperation tramples anger, and urgency cuts through the sharpness of my voice. "Please, Dad. Tell me. Why did you lie?"

Dad's eyes cut between me and Amanda.

She lays her hands on Dad's forearm. "It's okay. We can tell her."

He hesitates, shooting her a concerned look. "Are you sure?"

She flips her hand and shrugs her shoulder. "My standing at the Club was ruined when they towed Isaac's Mercedes away. This won't make it any worse."

She's worried about her standing at the Club? Are you kidding me? My hands twitch with the urge to slap her, and I literally have to bite my tongue to keep from screaming.

Dad points toward the couch. "Let's sit."

This is not a friendly get together. "I'll stand," I snap.

He shrugs and takes a seat on the couch. "Suit yourself."

Amanda perches on the leather chair across from him, ankles crossed.

"Amanda has been—I think I'm correct in my characterization—struggling."

She clasps her hands in her lap. "Entirely correct."

Struggling? With what? Wedding vows? How best to off your husband? This is beyond surreal. My stomach rolls with nausea, and a cold sweat coats my back.

Dad leans his elbows on his knees. "It wasn't planned, but we did have an instant connection, which grew stronger each time we met, so it just made sense."

Made sense to kill your rival? Oh my god, Dad, what are you even saying? My knees wobble, threatening to give out. I clench my teeth and press my fingers into my temples to keep from crying.

Sighing, Amanda swipes her hair behind her ears. "It's all so complicated. My emotions are all over the place. And, other than your father, no one seems to truly understand what's at stake. We're just a good fit."

I bite the inside of my mouth to keep from lashing out. Stakes? Her husband is hanging on by a thread. I could lose my business. Roddy could lose his business and maybe even his freedom. I can't believe she actually has the audacity to bring up stakes.

Amanda's voice trembles. "Your father listens. He doesn't judge. I don't know what I'd do without him."

Doesn't judge? Is she saying Dad knew about her plan to poison Isaac and did nothing to stop her? How could he? What kind of man is he? A crack splits straight through the center of me, splintering my heart.

"Amanda, give yourself the credit, not me. You are strong. You'd take one day at a time, like the Big Book says. With or without me, you *will* be okay."

Wait. My body freezes. I hold my breath. Big Book? What are they talking about?

Dad clasps his hands. "As your sponsor I can only share my experiences, strength, and hope. You're the one doing the work."

Sponsor? Air rushes into my lungs. Oh my god! This is not about PeanutGate. And Dad and Amanda are not lovers. They're in AA together. Just two people working on staying sober. I laugh, giddy with relief. Tears leak from my eyes.

Dad's brows knit with concern. "Ruby, are you okay?"

I collapse into the couch. "I'm fine. So, what you're telling me is you lied, to protect Amanda's anonymity."

Dad nods. "Yes. I hated not being honest, but anonymity is sacrosanct in AA."

Relief steps aside for shame. How could I even momentarily have thought Dad could've been involved in PeanutGate? My face burns with shame. I want to burrow under the couch cushions to hide my betrayal. What kind of daughter jumps to the worst possible conclusion about her own father?

Amanda's condescending voice breaks through my self-flagellation. "As you are well aware, I have many difficult issues in my life right now—chief among them a husband in a coma."

Anger flashes through me at her accusatory tone. Dad's hands are clean, but hers still seem stained. I'd love to throw what Millicent overheard in her face, but I don't. Roddy's case is top priority and I don't want to tip our hand.

She continues. "Despite the, shall we say, *complicated* circumstances regarding Isaac's condition, your father has been steadfast in his support."

Complicated is an understatement. Apparently, my dad is sponsoring the woman I believe is responsible for his son's arrest. I wonder if Dad's concern for Amanda is why he encouraged Roddy to accept that he might've made a mistake? Did Dad fear dragging the case into court would endanger her sobriety?

I can appreciate, even admire, Dad's loyalty to a fellow AA member, but what about his flesh and blood? Don't we deserve that unwavering faith? A heavy sadness drapes around me like a weighted blanket. I came here to apologize to Dad, but …

The silence stretches uneasily.

Amanda stands and collects her designer handbag from the coffee table. "I think it's best I leave. Donald, I'll see you at the hospital for tonight's AA meeting." She glances at me, tilting her chin slightly. "Ruby."

Dad stands and walks her to the door. When it shuts, he turns and leans against it. "Ruby, I *am* sorry I couldn't tell you."

I swallow the lump in my throat. "I know AA is important to you."

"Without it …" He sighs, slowly shaking his head. "Ruby, it saved my life. I owe the program and the people in it, everything. You and Roddy would not be in my life without it." He grimaces. "Hell, I probably wouldn't even be alive without it."

I fiddle with my fingers, unsure of my response. I'm hurt. It feels like he chose Amanda over us. Do I tell him that? Or do I just let it go?

I dredge up another Dr. Lauter quote (maybe I should carry her manual with me): "Silence may protect you for the moment, but only honesty will carry you forward." And then I dredge up some courage.

"Dad, I respect your commitment to AA and sponsoring Amanda, but it feels like you chose her over us."

His face crumples. "Oh, Ruby." He moves towards me, reaching for my hand. "I'm so sorry. The last thing I want to do is hurt you."

I lead him to the couch and we sit, side by side. "I hate to say it, Dad, but Amanda feels like the enemy. I'm sure you heard the accusation in her voice when she mentioned Isaac's coma."

He stares at his hands and nods. "I did."

"Well then, help me understand how supporting her doesn't come at the expense of us."

He blows out a long, slow breath. "I'm supporting her sobriety, not her. It's different. We steer clear of any conversations regarding the party or Isaac's condition. Our interactions focus on triggers and strategies to stay sober."

"So, you didn't urge Roddy to admit a mistake—that he most definitely did not make—to help her?"

Dad's face clouds with hurt. "Oh, Ruby. Absolutely not! Does he think that?" Dad drops his forehead in his hand. "And I thought Roddy and I had made real headway."

"No, no," I say, immediately trying to walk back my comment. "Roddy doesn't think that. He even said he appreciated your honesty."

Dad's smile crinkles the corners of his eyes. "That warms my heart to hear that. Roddy and I have come a long way in the past four years." He pauses, then sighs. "But that leaves us, doesn't it? Do you think I chose her needs over yours?"

I press my lips together and bow my head. "I do. I did. Oh, I don't know." The last word is barely a whisper.

He reaches his hand out, giving mine a squeeze. "It's okay to be honest. You don't have to whitewash your feelings with me."

I sniff back tears and raise my head. "Okay, yes. I wanted you to jump in and join the Peanut Posse without hesitation. Everyone else did—Gail, Millicent, even Marty. And when you didn't, it felt like a slap in the face."

"Ruby, I know what you wanted, but I also know what I had to give. Whether it's cynicism or wisdom, I can't say, but I believe it's always best to own up to mistakes. I'll be more than thrilled if Roddy is cleared. But more importantly, I wanted him to understand—to embrace the fact—that even if he made a mistake, he is not a mistake. And no matter what, I will be here for him. And for you." He meets my eyes. "Ruby, my support may not always be wrapped in the packaging you hoped for, but the gift always comes with love."

His words land, and the realization bursts like a cherry bomb on the sloppy sundae of my emotions. I don't just want his support; I want his *unquestioning* approval. And that's not fair. Okay, Dr. Lauter—how's that for some raw honesty?

A few tears slip from my eyes. I wipe them with the back of my hand and smile at my dad. "You're right. I've been equating approval with support, and they are not the same."

He squeezes my hand again. "Progress, not perfection. And this *is* a two-way street. Earlier you said Amanda felt like the enemy." He tilts his head. "I think we should talk about that. You clearly have concerns, and I want to understand them."

I tell him everything we learned about Amanda.

He presses his temple and shakes his head. "I admit it looks damning. It does. But you don't have the whole picture. What Amanda has shared with me was spoken in confidence—a trust I am not willing to break—but what I can tell you is you're barking up the wrong tree. If anything Amanda told me could exonerate Roddy, I swear I would tell you." His voice softens. "Please, Ruby, trust me on this."

"I do trust you, Dad. I always have. From the moment I met you at Green Dragon." I laugh. "In retrospect, I should have been wary, you did seem a little sketchy."

Dad rubs his beard as he nods his head. "I can't deny that."

I turn and hug him. "Thanks, Dad. I just … I guess I just needed to clear the air."

He hugs me back, chuckling. "Well, look at us. Having a breakthrough before lunch."

I pull back. "Speaking of lunch …" I stand and walk to the end table. "I brought ham loaf."

A crooked grin settles on his lips. "Nothing cuts family tension quite like ham loaf."

37 ~ Ruby

We're seated at a table for two in the front of Oriental Kitchen. Electric candles flicker inside red paper lanterns hanging from the ceiling. Mismatched handleless tea cups, and a black cast iron pot are delivered to our table by Mr. Khai (server, cook, and owner), quickly followed by eggrolls. Asian elevator music alternates with pop hits adding to the quirky, eclectic vibe.

Marty sips his hot jasmine tea, steam fogging his glasses. "Clearly, I'm mist-ified we don't come here more often."

I snicker and bite into my eggroll as he wipes his lenses with the red linen napkin. "They absolutely do have the best eggrolls."

"Hear, hear," he says, clinking his eggroll against mine in a crunchy toast. "Was Roddy's lawyer pleased with the new info about Amanda and Felix?"

Mouth full, I nod my head.

Marty brushes crumbs from his Hawaiian shirt. "After you filled me in on everything, I checked into life insurance policies. Though I can't access any specifics, like whether Isaac purchased any supplemental policies, I can tell you that as a coach at Myerstown University, he is eligible for a group policy through the Pennsylvania State System of Higher Education as part of his employee benefits. It's modest, but it does pay four times his annual salary."

I drain my tea and pour another. "Which would be a huge help in lessening Amanda's financial strain."

"It would," Marty agrees. "But unless there's a bigger supplemental policy, it hardly seems like enough for Felix and Amanda to be willing to kill for."

"Well, I haven't had a chance to update you or Roddy, but I talked with Dad. He and Amanda are …" I hesitate. I know Amanda isn't keen on others knowing she's in AA, but Marty and Roddy don't run in her circles. "Dad is Amanda's sponsor in AA, so he knows her pretty well and he says we're way off base in considering her a suspect. In general, Dad thinks we're spinning our wheels looking for suspects, but he wouldn't steer us wrong."

"Well, if the circumstantial evidence is convincing enough, it doesn't necessarily need to be true to add to Roddy's third-party defense."

"You're right. You know, it's fine to have all these theories, but I really would love to know what actually happened. I'm afraid even if Roddy beats the charges, the scandal will ruin our businesses. Finding the real guilty party would go a long way in restoring our reputations."

Marty gives me a reassuring smile. "Once the charges are dropped, I think it will be fairly easy to change the narrative."

I sigh. "I'm not so certain. Unless there's a clear resolution, there will be lingering doubts. And no one wants to take a chance on poisoned food or an event going wrong."

Marty cocks his head. "Hey there. Where are those rose-colored glasses your brother teases you mercilessly for wearing?"

I frown. "Tucked away in their case, unfortunately. This whole fiasco really has me on edge. My prospects for new jobs are slim to none. And some unknown person may have it out for my brother. We're assuming Isaac was the target, but in reality, if we don't find out who was really behind PeanutGate, we don't really know. Without a guilty party, I'm not sure I'll ever unclench."

He reaches across the table and grabs my hand. "I hear you. But right now, you're connecting dots that aren't even on the same page. Let's slow it down and focus on what we *do* know. You ruled Roddy out as a target for a reason. Motive. Other than you, Gail, Donald, and Millicent, the only person there who even knew Roddy was Hank—and they're buddies. Plus, we found no indication that anyone who attended the party owns or has connections to a rival business."

I draw in a deep breath and exhale slowly.

He rubs his thumb over my knuckles. "So, Roddy as a target is unlikely. Right?"

I nod. "Right."

He lets go of my hand and refills my tea cup. "As to your business, we will get it back on track. This dogged newspaper hound's got a lot up his sleeve. Okay?"

My smile is weak, but I feel less overwhelmed. "Okay."

"And, I'm not giving up. I will keep digging until we find the real culprit. Just call me Marty Mutt."

My heart swells with gratitude. *This* is what I wanted from Dad. No-questions-asked support. No limits. No hesitations. But even though Marty has always given me that, I doubted him and ended up pushing him away because he couldn't quiet all my fears.

I expect too much. The good ol' relationship manual taught me; no one person can meet *all* of my needs. Not Dad. Not Marty.

My conversation with Dad was a real eye-opener. His disagreement doesn't mean he loves me less, and it's not my place to dictate what his support looks like. And Marty wasn't a bad boyfriend just because he couldn't rid me of my doubts. The truth is, this is a *me* problem. I took responsibility for my relationship mistakes with Dad. Now, it's time I own up to where I went wrong with Marty.

I square my shoulders and charge in. "Marty, I need to apologize. I told you I've been reading self-help books and I know my abandonment issues and fears got the best of me, but I never said I'm sorry. And I really am. I know I was constantly nitpicking, constantly finding fault. You didn't deserve that. And I'm grateful that despite all that I put you through, you're here. And not only here, but invested—fully invested—in helping me. We've joked about you being a superhero since the day you rescued me from the bike accident, but it's no joke. You are my superhero. And my life is exponentially better because you're in it."

Mr. Khai brings our chicken and vegetable stir fry just as I finish my speech.

Marty grins and pats his stomach. "Perfect timing. Even superheroes need fuel to keep their powers up." His expression softens, growing earnest. "But seriously, I appreciate the apology. I did really feel like I was walking on eggshells. Like you were just waiting for me to screw up."

My shoulders hunch and I stare at my food. Guilt twists low in my stomach. "I guess I was."

"It's validating to hear you say that. It really is. By the time I ended it, I was pretty messed up in my head."

Regret fills me, stealing my appetite. I push the rice around on my plate.

His shoulders lift with his deep breath. "I'm not trying to heap all the blame onto you. I allowed it. I let myself get ground down."

I grimace at his words. "Ground down? Oh, Marty. That's how it felt? Like I was grinding you down?"

He takes a sip of his tea, and slowly nods his head. "It did. But I bought into it. And that's on me. I let myself feel like a failure, less than enough."

The word failure lands like a boulder on my heart.

His smile is weary. "I'm doing fine, now. But it took me a while to rebuild my self-esteem."

His vulnerability hits me hard. I never realized how deeply I'd hurt him. Tears catch in my eyelashes. "I'm so, so very sorry."

He reaches across the table, wiping the tears from my cheeks. "I know you are. I forgive you. Now it's your turn to forgive yourself."

I sniff and blink the tears away. “Forgive myself, huh? Looks like another trip to the self-help section at Waldenbooks is in order.”

Marty laughs. “I’ll tag along. With all the work you’ve done, I don’t want to be left behind in the emotional development dust.”

I shoot him a lopsided smile and nudge his foot under the table. “Emotional dust, huh? Don’t worry, I’ll slow down so you can catch up. Think of it as a three-legged race. We’re stuck running together whether you like it or not.”

Marty winks. “I like the sound of that.”

I do, too.

38 ~ Millicent

I settle my broad behind on Ruby's slip-covered couch, stuffing a polka dot throw pillow under my aching hip. Lucy rests her over-sized snout on my leg. The scent of fresh garden tomato wafts from a lit candle on the center of her coffee table. It's a tester from her friend Kelly's new side business—a line of garden-inspired soy candles called BotaniGlow.

"Kelly reminds me of my niece, Donna."

"Oh yeah?" Ruby says as she pours me a cup of tea from the pink kettle she's named Miss Bennet. "How so?"

"She's a dabbler."

Ruby chuckles. "That she is. I've got to say, I'm liking this dabble. These candles are amazing. You know, I'm super sensitive to smells, but the light scents don't bother me a bit."

"I used to like being Donna's guinea pig, too. Well, most of the time. The bath salts fiasco had me itching like I was wearing a wool sweater in July. Oh, and the lawn care business left my back-yard patchier than a crazy quilt. But the homemade cleaning supplies had my house spic and span. My all-time favorite was DoughNation, her fancy bread company. For every loaf she sold, she donated one to a local food pantry."

Ruby sits cross-legged (oh, to be young and limber) on the chair across from me. "How lovely. And what a clever name."

I sip my creamy, heavily sweetened (just the way I like it) Earl Grey. "I thought for sure that one would stick. But two years into it, she flitted to her next endeavor. Though I missed the constant supply of fresh-baked bread, she did gift me all her recipes and bread molds."

"I'm hoping candle-making is a keeper for Kelly. We've been planning a collaboration where she'll create custom-themed votive candles as party favors for some of my events. In fact, BotaniGlow was inspired by a garden tea party I've booked for next spring—assuming it doesn't get canceled like the majority of my other bookings."

"Oh, dear heart, once the charges against Roddy are dropped, your businesses will bounce right back. Yes indeedy! I'm sure of it. Who knows, the publicity might even give you a little boost. They say there's no such thing as bad publicity. Sometimes folks just love a story. I remember one time with Myrtle … Land's sake, there I go rambling again. Tell me, what did Roddy's lawyer say about Amanda and Felix?"

"I'm going to need more tea for this." Ruby unfolds her legs and heads to the kitchen. "Want a refill?"

"No siree, Bob. This old bladder holds water about as well as a leaky faucet."

As the kettle heats, Ruby fills me in on the lawyer's "cautious optimism" about the third-party defense.

"Dad assures me that Amanda can be crossed off our suspect list, but I'm not convinced."

My heart skips. I freeze, not sure what's safe to say. Does Ruby know that Donald and Amanda have been seeing each other?

"Um. Does he, uh, why would … Does he *know* Amanda?"

The kettle whistles and Ruby hops up to refill her cup. "He does. Very well, I'd say."

What does this mean? Have they made their relationship public? Does that mean Amanda's in the clear? Questions zoom around my brain, making me feel dizzy.

Ruby sits back on the chair, refilled tea in hand. "Dad is Amanda's sponsor. In AA."

My eyes pop open. "AA? Sponsor?"

Everything I thought I knew just flew out the window.

Ruby nods. "Yep."

So, they do have a relationship. Just not the kind I thought.

I feel worse than terrible that I suspected Donald. Here he is, quietly helping a woman in crisis and protecting her reputation, while I charge straight to adultery and attempted murder. It shames me that I jumped to such horrible conclusions when all along he was simply being kind.

My hand flutters to my chest. "I am such a bad friend. I had no idea she was struggling with alcohol. The signs were there. Definitely there, but I just didn't read them."

I'd like to say this revelation clears Amanda too, but if anything, it adds more kindling to the fire. Alcohol and good judgment don't usually go together.

Ruby twines a red curl around her finger. "Don't beat yourself up, Millicent. Amanda didn't want you to know. She didn't want anyone to know."

I wiggle around on the couch cushions, trying to get comfortable. Lucy, annoyed with the disturbance, hops off the couch, wanders over to her yellow checked dog bed, plops down, and resumes snoring within seconds.

"Ruby, Amanda's a friend and I'd love for her to be guilt free. I really would. But I have to tell you, even though Donald says we can cross her off the suspect list, I can't shake my doubts. She admitted she was seeing someone other than her husband. We know she's got financial troubles. And Felix is desperate for a baby. If this wasn't some sort of shenanigan between Felix and Amanda to get their hands on the life insurance, then why on earth would Felix be hoping Isaac dies soon? Jed wouldn't inherit a penny; Amanda and Ian would."

Ruby flips her palms up, shaking her head. "I don't know. And, as much as I would hate it, I guess we've got to accept that we may never know the whole truth about PeanutGate. We may have to be content with Roddy—fingers and toes crossed—winning the trial."

Lucy lifts her head, letting out a half-hearted ruff at the ring of the doorbell.

Ruby pops off the chair, stopping in her tracks at what she sees out the window. Her eyes snap wide open and her swallow is visible. "It's a sheriff."

My heart knocks on my ribs with worry.

Ruby swings the cottage door open.

"Good afternoon, ma'am," the officer says, removing his hat. "Are you Ruby Finch?"

"I am." I can hear the wariness in her voice.

His nod is curt. "I'm Sheriff Burns. I am here to serve you a summons and a complaint in a civil matter." He hands Ruby a sealed envelope. "The packet contains the summons, which requires you to respond within twenty days, and the complaint, which outlines the claims against you."

I can see Ruby's hand trembling as she accepts the envelope.

The sheriff replaces his hat. "I recommend you review the documents carefully and consult counsel. Failure to respond could result in judgment against you."

He offers another curt nod and steps off the porch. Poor, poor, Ruby. The thud of the cruiser door closing feels like a punch to my stomach.

Zombie-like she sits on the edge of the couch beside me and rips open the envelope. Her face turns as white as flour as she reads.

"Oh, Millicent! Amanda is suing both Make A Splash! and Chef's Secret."

"What?" Stunned, I grab the summons from her hand and read.

You are hereby notified that Amanda Stone has filed a civil action against you in the Lancaster County Court of Common Pleas. The complaint alleges negligence and seeks damages arising from the serving of food containing peanut powder after notice of a serious peanut allergy, which resulted in the plaintiff's husband suffering a coma.

I'm furious. Amanda knows Ruby and Roddy are like family to me. I can't believe she would blindside us like this. And what about Donald? After all he's done to help her, does she not give a fig for his children? I can't imagine how he'll feel when he finds out what she's done.

Ruby drops her face into her hands. "We're ruined. I guess I know where my share of Gigi's inheritance is going."

Lucy waddles over and nudges Ruby's leg. Ruby slides off the couch burying her face in Lucy's fur.

I scoot closer, patting Ruby's shoulder as she cries. "It's going to be okay. I'm sure the defense for Roddy's case will work in the civil suits, too."

Ruby lifts her head, horrified expression on her face. "Oh god! Do you think Dad knew what Amanda was planning? Do you think that's why she was at his townhouse yesterday, to tell him?"

I shake my head, furrowing my brows. "No. Absolutely not. He would've warned you. I'm sure he'll be as dumbfounded as we are."

"I've got to call him. And I've got to warn Roddy."

Her phone rings with uncanny timing. She leaps up, grabs it from the end table, and flips it open. "Roddy, I—yes, me too." Tears flow down her cheeks. "Okay. Okay. See you soon." She turns to me. "He got the summons too. He's on his way over."

I stand and wrap my squishy arms around her. She leans into me. As she trembles in my embrace, my anger sharpens into a hard edge. I may not have kids of my own, but Amanda's betrayal has stirred up some mama bear ferocity. She better clutch those cultured pearls, because she's going to get a piece of my mind.

39 ~ Ruby

Lucy whines at my bedside, ready for her morning walk. I drag myself out of bed, exhausted from my sleepless night. Both Roddy and Dad came over to talk me off the ledge after we got the summons, but their assurances did nothing to calm my worries. In fact, Roddy's newfound optimism bordered on creepy, like walking into a no-nonsense CEO's office to find it plastered with "Hang in There" kitty posters. Among other things, this role reversal has me rattled. I long for our status quo—rainbow and unicorns for me and Eeyore gloominess for Roddy.

I pad barefoot to the kitchen and push Mr. Coffee's on button. It normally shines at me like a chipper smile, but today it's as dim as I feel. As the coffee brews, I open my back door and let Lucy wander outside. The morning sun seems unusually harsh and I shield my eyes. My neighbor's flowers ooze their syrupy perfume, almost gagging me with sweetness. Luckily, as soon as Lucy's paws hit the grass, she squats, then lumbers back inside for breakfast.

I pour a cup of coffee adding less cream and sugar than normal and slug back a swallow. Its bitterness matches my mood. I'm beyond upset at having to fight this battle. Roddy and I did absolutely nothing wrong.

Although Dad mentioned the hefty medical bills piling up for Amanda's son Ian (and now Isaac's) as the possible impetus to her filing suit, he didn't defend her. I could tell he was struggling to rein in his anger at her decision—and her ambush. He was clueless to her intentions.

I throw a cup of kibble into Lucy's bowl. She sniffs it with disdain, then stares at me with her mournful eyes until I add warmed chicken broth. After wolfing it down, she climbs into her bed and promptly begins to snore.

I consider making myself breakfast, but settle for a second cup of coffee. Holding my mug, I pace my kitchen. We're going to have to double down on digging up more dirt on our suspects. Though Roddy's lawyer is confident, she warned us there is still the chance that the judge will exclude some or all of the circumstantial evidence, so we need as much as possible. Preferably, cold, hard facts. Something to indisputably point to one of our suspects.

My heart stutters warily at a knock on my door. Could this be more bad news?

I peek out the front window. When I see White Knight in my driveway, the stutter turns into a skip. I look down at my stained, oversized T-shirt and baggy boxer shorts and debate flying up the stairs to change.

"Anybody home?" Marty calls.

I tuck in my shirt, smooth my unruly hair, and open the door.

I needn't have bothered.

Marty's short-sleeved pink button-down shirt has a bit of dried egg yolk under the collar and his khaki pants are wrinklier than Lucy's skin. A portfolio bag is slung over his shoulder. He gives me a quick once over. "Still in pjs at ten?" He picks at the egg yolk stain. "Guess we're both dressed for success."

I groan and scowl dramatically. "It's too early for jokes." I turn and walk back into my living room.

Marty follows behind, dropping his bag on the coffee table. "Rough night?"

"You could say that. I'm being sued." I toss over my shoulder.

His mouth hits the floor. "What?"

"Oh yeah. Amanda is suing Chef's Secret and Make A Splash!"

Marty's baby face colors to lobster red. "As if the criminal charges against Roddy aren't enough."

"I guess she personally wants her pound of flesh."

"I'm really sorry, Ruby."

I want him to gather me in his arms and promise everything will be okay, but it's good that he doesn't. I wouldn't be able to hold back the tears.

I muster some false bravado and a less-than-convincing smile. "Coffee?"

"Sure."

"So, to what do I owe this pleasure?" I ask, as I pour him a cup of coffee, adding a dash of cinnamon, just the way he likes it.

He grabs his bag from the coffee table and we sit at the kitchen table. "Well, I've found some more interesting stuff that hopefully will help the defense." He takes a sip of his coffee. "Aww, you remembered the cinnamon."

"Just the way my superhero likes it."

Despite the heaviness of the morning, when our eyes connect, tingles zip down my spine. For a moment, I think he's going to kiss me, but instead, he clears his throat and opens his portfolio bag, pulling out a tablet filled with notes.

"I checked the public records at the county's Prothonotary's office and found a lien against Isaac and Amanda's property for unpaid taxes. Their financial troubles are substantial. I know your dad told you Amanda is not behind the poisoning—"

"He also had no clue she was filing suit against us," I interrupt. "So, obviously, he doesn't know her as well as he thinks he does."

Marty takes off his glasses, cleaning them with his shirttail. "If she and Felix are to blame, suing you and Roddy is a smart move. It not only deflects suspicion but also lets her play the role of the beleaguered wife, seeking justice for her husband. Plus, clearly, they need a cash infusion. As I mentioned before, unless Isaac has a supplemental policy, Isaac's life insurance payout isn't huge. A fat settlement would be welcome."

I palm my face as the realization washes over me. "Oh my god. I bet suing us was always part of the plan. Murder Isaac, collect the life insurance, sue us for pain and suffering. She and Felix are diabolical."

Marty taps her name on his tablet. "Her motives *are* textbook: Isaac's infidelity has humiliated her for years, a new love begs for a fresh start, and she's staring down financial ruin. It's practically a dot-to-dot of murder mysteries."

I pull at my unruly curls, sighing. "I desperately hope the judge agrees. In the meantime, will you keep digging?"

He taps his finger on his chest. "Marty Mutt. Remember?" He pulls a poster board from his portfolio. "I also have something else to show you. I know when you plan your events using a storyboard always helps you feel prepared and grounded. So, I thought maybe a visual plan of ideas for how to get your business back on track might ease some of the uncertainty."

He points to the first square, with ad mock-ups. "I asked the comp team at the paper to lay out some options for a campaign." He moves his finger to the second square. "Here are some ideas for testimonials. I'm sure some of your past clients—my sister, for one—would be more than happy to give you recommendations."

He slides his finger to a list of organizations. "I thought you could call on some of these non-profits and volunteer to organize fund raisers, or galas, or volunteer appreciation lunches. I mean I know that would be a lot of work for no money, but once word spread about how creative and amazing your events are it would hopefully translate to paid bookings."

Gratitude knots in my throat, and tears trail down my cheeks. Why did I ever let this caring, supportive, loving man slip through my fingers?

Marty's gentle eyes widen in alarm. "It's too much, isn't it?" He fumbles to shove the board back into the portfolio. "I was afraid I was overstepping. I'm so sorry. I thought I could help."

I cup his cheeks, lean in, and kiss him full on the mouth. He stiffens and I pull away.

"Oh, Marty." Ashamed of my impulsiveness, I cover my face with my hands. "*That*—my kissing you—was too much. I shouldn't have … I, uh, what you did was so kind. I just …"

He pulls my hands away from my face and holds them, then leans his forehead against mine. "Ruby, you mean more to me than anyone ever has, but you also hurt me more than anyone ever has. I'm not sure I can dive back into us." He leans back and brushes a stray curl off my forehead. "What I am sure of is that I want you in my life. If we can start there, maybe we'll find our way."

He didn't open the door, but he didn't close it either. Regaining a spark of my positivity, I pull the storyboard back out. "This is amazing and it'll work. Step by step, day by day—with a little help from friends like you—I can rebuild my brand. And as for us … We can take that slow, too." I blink and look down at the table. "You know I want to be more than friends. I want to get back to where we were before I messed everything up." I reach out and grab his hand. "But there's no hurry. I can give us all the time we need to rebuild our friendship into more."

Marty watches his own thumb trace the back of my hand. His silence is ambiguous. I'm on pins and needles waiting for him to respond. Finally, he exhales. "Ruby, I need you to understand there may not be more." He lifts his head, his blue eyes catching mine. "But let's see where step by step leads."

He offers no promise. But his eyes and gentle touch tell me there's space for something new to grow.

40 ~ Millicent

Neither a bout of furious weeding, a six-cookie breakfast, nor a morning tirade to Liza about Amanda's heartlessness has managed to douse my anger. In fact, I may be more disgruntled now than when Ruby received the summons because I've had time to stew. At the very least, Amanda could have given me a warning about her intentions.

Liza, wanting to avoid a Three-Mile-Island level meltdown, has insisted she go with me to speak with Amanda. Probably a good thing. I don't get roaring mad often, but when I do my words leave blisters.

The last time I breathed fire was when I tagged along with my nephew Dale to buy a puppy for his kids. Dale's friend recommended an Amish breeder, but mercy me, when we arrived it was clear we stumbled onto a puppy mill: crammed cages, matted fur, and skin-and-bones dogs.

That man got such a tongue-lashing from me his ears must be scarred from the burns. Dale threw the money at the man and scooped up the poor Labrador pup. I snapped a few photos of the dreadful mess, and off we went. Once we were safely away, I reported the whole sorry affair. The dogs and puppies were rescued and the breeder was arrested for animal cruelty a week later. As for me, I had the satisfaction of knowing my sharp words did more than scald his ears—they helped set things right. And that's what I intend to do when I talk to Amanda.

I'm done pussy-footing around. Best case, Amanda is using the situation to ease her financial troubles at the expense of Roddy and Ruby. Worst case, she and Felix are behind this whole fiasco and scapegoating Roddy and Ruby. Either way, I won't sit here like a bump on a log.

Even if Amanda truly believes Roddy made the mistake, what sense is there in dragging Ruby into it? Isn't it punishment enough that Roddy faces jail time and the ruin of his business? To sue Ruby is not only unfair—it's downright cruel.

My heart is pounding in my ears. The more I think about it, the more worked up I get. Liza better pick me up soon or I just may march over to Amanda's without her.

The rap of knuckles on my door comes just in time. I grab house keys, planning to leave, but Liza strolls inside. As Liza strides into my kitchen, the flowing hem of her long skirt serves as a plaything for Pizelle.

Liza's holding two muslin tea bags in her hand. "I brought us each a SereniTea. By the steam coming out of your ears, I think you can use it. I thought I'd also do a reading before we confront Amanda."

My forceful huff lifts my frizzy bangs, but does nothing to dissuade Liza. After turning the burner on beneath the tea kettle, she drops the specialty tea bags into two mugs, then fans four tarot cards out on my dining room table.

She sweeps her gunmetal locks behind her ear. A line of gold star earrings follows the curve of her ear. "Hmm." She considers the cards. "Quite an interesting spread." She taps her long, burgundy fingernail on a card that looks like a crumbling tower. "We may be in for a surprise. But it should clear away false assumptions and reveal the truth."

I pick up the Tower card. "Wait a darn minute. I've seen this card before. And last time you told me it meant we needed to have a confrontation."

"Millicent, the cards don't work in isolation." Liza's tone is patient, like she's explaining subtraction to an elementary school child. "They talk to each other. It's kind of like baking. Each ingredient has its own flavor, but together they create something entirely new."

"Okay, now that's something I understand." I lay the Tower card back in the row and, despite my skepticism, am drawn in. "What kind of surprise?"

She traces a pale moon on the next card. "Things are not as they seem. The surprise may be that what we think we know has never been quite true."

The kettle whistles. As I pour hot water over the tea bags, adding cream and lots of sugar to mine, I mull her words. Could Donald be right about Amanda's innocence? I was wrong about the nature of his and Amanda's relationship. Could I be wrong about what I overheard Felix say?

I set the mugs on the table and ease into the chair. "So, the cards are telling us we've been looking in the wrong direction?"

She tilts her head. "It appears so. But the Ace of Swords is here—"

"I've seen this one before, too."

She nods. "You have. It's a powerful card—cutting through lies, bringing mental clarity, revealing truths."

I prop my elbow on the table. "It didn't work last time."

"The cards don't 'work' the way you mean. They're not causing things to happen. They're a tool for insight and guidance. And this spread strongly suggests we'll uncover new information when we visit Amanda. It may be unexpected, but it will move us closer to the truth."

Hmm. If the cards are right, I'd better holster my blazing guns.

The moment the thought crosses my mind, I give myself an inward eye roll. For crying in a bucket. Here I go again, letting Liza's tarot reading sway me.

I cross my arms huffily. "Will the truth convince Amanda to drop her lawsuit against the twins? Because that's all I'm interested in."

Liza picks up a card with a sky full of stars and smiles. "This is the card of light returning. It's a good sign of healing and hope. I think the path will be brighter."

I empty my cup in one long swallow. "Surprise or no surprise, nothing *concrete* is being revealed at our little tea party. Can we go?"

She holds up one elegant finger, then savors the last sips of her tea.

As she moves towards the sink to wash her cup, I grab it out of her hands. "I'll wash them later. Let's go."

"Millicent, take a breath. Your energy is combative. I know you're angry, and rightfully so. At the very least, a heads up would've been appropriate. But I think the conversation will go a lot better if you're approaching the situation from a place of compassion."

"Where is her compassion for Ruby and Roddy?"

"If you respond to darkness with more darkness, no one can find the way forward."

I grit my teeth, knowing Liza's right. You get more flies with honey … If I charge in like a bull, I'm not likely to convince Amanda to drop the suit.

"Fine." I say, with a huff of frustration. "I'll wrangle my anger on the ride over. Promise."

As we pull out of my driveway, Liza slides a CD into her Volvo's player. The bong of a low-toned bell fills the air. The sound continues to hum and I feel the vibration in my chest. More bells, with various tones ring out is some peculiar kind of music.

"What kind of music is this?"

Liza's smile is serene. "Singing bowls. A sound meditation to cultivate calm."

"Bowls?"

Liza's sideswept long bangs fall across her cheek when she nods. "Himalayan singing bowls. They're lovely, aren't they?"

My jaw and fists have unclenched and I feel like there's more space for me to breathe. "Not bad."

Sometimes Liza's woo woo stuff really does work. By the time we're on Amanda's street, my murder-hornet energy has simmered to a low buzz.

Liza turns into the circular driveway. It's packed with cars. Jed and Felix are stepping out of Felix's Mazda as Liza shifts into park. They notice us and wait for me to heft myself out of the car.

Jed walks up and hugs me. His eyes are red-rimmed and the thick stubble on his face, scratches my cheeks. "Millie, thanks so much for coming. It means a lot."

I haven't the foggiest idea what he's talking about, but I hug him back. "Of course," I say, winging it.

A Lexus parks behind Liza's Volvo and a middle-aged woman in a somber dress hops out. She hurries over to Jed, grabbing his hands. "I'm so sorry for your loss."

Loss? Oh my stars! Isaac is dead.

My knees buckle. I grab the hood of the Volvo to keep from falling.

Jed and Lexus woman lurch towards me, but Felix beats them, weaving his arm around my waist to steady me. "Can't have one of the Golden Girls breaking a hip."

My breath is coming in pants. If Isaac is dead, Roddy will very likely be charged with homicide.

Felix flicks his hand towards the front door. "Go on in, you two. We'll follow in a few."

Jed's eyebrows furrow. "If you're sure …"

Felix nods. "I've got this. Go."

Jed and the woman walk into Amanda's front door.

"Your wobble came at a good time. I need a minute to staple on my grieving face." Sighing, he runs his fingers through his thick black locks. "Truly, I don't know how Jed has been able to be so forgiving. The man was a vile, nasty queer-hating bigot, who always treated Jed as a disappointment and me as nothing more than the revolting evidence of Jed's failings. I'm glad he's gone."

Liza's eyebrows shoot so high they almost leave her face, and my jaw nearly hits the driveway. I had *no* idea Isaac had been so cruel to Jed and Felix. That earth-shaker hits like a cold, hard slap. Was that Felix's justification for poisoning him?

Liza and I stand silent, stunned into speechlessness.

Felix shrugs his shoulders. "I swear he hung on out of pure spite, just to keep Jed from inheriting. We had asked for a loan to fund our baby dreams, but all we got was a resounding no." He slides his hands into the pockets of his skin-tight jeans. "Now that he's croaked, we'll be able to afford it."

I gasp at his heartlessness. "Heavens to Betsy, Felix! You wished for his death just because he wouldn't loan you money? Maybe it had nothing to do with Jed being gay. Maybe he didn't have it to give. Have you ever thought of that?"

He scoffs. "Judge me if you want, but I'm not the monster. He was. He was cruel and selfish. He belittled and berated every chance he got. And he had millions—millions—and refused to help."

Millions? Isaac and Amanda have a lien on their house. His car was repossessed. Why would Felix think Isaac has millions?

Felix crosses his arms and raises his voice. "Just because he's dead, doesn't mean he was a good person. I mean look at what he did—or should I say, didn't do—for Amanda and Isaac. They are drowning in debt, partially caused by overwhelming medical bills for Ian, and Old Ivan wouldn't lift a finger to help."

Ivan?

"So, Isaac is still alive?" I blurt out.

Felix's face crinkles in confusion. "Yeah? Of course he is. And when he wakes up from the coma, he'll probably be heartbroken he didn't get to tell his nasty old father goodbye. Forgiveness must be in the Stone brothers' DNA. It's not in mine. I can tell you that."

Uncontrolled laughter burbles out of me. Roddy is not facing homicide charges. Amanda and Felix were talking about Ivan, not Isaac. And maybe with the impending inheritance I'll have a better chance of talking Amanda out of suing Roddy and Ruby.

"Millicent, what's happening? Is this some kooky Golden-Girl-grief-coping ritual I should know about?"

I fan my hand in front of me. "Just the heat getting to me."

He gently pinches my cheek. "You look a little peaked."

Weak with relief is more accurate.

Liza pipes up. "Millicent, let's pay our respects later. I think I should get you home."

Felix blows a storm of kisses to us. "Take care, lovies. I'll let Amanda know you're planning to stop by in a few days."

He waves goodbye as Liza and I zip out of the driveway.

"As expected, the cards were right," Liza says.

"Can't argue that. It was a big surprise and we got clarity."

She shoots me a smile. "And don't forget The Star card. A card of hope and returning light."

I nod along, but my worry is sticking around. Felix may be in the clear—but is Amanda? Money's not the only thing that motivates. Years of humiliation and a shiny new man can do strange things to a person. Poison-your-husband things.

Ruby may talk herself into being content with Roddy beating the charges, but I need the truth. Because if I don't find it… I'm not sure how I'll ever sit across from my friend again.

41 ~ Ruby

Marty's words caution that friendship may be where we land, but his actions speak louder. Clearly, he spent hours creating the vision board to resuscitate my business. And his plan is solid. I really think it will work. I haven't fully embraced the bubblegum and cotton candy mindset yet, but between this bang-up marketing strategy and Marty's forward movement in the relationship department, my mood is tinted with a hint of pink.

As he suggested, I'm trying to compose a letter asking previous clients for a testimonial. My poor, helpless pencil—wood gnawed and metal band mangled by my relentless teeth—is seeing none of that rosy mood. I'm mid-chew when my ringing phone offers it a reprieve.

I—and my trusty #2—welcome the break. "Hello."

"Ruby, it's Amanda Stone."

I pull back, stunned. Why is *she* calling me? The happy hint of pink, turns to fiery red as anger sizzles through me. "I received the summons," I say through gritted teeth.

"I had no choice. I hope you can understand." Her tone is clipped.

I stifle a scoff. I understand you had no choice because you wanted to cover your tracks.

Learning that Ivan was the man Felix and Amanda had been talking about did nothing to ease my suspicions. Amanda has a philandering husband. Amanda has a new lover. Amanda is neck-deep in debt. Even if she knew a large inheritance was on the horizon, money could still be a motive—because once the debts are cleared, a divorce might leave very little left to divide.

Someone poisoned Isaac. My money's on Amanda.

"Ruby? Are you there?"

I want to fling all the evidence in her face. I want to berate her for filing suit against us. I want to shame her for relying on my dad but not even giving him the courtesy of a heads up. But I clench my jaw, locking the words behind my teeth. The lawyer warned Roddy and me to absolutely, positively *not* confront her.

"Ruby?"

I exhale slowly, reducing my heat level to simmer. Keeping my tone flat, I ask, "Why are you calling?"

"Isaac is awake."

I slide right off my kitchen chair, slumping with relief. The debilitating fear—barely held at bay—that I'd be visiting my brother behind bars drains out of me, leaving me a teary, boneless heap. Negligent homicide is off the table. Jail should be, too.

My senses go muzzy as weeks of unrelenting vigilance finally let go.

Amanda's voice reaches me as if from inside a tin can. "He's awake and asking for his jacket. The one from the night of the party. I've torn the house apart, but it must've been left there. Do you have it?"

I blink, still foggy. A jacket? He wants his jacket?

"Ruby!" Amanda's impatience barges through the haze. "Are you listening to me? Do you have Isaac's jacket?"

I push myself off the floor, the room settling back into focus. Isaac wakes from a coma and is worried about a jacket? Strange.

"Ruby?"

"No, I—" I stop, remembering the box Marty and I collected from the bank. "I might. I still have a box of things from that night. I can look through it."

"Do." Her imperiousness tone cuts through any lingering fuzziness.

I can't believe I forgot about the box. Though the worst outcome is off the table, Roddy and I are still facing financial devastation. I wonder if anything in it could be useful to solving PeanutGate. I move to my front door, sliding into my Chucks as I talk. "I'll look through it as soon as we hang up."

"Good. For whatever reason, Isaac is adamant I bring it to him. The doctor said his obsessiveness could be a symptom of brain trauma."

Brain trauma? My throat tightens. Compassion twists with panic. I feel awful for Isaac, and even worse that my survival instinct is already whispering about lawsuits and damages. When Amanda said he was awake, I thought he *and* Roddy were out of the woods.

"Amanda, I really am happy he's awake."

"I'm sure you are." Snideness is clear in her tone. "I'll be at the hospital all day. I'd appreciate it if you'd bring it in if you find it."

Despite her sarcasm, I keep my tone polite. "I can do that. I'll call you and let you know, either way."

She ends the call without saying goodbye. Her rudeness adds fuel to the simmering fire, but I don't have time to stew. The box may contain something helpful.

Lucy follows me out to Sally, sniffing under bushes along the way. The sweet-vanilla scent of the clematis climbing my neighbor's trellis prickles my nose as I pop open the front hood and tear into the box. Inside is a hodgepodge of leftovers from that night—Gail's wig, a spatula, a half-empty bag of gold confetti, a clip-on earring, a pair of handcuffs, and Isaac's jacket, crumpled at the bottom. Nothing that blows this case wide open.

Lucy nudges my leg, probably sensing my disappointment. I pull Isaac's jacket from the box and lay it on Sally's front passenger seat. After allowing Lucy a few more minutes to sniff and pee,

I corral her back into the house, give Amanda a quick call to get the room number, and head to the hospital.

Driving seems like a chore. I'm emotionally exhausted. Wrung out. Between the PeanutGate rollercoaster and the hills and valleys of the Marty-train, I don't know if I'm going forward or backward. And we still have months before Roddy's criminal trial. Before the chaos resolves, one way or the other. Add in the civil suits and we're facing at least a year of uncertainty. I need to buck up if I'm going to make it through.

During the elevator ride to Isaac's floor, I take a few deep breaths. My charged emotions are seeping out all over and I'm finding it very difficult to mask my suspicions and resentment. But I intend to keep my promise to my lawyer. I certainly don't want to make anything worse than it already is. And antagonizing the woman who has filed a lawsuit against me and Roddy isn't a brilliant strategy.

The hall bustles with activity and the sharp antiseptic smell gives me a headache. When I reach Isaac's room, I square my shoulders and tap on the doorframe to announce my arrival. Amanda looks up from paging through a *House Beautiful* magazine. Her face turns stony. Isaac's eyes catch mine for a second, then dart away.

"Hi Isaac. I don't know if you remember me. I'm Ruby Finch, the party planner. I've brought your jacket. Amanda said you wanted it."

He clears his throat and avoids my gaze. "Um, uh, yeah. I think I remember you." His fingers twitch at the edge of the blanket like a nervous stutter.

"Hmph, as if I could ever forget." Amanda reaches across Isaac's bed. "Just give me the jacket."

As I'm handing it to her, Isaac lunges forward, snatching it away. His wallet and a tin fly out of the pockets, skittering across the floor. Amanda grabs the wallet, stuffing it back in the jacket pocket, then picks up the tin. Her forehead wrinkles. "Isaac, why do you have a cigar tin? You detest smoking."

Isaac's face pales whiter than the hospital sheets. "Give that to me!" he snaps, straining to get out of bed despite the IV, tubes, and electrodes attached to him.

Amanda flips open the tin. "What is this?" Her brows knit in confusion.

"Give it to me! Now!" Isaac yells, pulling the IV pole so hard it topples over.

I jump at the crash, but Amanda ignores it. Her wide eyes stare into the tin with what looks like horror. She touches her pinky to her tongue, dips it into the tin, then slips the coated finger into her mouth.

Panic floods her features. For a heartbeat she freezes, like she's too overwhelmed to react. Then her hands fly to her mouth, muffling a sharp gasp. When she speaks her words come out thin and shaking. "Dear god, Isaac… what have you done?"

He collapses back into the bed, face pulled into a pained grimace. A strangled sob bubbles up, and tears slide down his face onto the pillow. "I'm so sorry," he chokes out. "I'm so sorry. I did it for us. For Ian." His voice cracks on his son's name. "The bills, the bills just kept piling up. I had to do something." He hides his face behind his hands, as if he can't bear to let either of us see him.

My eyes shift from Amanda to Isaac, a whir of cold confusion revving in my chest. What is happening? What is he talking about?

Amanda's demeanor turns robotic, her expression flat and tightly controlled. "Oh, Isaac. How could you?"

Churning dread twists my stomach. My voice sparks with unease. "Tell me! I don't understand. What are you saying?"

Amanda hands me the tin. "Taste it." Her voice quivers, like she's barely holding herself together.

I shake a bit of the powder onto my palm and lick it. Peanut. In Isaac's jacket. My brain misfires. My eyes blink in rapid succession, like they're trying to reboot. Isaac had a tin of peanut powder in his jacket pocket.

Oh. My. God.

He poisoned himself.

I'm reeling. We went in circles, suspecting everyone—Janelle, Hank, Felix, Amanda—Isaac never once crossed my mind.

"Ruby, I am so sorry. So deeply, deeply sorry." Amanda's face is blotchy, her eyes shining with humiliation. The mortification rolling off her is palpable. Her eyes cut to Isaac, who's mumbling rambling apologies, and her hands curl into fists at her side, knuckles whitening. "You're a pathetic excuse for a man."

My shock and horror turn ferocious, igniting into something much hotter. My pulse spikes. I grip the siderail of the hospital bed to keep from slapping him. Spit flies as I shout, "You heartless brute! You cold, unfeeling monster! My brother went to jail. Our businesses ground to a halt. How could you set us up like that? How could you wreck our lives?"

Isaac drops his face in his hand. "I was just so desperate. Ian needs so much medical care. There's a lien on the house. We're late paying everything else. I didn't know what else to do. How else to provide for my family. My father wouldn't lend me the money—"

His pitiful, whiny voice snaps the last thread of my self-control. I shake the bedrail so hard it rattles. "Don't make excuses!"

"He's dead," Amanda says, her voice cold as steel. "Your father is dead."

Isaac's body slams back against the bed like he was punched. "What?" His face crumples. "No …"

"Yes! And I'm glad," she yells. "I'm glad he didn't live long enough to find out his son tried to kill himself."

"Amanda, no. You've got it all wrong." He strains forward, hands gripping the bedsheets. "I wasn't trying to kill myself. I had my EpiPen, but it must've fallen out in the scuffle. I, I didn't think it would go this far. Listen to me." He shakes his fist in the air, frantic. "Both of you. I thought it'd be simple. A lawsuit and quick settlement. Ruby, I swear, I thought your business liability insurance would cover the costs. I thought … I thought it'd be nothing more than a blip."

Anger flares—volcanic, blistering. My body is on fire, burning from the inside out. I shove my face inches from his, rage-fueled tears streaming down my cheeks. "A blip? A blip? We have worked so hard to build our businesses, and your *simple* little scheme has smashed our dreams. Our livelihood. Every job we had booked has canceled. You've ruined our reputations. My brother was facing jail time for god's sake. You're despicable." I punch the side of the mattress, fist skimming his ribs, and turn my back on him, leaning my forehead against the wall to catch my breath.

Amanda's voice is tight and menacing. "Ruby is right. You are despicable."

I turn around to face the two of them.

Amanda skewers him with her glare. "First your string of coeds. Then Connie. I didn't think you could sink any lower. But I was wrong. You deliberately tried to ruin two innocent lives just to save your own skin."

"I did it for you. For you and Ian," he snivels.

"Liar! You did it to protect your standing. To protect your lifestyle." Her scoff is hard and unforgiving. "You don't have selfless in you, Isaac." She flips the strap of her purse over her shoulder. "I'm done."

Striding to me, she wraps her hand into the crook of my elbow, and guides me towards the door. "Ruby, we're going to the police station together right now and straighten out this whole mess."

"No, please! Please! I'm sorry. I'm sorry! You can't mean that, Amanda. Don't go to the police. We'll be ruined!"

Isaac's pleas for forgiveness follow us into the hallway as we wait for the elevator, but Amanda and I don't so much as flinch.

Only when the doors slide shut and his voice finally fades does the adrenaline begin to ebb. That's when the realization sinks in. The undeniable proof of Roddy's innocence had been sitting in Sally's trunk this whole time, within my reach. My stomach twists. If only I had remembered the box, we could have been spared so much fear, so many sleepless nights. The thought stings.

In the elevator, Amanda turns towards me, spine ramrod straight. "I am humiliated by Isaac's actions and profoundly sorry for filing the lawsuit." Her words are clipped, as if letting any emotion through might shatter her composure. "I hope you can find it in your heart to forgive me. I promise you I will do everything in my power to restore you and your brother's reputation. I promise, I will try to make it right."

I release a long, slow breath. Depleted, my body trembles. The outrage is still there, disgust too, but underneath it a calmness settles in. The whirring anxiety of the past few weeks quiets, and a familiar brightness nudges at my raw edges.

Everything will be okay.

The charges and lawsuits will be dropped. Our businesses will rebound. And I'm ready to use what I've learned in all those dog-eared self-help books.

There's a spring in my step as we exit the elevator.

The new-and-improved Ruby is here—wearing a fresh pair of rose-colored shades.

42 ~ Millicent

Liza, Shampoodles, and I turn onto Endurance Lane in Lititz's newest development. Considering what Amanda has been through in the past few months, it seems an appropriate street for her to call home.

Liza parks her Volvo and lifts Shammie out of the car. I'm still hefting myself out of the passenger seat as Shammie finds the perfect spot to whizzy. Leaves crunch under my feet, and autumn's chill worms it's way past my crocheted sweater, goosebumping my arms. Vibrant pink and yellow mums line the walkway leading to Amanda's townhouse. A harvest-themed wreath decorates her front door.

Before we can even knock, Amanda flings the door open, embracing Liza and me in a group hug. "I am so excited you're here!"

Her pearls, tailored dresses, and not-a-hair-out-of-place bob are gone—along with Isaac. She filed for divorce, packed up, and moved out with Ian. Her new look is relaxed and casual: fuzzy sweaters, jeans, and a pixie haircut that makes her look ten years younger. The McMansion is on the market. She's given up her country club membership (after spreading the good word about Ruby and Roddy's businesses). She's working as a receptionist in a doctor's office. And she's happier than a robin after a rainstorm.

She motions towards the kitchen at the back of the townhouse, as if the smell of bacon and cheese didn't already have me moving in that direction.

A round kitchen table for four is set with leaf shaped plates, an umber table cloth, and a gourd centerpiece.

Amanda pulls a bacon quiche from the oven, setting it on the stovetop. "I have sparkling apple cider for virgin mimosas." She pours the bubbly liquid into champagne flutes, adding a splash of orange juice.

Since the whole PeanutGate debacle, Amanda has really opened up to Liza and me about her struggles with alcoholism. It's as if having her husband's crimes splashed across the front page of the newspaper (no doubt thanks to Marty's nudging) finally freed her from her perfectionism.

She moves to the table and raises her glass. "Let's toast to our friendship."

We clink our glasses, genuinely relieved we can toast to that without anyone side-eyeing anyone else. After we finally learned who actually laced Roddy's food, Liza and I came clean to Amanda about our earlier suspicions.

One thing I learned long ago, secrets will sour a relationship faster than milk left out at a summer picnic. One doozy of a secret had Myrtle and me not talking for over a week. (That's basically like a year for non-twins.) We were thirteen, no wait, maybe fourteen or fifteen. Doesn't matter. Anyhow, I liked this boy named Martin, and that was kind of unusual for me. Normally, I preferred books to boys, but Martin had these cute little dimples that made me feel like warm caramel sauce.

Myrtle knew I liked him, so matchmaker-wannabe that she was—well, still is—she passed him a note trying to gauge his interest in me. His response was interest in *her*. Not wanting to hurt my feelings, she kept it quiet, but Nasty Nancy O'Donnell—always one to stir up trouble, hence the nickname—found the note and made it public knowledge. I was furious with Myrtle for keeping it from me, and for keeping the darn note. Took me a whole week and the bribe of a new book to start talking to her again. So yes, I know firsthand how damaging secrets can be.

Anyhow, when we fessed up, Amanda was, understandably, miffed that we'd thought her capable of it. But once we walked her through the (admittedly circumstantial) evidence, and gently pointed out the *small* detail that her husband was indeed the one who committed the fraud, she forgave us.

After our toast, Amanda brings the quiche, fresh fruit, and dressed greens to the table. "Help yourselves."

Liza shares an orange slice with Shammie. "Supports her immune system."

I help a strand of melted cheese into my mouth. (Supports my backside.) "Delicious."

Amanda dabs the corner of her mouth with an orange linen napkin. "Not as scrumptious as Roddy's food. I am really thrilled that, even after I filed a lawsuit against him, he was still willing to volunteer his catering company to provide the food for the Friendsgiving Gala at Violet House."

I smile. "He's not vindictive. He understands why you thought he was to blame and why you felt like you needed to do what you did."

"And Ruby's a gem, too. How kind of her to arrange the enormous gift raffles and provide the photo booth for the women to have a remembrance of the special night. Again, I'm not sure I could be so magnanimous."

I pat Amanda's hand. "Let yourself off the hook. Both of their businesses are booming again, thanks in part to your and Clarice's glowing recommendations to the country club members."

Liza slides an apple to Shammie. "It's hard to believe the gala is only two weeks away."

Amanda adds a heaping serving of greens to her plate. "I'm really looking forward to introducing Adam to all of you."

I chuckle. "Your new man's debut night in society—if you can call us society."

Amanda's smile is wide and genuine. "It's the only society I'm interested in."

Turns out Isaac was the one scrambling up the social ladder. And, mercy me, I couldn't be happier that Amanda stepped off the rungs.

Liza nudges my elbow with a grin. "You know what I'm looking forward to?"

"What?" Amanda and I ask in unison.

"Millicent's makeover!"

Amanda's eyebrows shoot up. "What?"

I press my lips together and nod my head. "Yes siree, Bob. I agreed to let Liza have full creative control. New haircut, makeup, manicure, the works. She's even picked out a dress for me. I'll be all gussied up."

Amanda leans her elbows on the table and leans towards me. "What brought this on? Is there something you're not telling me?"

"She has a date," Liza says in a teasing sing-song voice.

I flare my nostrils and pretend to be annoyed. "I one-hundred percent do not have a date. Donald and I are simply going together. That is *not* a date."

"That's not what the cards said," Liza volunteers. "Millicent pulled the Ace of Cups, the classic new love card."

Even though I asked Liza for insight on the state of my love life—tarot is downright addictive—I roll my eyes. "Pff. Who believes in those cards anyways?"

"Millicent Wagner," Liza places her hands on her hips indignantly. "You have to admit they've been dead on throughout the whole PeanutGate situation."

"Wait." Amanda lays her napkin on the table. "You were doing tarot readings about Isaac's anaphylaxis?"

Shamefaced, Liza and I stop our sassy sparring.

We hang our heads until Amanda cracks up laughing. "That's hilarious. No holding back. You've got to fill me in on the readings."

Liza scoops Shammie onto her lap. "Scoff if you want, but the readings were quite accurate."

"Oh Liza, I'm not laughing about the readings. Clearly, the one you gave me well before Clarice's party was spot-on, right down to Isaac's cheating and the whole 'traumatic events will lead to a new beginning.' I'm laughing because the cards helped precipitate his downfall. Isaac is so judgmental and close-minded, it feels like poetic justice."

Feathers unruffled, Liza kisses the top of Shampoodles' head before setting her back on the floor.

Amanda fixes another round of virgin Mimosas. "So, really, fill me in on the readings. What insight did the universe provide?"

"The kicker for me," I say, "was the reading when Liza and I dug our heels in to figure out what truly happened. I can't remember the names of the cards, but I remember the gist. Love for a child, financial strain, deception."

Liza leans back in her chair. "After overhearing Felix at your house, we misinterpreted the reading as an overwhelming desire to have a baby. But, as they say, hindsight is twenty twenty. It's now obvious the cards alluded to Isaac's love for Ian and his misguided attempts to provide for him."

Amanda sighs. "Misguided is a generous word for what Isaac did." She sips her fizzy drink. "On a happier note, Felix and Jed are pregnant!"

I clap my hands with delight. "Oh, how wonderful!"

"Jed's share of his father's estate will more than cover the costs. Their surrogate is due in late April. I can't wait to be an auntie."

I pop a strawberry in my mouth. "It's the best. I have a baseball team full of nieces and nephews."

Liza's bangles clink when she brushes her long bangs from her face. "So, you and Jed are still close? Even now that you and Isaac are headed towards divorce?"

"He and Isaac were never tight."

"Because of Jed's relationship with Felix?" Liza asks.

"No. I'll give Isaac credit for that. He never tolerated Ivan's digs about Jed being gay. But he had his own way of cutting him down. He made Jed feel like a screw-up for daring to chase his dreams instead of taking some 'respectable' job."

"The three of us should make a plan to go and see Jed play," I suggest.

"Oh, you will! He volunteered to play one set at the Friendsgiving Gala. He's quite talented. I'm really glad the inheritance will also give him a little breathing room to build his career."

Liza slips Shammie the last bit of her fruit. "A baby and launching a career. He's got a lot to look forward to."

Amanda nods her head. "He does. And so do I. Isaac's share of the inheritance will get us out of debt. I should even end up with a nice little nest egg when the house sells. And bless Roddy and Ruby—they only asked for their legal fees after everything Isaac *and I* put them through."

She ducks her head, straightening the napkin on her lap, then looks up with a meek, remorseful smile. "Truly, after Isaac dragged them through the mud, they could've sued us into next year. But they didn't. They showed more grace than we deserved." Her laugh is dry and self-mocking. "We all know, if I'd been in their place, I'd have slapped him with a defamation suit before breakfast."

I finish the last sip of my mimosa. "In a funny twist of fate, the notoriety topped off with a full exoneration skyrocketed their businesses." I shrug. "Like they say, there's no such thing as bad publicity."

"That's marvelous. I am thrilled—and relieved—that their businesses bounced back. I'm just sorry we all had to go through so much to get here." She presses a hand over her heart, smiling wide. "But I guess it's all worked out in the end. Isaac will face the consequences. And everyone else's futures look bright."

I offer Liza a validating nod. "Just like The Star card predicted."

Her smile holds the slightest glimmer of satisfaction. "The cards never lie."

43 ~ Ruby

The smell of cinnamon and cloves wafts through Roddy's commercial kitchen. He's baking a test batch of mince pies for the book club's Dickensian Christmas party we've been hired to plan and cater.

I inhale, savoring the homey scent. "The pies smell delicious. And to think I was worried there'd be gruel."

Roddy snorts. "Gruel is *underrated.* Very minimalist. Very avant-garde."

I laugh. "I'm pretty certain our clients are not looking for that level of authenticity."

He sighs dramatically. "Fine. No gruel. But I'm keeping the option of oatcakes on the table.

I pretend to wince. "Absolutely not."

"Just one tiny biscuit of despair?"

"Roddy. Be serious. We have five holiday parties to plan."

He pulls the mince pie from the oven. "You're no fun."

I shoot him a look of mock indignation. "How dare you! I'm the architect of fun. The Frank Lloyd Wright of parties. All I'm saying is, let's not traumatize the guests before dessert."

He throws me a wink. "Valid point. What's on the agenda for activities?"

"I'm going to have some classic Victorian parlor games, charades with proverbs. Blind Man's Bluff, Hunt the Thimble, along with a few modern additions. Oh, and did I mention we all will dress in period fashion?"

"You most certainly did not. I guess I'll bust out my waistcoat and cravat."

"What do you think your new employees will think of dressing up?"

He cuts us each a slice of pie and sets them on the stainless-steel counter. "They'll think you're over the top—just like I do."

"Details matter!" I say, shaking my hands for emphasis. "That's what makes Make A Splash! so different."

"And topnotch!"

"Aww. Thanks, brother. Chef's Secret is stellar too." I take a bite of the warm pie. "Ooh, that's velvety. And I like the warmth the brandy added. It's beyond stellar!"

He mulls the flavors. "Not bad, but I think more currants and raisins would deepen the sweetness." He scratches a few notes on his recipe card. "Alright, I think I'm good for Dickensian Christmas. Let's move onto the cozy apocalypse party—where do you even come up with these ideas?"

"Well, this event is for a die-hard *28 Days Later* fan's seventeenth birthday party. His mom was game to an apocalypse party as long as I toned down the horror. Hence, the cozy-apocalypse theme was born."

Roddy runs his hands through his shaggy hair. "So, I'm offering rations served in rusty cups with hand-crocheted cozies?"

I crack up. "Exactly. And maybe a communal cast-iron pot of hot chocolate heated over a trash-can fire."

"You stretch my imagination—in the very best way possible. Crazy to think that just a few months ago it looked like both our businesses were going to tank? And now we're swamped and I'm hiring employees."

"Yeah. It's downright prodigious."

Roddy raises his hands for a high five. "Good word, even if it is a bit magniloquent."

I brush his hand aside, pretending to be annoyed. "Is that even a real word."

Roddy's smile is smug. "It most certainly is."

I groan. "Oh man, you've been saving that one. I give up, what's it mean?"

"Pompous or grandiose. And yes, I've been keeping it in my back pocket since you won the first annual Sesquipedalian crown."

I take another bite of pie. "Gail was right. She's in for many more word nerd contests."

Roddy laughs as he washes the baking pan. "I hope so!" He slides the pan into the drying rack. "Should we let Gail and Marty participate or keep it between us?"

"Is that your sly way of asking where Marty and I stand?"

His grin dimples his cheeks. "Not so sly, huh?"

"A smooth operator you're not." I take my last bite of pie and think about my response. "I'm all in. Marty's got his foot in the door, but he's not ready to step over the threshold. I can't say that I blame him. I was pretty rough on him."

"Well, if you want my two cents—"

"By all means," I deadpan.

"Marty and you are a perfect fit, so stay the course. If you're patient I know he'll come around."

"Noted." I pretend to hand him pennies. "And here's my two cents. Gail is a keeper. I think you know that. When do *you* plan to take the next step?"

His cheeks blush. "Well, actually …"

"Actually, what? Don't leave me hanging."

"I think I'm going to ask her to move in." He sucks his bottom lip behind his teeth. "Are you okay with that? I mean, technically this house is half yours."

I blink, surprised he even felt the need to ask, then clap my hands excitedly. "Yes! Yes! A thousand times yes!"

"Whew," he says, wiping his forehead. "I didn't want you to feel like I was stepping on your toes."

"Not at all. You know I consider Mirabella *your* house."

He leans towards me and kisses my forehead. "You're the best."

I loop my arm around his waist and lean my head on his chest. "You're not so bad either."

We stand there, arm in arm, the sweet smell of pie grounding us as we take in our blessings. A few months ago, everything was slipping through our fingers. Now here we are: planning cozy-apocalypse parties, moving forward in relationships, and talking about next steps and new beginnings.

I bump my shoulder against him. "Big changes coming."

He smiles. "The good kind."

I give him a crooked, smart-aleck grin. "The prodigious kind."

44 ~ Ruby

The sun reaches past the downy white clouds, warming our faces. The autumn breeze holds an invigorating chill and sends flecks of papery corn leaf dancing around us. Marty sneezes as we move deeper into the corn maze.

He wipes his nose. "Why doesn't Sneezy ever get invited to a second date?"

"He blows it every time," I answer, shooting him a you-gotta-do-better-than-that look.

Marty staggers back, wounded that I beat him to his own joke.

We come to yet another choice: left, right, or straight. Somewhere I heard or read the best way to get out of a maze is to take all right turns. So, we turn right.

Marty stops to clean his glasses. "Didn't we come this way before?"

I look around. Drying corn stalks and a dusty dirt path. It all looks the same to me. "How would we ever know?"

Marty points to a gum wrapper caught in one of the husks. "I noticed that earlier. I think we're walking in circles. And we've got to get out of here soon."

"Because of the sneezing?"

He shakes his head. "Nope. Because I'm going to run out of *corny* jokes."

I groan. "I think you just did."

He winks and grabs my hand, sending a happy little zing through me. In the past month I've noticed an increase in PDA. Nothing earth-shattering, but enough to fan my hopes we're edging out of friendship territory.

"Righto," he says, mopping his sweaty head despite the chilly air. "I think your all-rights strategy has gone off the rails. Let's go left."

"Lead the way."

I'm thrilled that he doesn't let go of my hand until we stop for a water break. I pull a bottle of water for each of us out of my neon fanny pack, a find I kept from an '80s themed party I organized before PeanutGate.

I crack open the bottle and draw a long swallow. "Did I tell you I'm setting up a photo booth for Violet House's Friendsgiving Gala?"

"With masks and moustaches?"

My curls bounce when I shake my head. "No. More like you'd see at a prom."

"Aah," he says, rubbing his chin. "This may ruin my masculine mystique, but I didn't go to my prom. With a full metal mouth and early-onset balding, it's hard to believe I wasn't a hot commodity. Even the dorkiest girl said yes to Lenny Waters—a string bean with halitosis—over me."

"Well then, good thing I am asking you to be my date."

He bats his eyelashes and puts his hands on his chest. "Little ol' me? I accept. I'm pretty sure I can rustle up a ruffled shirt, bow tie, and powder blue tuxedo."

"Please don't," I say, laughing. "I'm helping Dad with his outfit. I'd be more than happy to help you, too."

"Your dad is going, too?"

"Yes, and get this," I say, flicking the back of my hand against his arm. "He's going with Millicent."

"Brilliant." He hooks a loose curl behind my ear. "It seems romance is a bumper crop."

My stomach does a backflip. Does this mean we're beyond friends?

I take another sip of water to cool the heat building inside me, then wiggle our bottles back into my fanny pack. "Onward."

Marty leads the charge.

"Ta-da," he says bowing, when we enter a clearing. A deer stand manned by a highschooler serves as the maze's rescue station for lost travelers.

I put my hands on my hips and give him the hairy eyeball. "Ta-da? You do know the rescue station is always positioned dead in the middle of the cornfield."

"As I am not a maze corn-oisseur, I know no such thing."

I laugh. "Look at you being ear-resistably clever."

He leans towards me, popping a kiss on my startled lips. "You're the one who is irresistible."

I'm halfway to kissing him again when the teen yells, "Hey, you two need any help? You've been stuck in the maze for a while."

Marty teasingly rubs his nose against mine and whispers, "To be continued." Then he waves at the boy. "Nah. We're just corn-fused. Not ready to quit."

Marty twines his fingers with mine, and we wander left and right, paying no attention to finding the exit. Just quietly content to savor the wonder of the romance blooming between us again.

Somehow, we reach the exit. The maze opens up, spilling us into an expansive field of pumpkins, bathed in the pastel light of the setting sun. Marty moves behind me, wrapping his arms around me. I lean into him as we watch the sun's artistry paint the sky.

He turns me to face him. His hand cradles my chin as his lips touch mine. His kiss stirs sweetness through me.

"I'm ready, Ruby."

My heart rises, full and grateful. Even after every wrong turn and dead end, we found our way through.

ACKNOWLEDGMENTS

I am extraordinarily lucky to have had a team of wonderful people (and one adorable Basset Hound) help me bring *Banking on the Truth* into the world.

To my awesome beta readers—Deb Carson, Cindy Hospador, Melissa Roos, and Jennifer Ericson—your sharp eyes, thoughtful notes, and uncanny ability to spot every tiny clue (and misbehaving comma) were truly invaluable.

To Darin Miller—thank you for being the kindest, most generous, wildly talented friend and author. Having you on my side is a puissant prerogative. (Five points for obscurity, with a bonus ten for alliteration.)

To my author friends and the online writing community: thank you for the wisdom, the pep talks, the commiseration, and for helping spread the word about my books. You make this journey feel a lot less like wandering through a corn maze alone in the dark.

And last, but certainly not least … a huge, heartfelt thank you to my family. You never bat an eye when I mutter about suspects mid-paddleboard adventure, and you cheerfully (only occasionally grudgingly) talk through plots and red herrings with me ad nauseam. Your tolerance for my fictional chaos is admirable

A LETTER TO MY READERS

When I need a little lighthearted fun, I snuggle beside my Basset Hound, Annie, and dive into the world of Ruby Finch. My cast of characters—bless their quirky hearts—keep me guessing. I hope they've brought you the same delight they bring me. Sharing my love of Lancaster County—with its rural beauty and small-town charm—has been a privilege.

I'm also thrilled you've embraced the puzzling fun of the **Secrets Society**, my free members-only page. I love crafting puzzles for you to test your solving skills.

New to **Secrets Society**? Join and around four times per year you'll receive a week's worth of puzzles to solve using copies of the Ruby Finch Mystery books. Each correct answer is entered into a drawing to win fantastic prizes. Sign up for FREE at **MelissaNordhoff.com**.

With the millions of amazing books available, I am humbled you chose to read mine. I truly hope you enjoyed it. It absolutely makes my day to hear from readers, so feel free to connect with me on Facebook, Instagram, or through my website **MelissaNordhoff.com**.

And please—if you have a moment—write a review. Your words have power. Reviews are the very best way to support authors.

Gratefully yours,
Melissa

www.ingramcontent.com/pod-product-compliance
Lightning Source LLC
LaVergne TN
LVHW090558110826
845146LV00001B/176

* 9 7 9 8 9 9 5 4 1 3 1 0 3 *